THE TALE OF TWO SHAGGING MONKEYS

"The Siege of El Rancho"

ANTHONY BUNKO

First published 2004 by A. Bunko, 17 Cyfarthfa Gardens,
Merthyr. CF48 2SE

Printed and Bound by:- Creative Print and Design, Wales

Email:- anthony@bunko.freeserve.co.uk

Dedicated to:-

"The town that invited me to sit at its table and feast on a selection of steam pies covered with watered-down brown sauce."

Anthony Bunko

The author was manufactured in 1962 in a rough old industrial town in the Welsh valleys. While some people got born into wealth and riches, he was given a simple nickname (that no one understood) and a great upbringing.

Looking back, he has been influenced by many people down the years, (some good, many bad). But he recalls that the biggest, and the strangest, was the night the cockle-man informed him that... 'You can walk tirelessly around the world in search of comfortable shoes... only to find a pair already under the bed.'

The author immediately bought ten slightly frozen crabsticks and a big bag of fish eyes. He is still addicted!

4

"It was cold, and it rained and I felt like an actor"

David Bowie

Also by Anthony Bunko

The Tale of the Shagging Monkeys
(see back for details)

Prologue
August time 2003

'I don't like Sunny days'

Chris Kemish crammed his family saloon car up to the rafters with all the equipment that he required for his day trip. He reversed out of the narrow tarmac drive, waving goodbye to his wife and kids who had all nestled around one of the upstairs windows. He shifted the gear stick into first, just as the smooth voice on the radio informed him, and the rest of the world, that a gang of teenage yobs had beaten an innocent man to death in broad daylight in an unprovoked attack, yesterday afternoon. The voice also declared, that the month long car dispute in the Midlands had predictably reached a stalemate between the warring factions. The report ended on a more pleasant note, because it had just been announced that 2003 had been the hottest year since records had been introduced.

Chris switched the talking box off, and started winding himself down for what he hoped would be a thoroughly relaxing and therapeutic full day of fishing. He pointed his old trusty car in the direction of the mountainside while sampling one of the cheese and tomato sandwiches, which his wife had lovingly prepared for him the night before.

Twenty-five minutes later, he was out of his vehicle and staring in sheer disbelief at the sight of a bed of mud and clay that had somehow replaced the blanket of water that normally covered the top of the lake. He hadn't realised how bloody hot it had been during the long summer months. But, when you work in a factory, supervising the manufacture of millions of light bulbs in a building with no natural light, from six in the morning to seven in the evening, then sometimes, little things like that, can just pass you by.

'What a bloody waste of a lieu day,' he said to himself as he started to put his brand new rod back into the boot of the car. This unexpected event had been a shock to his system, and he now wondered what the hell he was going to do for the rest of the time.

Suddenly he heard a noise somewhere off in the distance. It was very faint but it sounded like the cry of a man who had more than a hint of a tremor in his voice. The sound travelled eerily across the morning mist. Chris looked around expecting to see another disgruntled fisherman cursing to himself on the bank. But, there was no one in sight. He then caught a glimpse of something out in the middle of the dried up water bed. He looked twice, rubbing his eyes just in case it was a mirage. Yes, there was definitely something there poking out from the freshly exposed earth.

His curiosity soon came alive and jumped out of its bed. Any second thoughts of him driving home and just ignoring the strange vision, were dismissed, as he immediately succumbed to the temptation of the strange sight. He had always been a nosy person. It stemmed from his mother's side of the family. Even as a boy, he would always be sticking his fingers into dark holes, or climbing over rocks, or squeezing through caves to satisfy his desire for adventure. So, he didn't think twice of sliding down the bank to go and investigate the interesting object that reached out into the bright morning sky.

As he carefully strolled towards the middle of the dried up bowl, that was sadly littered with the skeletal corpses of unwanted dogs, whose owners had declared them to be past their sell by date and had sentenced the poor creatures to a relatively cheap, but inhumane death, he wondered where all the water had gone? He pondered if the real reason for its disappearance had been because the sun had needed a long refreshing drink, and had decided to suck all the liquid up from the lake with a long straw.

'You greedy yellow shiny ball, you could have left a drop for me to do a spot of fishing,' he taunted and shook his fist in jest, at the slowly rising sun.

As he continued on his quest, the logical part of his mind started to ask more fundamental questions like, where had all the fish and other pond-like creatures gone to? Had they too been sucked up by old shiny face, and were they at that precise moment, swimming around inside its stomach, kitted out in asbestos swim suits to protect them from the boiling water? Or, perhaps they had all taken a package holiday to another part of the world. In his mind, he pictured a plane full of Pike and Salmon in union jack shorts, necking bottles of miniature spirits and completely ignoring the pretty trout-stewardess going through the safety routine. He wished he hadn't had that job working next door to the magic mushroom farm when he was growing up. He shook the psychedelic thoughts, that had surfaced out of his head, as he continued with his journey.

As he got closer, he noticed that the object at the centre of the lake, appeared to be a thin dark piece of wood of some kind, with something metal on the tip which stuck up approximately two feet in the air. He waded through the foot or so of surviving water that clung onto the object for dear life. He stepped over a freshly deceased Jack Russell bitch which had been modelling a new range of Tesco shopping bag, tied firmly around its head, Suffocation Summer Wear.

When he reached his goal, he saw that the thing at the centre, appeared to be an old walking cane with a silver handle in the shape of a horse's head.

'Where the hell had that come from?' He said aloud, looking up to the heavens. 'Perhaps it was one of God's tooth picks, that he had abandoned and dropped from the sky after dislodging a tough piece of pork from his teeth.' Chris hoped that his vision, wasn't at all linked with the dogs that lay dead in the mud.

He finally reached the mysterious item; he gently placed his hand on the wood. A cold shiver awoke inside him, then, ran blindly through his body bumping into every nerve ending in its path. He felt a sudden sense of abandonment and loneliness enter his mind. He couldn't release his grasp of the cane. Invisible fingers of past ghosts seemed to stop him from letting go. Then suddenly the Velcro grip loosened, and Chris pulled away slipping into the lukewarm water. He landed on the deceased dog. The stench of death raced up and bit the back of his throat. He then heard the voice again. It wasn't clear as it drifted on the wind, but it sounded to him like; 'It wasn't my fault.....I didn't mean for it to happen!'

Chris scrambled to his feet. He moved fast over the mud slipping occasionally. Once he reached the relative safety of the car he quickly locked the doors, taking a long look at the strange object before speeding off back to the town.

Later on that night, he sat in the Station Arms Hotel, which he called his local, (even though he still knew that most of the locals that drunk there, hadn't accepted him as one of their own). They still referred to him as 'Chris from over the bridge.' He rubbed his hands fervently, and thought back to the bizarre experience he had encountered that day.

As the beer flowed, and the conversation between the regulars turned to light-hearted banter about football or reincarnated lesbians, Chris interrupted the debate and asked the men on his table, were they aware of the strange walking stick in the middle of Doggy Lake.

Old Gary Churchill, as always, was the first to speak. He was the type of man whose head would have fitted just as well on the shoulders of a wise old owl, and was the proud owner of a mind that housed a thousand stories for a thousand cold nights. 'Look Chris, we would tell you, but you are a stranger around these parts.'

'I've been living here for four bloody years, and you lot still don't consider me one of the community. I bet I know more about you lot than you do yourselves!' Chris replied, obviously upset.

The pub could sense a challenge in the air, and whatever people said about the little tavern, it loved a good challenge. Everyone stopped what they were doing, including the rowdy table of football players celebrating their cup success, and they turned towards the round table by the log fire.

'Let's just see if you are right then..... Mister Outsider.' The old man's voice dropped a notch, but didn't lose any of its purpose.

He then smirked and the rest of the regulars closed in.

'Ok, a test for you. If you pass, by answering one of the following questions, I will personally tell you the tale behind the legend of Old Cherry-nose, and the reason why the Looooord Almighty himself, sent down his angels of death, that cold winter night, many many years agooooooo.'

Chris was now even more intrigued by the words that came floating out of the old man's mouth. He had to admire the passion that Gary could put into any sentence, and he now appreciated, how he had won the 'Best Storyteller of the Year' award for the last three years running. Everyone in the room knew that when Gary was on top form he could, (and normally would), make even the most basic throw-away comment, into an all day story epic.

'And what if I don't pass the test?' he said slowly, suddenly conscious of the many faces that surrounded him.

'That's simple; you buy the curry and chips from Sammy's on the way home.'

Chris nodded his head in approval and the scene was set. The two men looked at each other from across the table, two chess players, waiting for their opponent to make the first vital move.

'Ok! First question,' Gary bellowed loudly, speaking as much to the audience as the person facing him. 'What is my favourite colour?'

'That's unfair. How the hell do I know?' Chris pleaded an inquisitive expression on his face.

'Come on, Mister big factory supervisor. If you were from around these parts, you would know that.' Gary waited a minute, and then shouted over to Ronny Mouth-organ, who was sitting by the bar, and asked him the same question.

'Black,' came back the instantaneous reply, followed by a quick musical blast from his ever present and worn out harmonica.

'Correct answer, Mr Mouth-organ. Right then Mr Kemish…. that's one wrong, and only two more left to go. Are you ready for the next one?' He left an awkward pause. 'Ok what is Ronny's favourite colour?'

'I don't fucking know!' Chris stated, starting to wonder if he had been transported deep inside the Twilight Zone. 'What type of question is that anyway?'

'A fucking good one.' said the young bartender who had a stupid grin occupying his usually sour looking face.

'Come on, I'm waiting,' said Gary impatiently. 'Go on have a guess. And by the way tell Lydia from Sammy's, to put lots of salt and vinegar on my chips,' he jokingly added.

'Shush, give us a minute, I haven't lost yet.' The heat from the logs was starting to burn into his skin. He was trying hard not to scowl.

Chris stared at Ronny for a few moments. 'Now what colour would a second rate painter and decorator, whose wife had left him for a bus conductor, like?' He sighed, loudly.

He then noticed, that the man sitting by the bar twirling his mouth-organ, had a pattern of little purple squares in his white socks.

'A sign,' Chris thought, but before he answered he double checked to see what the rest of the regulars in the bar were wearing. The smile returned triumphantly to his face because, wherever he looked, he could see the normal plain white socks which had become the uniform of the men-folk of the town.

'This was definitely a sign.' He said inwardly. Finally he turned with confidence at his detective work and spurted out, 'Purple.' The pride was evident in his voice.

The whole pub burst out laughing.

'Ronny…Ronny,' Gary shouted out with great delight. 'Chris here, thinks that your favourite colour is …..PURPLE.'

'Fucking PURPLE. I'll give him fucking PURPLE. Does he think I'm a nancy boy? I'll come over there and give the cheeky foreign bastard a bunch of fives in a minute.' He breathed out angrily on his instrument.

'Ok last chance,' Gary goaded. 'I can hear them chips dancing in the batter.' He licked his lips.

'What is Ronny's favourite colour anyway?' Chris asked bemused.

'It doesn't matter.' Gary ignored his question. 'Last go. What is…..' he again left time for a deadly pause before adding, 'your favourite colour?'

'Was this a trick?' Chris thought. 'Were the sadistic bastards playing another game with him?' He felt that he was in a room full of alley cats who were content to torture a defenceless mouse before the inevitable.

'Ok, you win. My favourite colour is green, which is obviously the wrong answer,' he conceded, and looked despondent. He reached into his pocket and threw enough

13

change onto the table to more than cover his side of the bargain.

'On the contrary, Mr Kemish. It is the correct answer, your favourite colour is in fact green,' Gary informed him and the rest of the pub. 'Now if you're still like to hear the true story of what happened to Old Cherry-nose and how he came to lose his walking cane, get the beer in and settle down.'

The pub lights were dimmed, and extra logs were put on the fire as Gary took them all back in time to Christmas Eve 1986; to the beginning of the legendary story in the town's history that was simply known as:

'The Siege of El Rancho.'

Chapter 1
Christmas Eve 1986

'Pablo's last stand'

The front room of 32 Acacia Avenue was filled with a strange and pungent odour. Old man Pozzoni stared into the mirror above the fireplace, hands trembling in anticipation. He picked up the tube of cherry red No.7 lipstick he had half-inched from Boots the chemist shop the previous day, and slowly unscrewed the cap.

Upstairs, he could hear the muffled moans from the master bedroom. He purposely ignored the cries for help, and carried on with the ceremony that could only take place behind the security of, thick faux velvet curtains.

Nervously, he sniffed the sticky bullet of lipstick housed in the plastic container. It was a weird smell. He wondered what exotic ingredients, or small furry animals, the cosmetic companies must have squashed into that tub to get it to pong like that.

He unplugged the phone, and checked that the front door was shut. He snatched at the one page leaflet that someone had left in his letterbox. He cursed as he glanced at the flyer which informed him, that Old Cherry-nose would again be performing at the Buffaloes pub on New Years Day.

'Bloody voodoo mumbo jumbo,' Pablo sneered and screwed the paper up as he stomped back into the front room.

As the lipstick got nearer to his rugged and chubby face, he imagined what the old boys in the Labour Club would say if they could see him now. If he had realised just how bad their reaction to the news would have been, he would never had come out of the closet in the first place. Since the day he had bared his soul to them in confidence, they had mocked and bombarded him constantly. He had become the butt of many of their immature jokes.

'You're a bloody idiot Pablo,' they had all shouted at him in unison.

That was quickly followed by 'You're a big teacher Bessie... we always knew that you were a weirdo,' He could still hear their taunts directed straight at him, during the Wednesday afternoon Sausage and Mash Bingo which was held in the lounge.

'But what did they know?' he said to his reflection. 'They wouldn't understand. They're all John Wayne fans anyway. Bloody council estate cowboys through and through, with their cheap leather Stetsons and fisherman's waders,' he muttered insanely to himself.

He was proud of what he was. He couldn't help it. It was just part of him. It made him feel good. He faced the mirror and applied a thick cherry red stripe from his one cheek, across the bridge of his nose, and over to the other cheek.

He looked like a slightly older Adam Ant. Well, a fifty-two year old bald Adam Ant actually, with his front teeth missing, earrings in each ear, and large portions of his face covered in blue scars from a brief spell of nicking coal from the open cast mines that were dotted around the mountainside.

He stood proud and erect to reveal a barrel-shaped bare chest, which had already been dabbed in war paint, and with his privates covered in a loin cloth. This he had

16

made, by cutting the front of his Woolworth's white underpants in half, and pulling the rest up, until it disappeared somewhere up the cavernous crack of his arse. He placed the last piece of the jigsaw on his head; this consisted of an Indian headdress made up of pigeon feathers and a snake belt. He was now transformed from Pablo Pozzoni, recently crowned King of the Scroungers, into Great Chief Giro-cheque of El Rancho.

'Ooh ooh ooh ooh,' He made child-like Indian noises, as he danced around the small room holding a rusty hatchet from the coal shed.

He took the last drag on the peace pipe, which was filled with herbs from the kitchen rack. The smoke which bellowed from the clay pipe, was a mixture of basil, coriander, and half an OXO cube. Slightly light headed, he jumped on his imaginary saddle-less stallion and motioned it towards the stairs.

He dismounted on the landing, tied his invisible horse, Champion to the veranda, and crawled on his belly towards the master bedroom, like an overweight tattooed snake that had just come back from eating a litter of succulent baby pigs. His progress was halted suddenly on hearing heavy voices break the silence. He hid for cover behind the radiator, thanking his lucky stars that his wife had been drying some mean hombre beach towels at the time, which meant, that he could blend into the woollen surroundings. He then saw two cavalry officers parading next to the yellow glossed bedroom door. They were obviously keeping guard on the prisoner locked up inside.

Old Man Pozzoni moved as fast as a laboratory mouse on a triple dose of amphetamines, as he sneaked up and took the first guard by complete surprise. With one blow from his fist he knocked him out cold, sending him hurling down the lino covered stairwell. In the same movement he jumped on the second one, wrestling him to the ground. After a brief struggle, Great Chief Giro-cheque had the better of the cavalry officer. He unleashed the hatchet from out of his pants, and proceeded to scalp the defenceless white man, who was in fact, a shop window dummy which his son, (Luke or Luke Geronimo Tomahawk Pozzoni, to give him his full title) had acquired for his old man, by ram raiding the local Fosters menswear store.

He tucked the scalp into his briefs, and slowly opened the door to the small ten by ten bedroom. There he found his long lost squaw, or to be exact, his long suffering wife, tied to the real tree that he had set-up in the corner of the room. She, was also dressed in full Indian regalia, including a very new, and extremely sexy otter skin peek-a-boo bra with a pair of matching crotch-less panties.

At that precise moment, she was not Doris Pozzoni the mother of two with another little cherub, probably to be named Wayne Wig Wham Pozzoni, expected to pop out in two months time. No, she was Thunderfoot, daughter of the warrior Sitting Bull, head of the Sioux Ann tribe, captured and imprisoned in Fort Worthlessness by the demon white man with forked tongue.

Pablo rain danced around her, parading his manly stuff just as a male peacock would flex his colourful kaleidoscope plumage to impress his female counterpart.

'Ooh ooh ooh ooh ooh ooh ooh' He smouldered at her with a passion far beyond his normal below average education in the lesson of love.

She puckered her lips, feeling herself getting moist down below, as he bounced up and down on the bed nearly losing his balance after hitting his head on the light shade.

She stared back coyly, hoping that this time the tree which he had screwed to the plasterboard would not fall over like before. That episode had ended with her nearly getting squashed by the stump of the tree, and the brave warrior getting rushed to the casualty department for a tetanus jab, after the rusty hatchet gnashed the inside of his thigh. To add insult to his injury, he got arrested after attacking a cocky porter, who just happened to called him 'Little Pablo Plum' while wheeling him to the cubicle.

Back in the bedroom, lust was firmly on the agenda, as Pablo puffed out his chest, showed her the fresh scalp, and kicked the door closed. He smiled as he touched her. He loved the feel of otter skin.

Cyril Beaverman sat upright in his supposedly disguised TV detector van outside 32 Acacia Avenue, waiting, for his moment to pounce. The driving rain that splattered on the windscreen, made his job of observing all suspicious movements in the run down council house, very difficult and dangerous.

But Cyril loved his job. He liked the chase, and although some criminals could dodge paying the very reasonable licence fee for a while, he would inevitably collar them in the end. He was renowned amongst the detector van fraternity, for, always getting 'His man.' This had made him the number one tracker of all time. During his six years on the force, he had been solely responsible for the conviction of 132 suspected TV freeloaders, and at one time, had even helped bring to justice a gang of diamond smugglers, who, he thought, were a family watching an illegal gangster movie.

Unfortunately for Cyril when he wasn't busy snooping at work, and found himself outside the environment of ultimate power, he was a nothing sort of bloke. A person that could walk into a room and no one would notice or remember that he had been there. It had taken him nearly forty-two years to develop himself into an interesting character, but all he could come up with in that time, was an ability to recall the precise rain fall in every major city across the globe and, own a substantial collection of Matt Monroe records.

He had been camped outside the Pozzoni household for sixteen long days, and even longer nights, living off fish and chips and packets of cup-a-soup, ever since his work colleagues had bet him that he would never collar Pablo

Pozzoni. So, with his sophisticated sound equipment which consisted of nothing more than a pair of record player headphones, and a large microphone covered with his grandmothers old woolly bed-sock, he listened with all his might for that one tell tale noise that would enable him to search the premises.

During his mission to complete 'Operation Nail The Big Cheese' successfully, (he always gave his missions code names), he had heard, and witnessed, some very strange goings on from the other houses in the street.

The couple who lived in number 31, who didn't have any kids, would entertain married couples every night. These pre-arranged meetings would start with an introductory round of sherry, a finger buffet consisting of penis-shaped sausage rolls, and fish flavoured vol-au-vents. The snack would be quickly followed by a warm starter of French kissing, which soon disintegrated into some depraved Roman orgy with a touch of Greek thrown in. Cyril forced himself to listen to every gruesome detail as bodies of every shape and size would intermingle into every available crevice, searching out the ultimate suburban pleasure. Cyril actually sneaked into the party one night amongst a minibus of swingers from Nelson, but soon got thrown out when he refused to throw his company issue van keys onto the table, and kept asking questions like, how long had they had a coloured television set? He knew full well from his personal records, that they had only purchased a licence to cover the use of a black and white one the previous week.

Cyril often sympathised with the poor soul who lived, or to be more accurate, survived at number thirty-six opposite the Pozzoni's household, along with his overpowering and demanding wife. Percy Norman was so far under his fat wife's thumb, he had developed calluses on his rapidly receding hairline.

Cyril tuned in nightly for another gripping instalment, as Percy would get physically and mentally abused by his overweight beast of a spouse. Complaints and constant put-downs on a daily basis, had stripped all self-confidence away from this once proud man. Cyril would scream through his head phones at the pathetic individual for him to stick up for himself, but each day just brought with it a bigger misery pill for Percy to swallow without as much as a mouthful of water.

Cyril prayed that he would catch his prey soon and get out of this evil place. This mission was slowly driving him stir-crazy, and he found himself making regular small talk with the gear stick, until they had a disagreement about the practical use of rain gauges.

During all this time of listening, unbelievably, there was nothing from house number 32. There was no suggestion of any illegal goings on whatsoever. Not even a sound bite of daytime television, or a mention of the weather forecast by some leggy blonde could be heard coming out of the four walls.

'Perhaps his colleagues were wrong,' he told the indicator lever. He still wasn't talking to the gear stick and had put the woolly sock over it in spite. 'Perhaps the Pozzonis' don't have a TV. Perhaps they are the outdoor types, walking or rambling all day in the forest.'

But the reason for the lack of noise through the airwaves, was because all twelve television sets, dotted around Pablo's house, were wired up with personal headsets. He even had two TVs in the toilet. One tele was positioned over the bath, and the other was facing west, for when one was shitting on the throne.

So, while Cyril sat out in the cold and the rain, Pablo flaunted shamelessly in the warmth, fully in charge of the remote control of life, which was being funded by the very understanding people from social security.

What Cyril didn't know was that although Pablo was a massive closet Red Indian, he was also a great film buff. He watched films until his eyes were the shape of imported tangerine boxes. When it came to his best ever movie, there was only one that rocked his boat. That cinema epic was 'Jaws' which he watched everyday since his son had stolen him a Betamax video for his birthday. He knew every word and every piece of action that made up the classic movie. He would even tip his settee upside down, pretend that it was a boat and that he was Shark-hunter Quint, on the trail of the naughty man-eating fish. On occasions when his Misses was out, he would have his daughter, (Romana White Wolf Pozzoni), throw buckets of water mixed with fish shaped candy sweets at him during the climatic end scene. He would then have to race against time to tidy the room up before his wife came home from a hard day, eight hour shift playing the slot machines in Happy Valley.

Cyril rubbed his tired eyes, as he watched the Mayor's car pass with a waving Cherry-nose sitting in the back. He then heard the sound that he had prayed to God for.

'Ooh ooh ooh ooh ooh... me big chief...you my woman.' the loud words snaked through his headset.

Cyril quickly reached over to the glove compartment for the TV times to check the programme listing for that day.

'Please be gentle with me... big chief... or should I say very, very big chief.' The reply echoed down the reception wire.

Cyril checked BBC2. 'Yes... got the bastard,' he said excitedly to himself on finding out that the afternoon matinee was an old cowboy film called 'Custer's Last Stand.' He quickly phoned into head office and told them to break out the bubbly, because he was coming home with... the Money. He boasted to himself that 'Operation Nail The Big Cheese', would be written in detector folk law, and told to all new recruits for years to come. 'Perhaps they'll make a film about it,' he laughed.

He punched the roof of the van, took off his slippers, and replaced them with his works issue steel toe-capped boots and his clipboard. He removed the sock off the gear stick and poked his tongue out at it. He marched up toward the door, warrant in hand, while all the other curtains in the street were pulled back far enough for curious eyeballs to peek through.

Upstairs in the bedroom, beneath the backdrop of the great outdoors, things were getting steamy. Old man Pozzoni could really move for an older guy and bit savagely into his wife's exposed neck.

Then, all of a sudden, Cyril burst through the bedroom door flashing his TV detector man badge, fully expecting to see Pablo holding a mug of tea and perhaps some jammy dodgers while watching how General Custer had lost his fashionable yellow locks, illegally on a 24" colour TV set. What he didn't envisage seeing in a million years was a real-life, half naked Indian, covered in bird feathers, humping a dyed-blonde haired, heavily pregnant squaw, who was fastened to a conker tree, and a male mannequin, with no hair, tied faced down on the bed.

The uninvited guest realising his mistake, turned and fled. But, Great Chief Giro-cheque was too fast, and lassoed the detector man with the string of his dressing gown. The screaming man dug his nails into the lino, but was dragged in like a helpless fly towards a table of irritable and extremely hungry daddy long-legged spiders, who had just finished fasting for lent.

It was all too much for Cyril, who fainted, and woke up twenty minutes later dressed in a cavalry outfit with a wig on, and secured tightly to the tree.

Outside, his screams and yells could be clearly heard throughout the four corners of the street. Even the sweaty bodies in number 31 stopped hunting for wet patches between each others thighs, and went to the window to see what the hell was going on.

Then, all at once, the mob quickly appeared from behind closed doors. Gangs of streetwise hyenas who instantly knew that someone had kindly left them, a big bag of goodies on their doorstep. Their calculated, measured footsteps, turned to mad gallops as they all descended on the vacated detector van, stripping it clean before taking it for a one way journey up on the mountain to Fire-town!

Two hours later, Cyril held his breath and tried to listen to the voices that were climbing up through the floor boards.

'Alive Alive oh.... my sweet Spanish lady... Alive Alive oh... your ladies of Spain,' drifted up from the front room below, followed by the sound of water and candy sweets splashing, against the damp proofed wall.

Chapter 2
New Years Eve

'Ghosts of Fist-fights in Tiffany's'

The disc jockey interrupted the music to announce to the revellers, that Cherry-nose had just entered the nightclub and was signing autographs until eleven 'o' clock. People cheered and clapped, as the old hobo limped across the stage waving his walking stick.

As the commotion died down, Alex Davies used his elbows on the table to stop his head from slumping as he surveyed the majestic splendour of Tiffany's nightclub. This he did in a similar fashion, to how a professional photographer would use a camera stand to capture a large family wedding. He was sitting next to his mate Jac Morgan, who was sporting, a newly received black eye. It had been an unwanted Christmas present, off his father.

Both the nineteen year olds had arrived at the club slightly drunk, but had the full intention of jumping on the train to the well visited station called 'Absolutely Plastered'. They had devised their legless route with cans of 'Vat 69' cider, followed by 'rum and black' chasers, which they felt, were sufficient enough fuel to get them quickly to their desired destination.

Alex's eyes took everything in. The place fascinated him to the point of obsession. He loved everything about it. The artificial trees, the joyful atmosphere which could turn nasty with the flick of an emotional switch, and the plastic glasses. He found it ironic that someone had the cheek to actually call plastic glasses…plastic glasses.

'There are some strange sarcastic twats in the world,' he tried to shout, over the thick bass beat which had made a wall of sound in front of his face.

'Urrgg,' Jac shook his head. He could see his mates lips move but was unable to make out the words.

'Strange sarcastic twats,' he yelled louder. 'Someone calling plastic glasses… plastic glasses.'

'Yeah there are some strange looking bastards in here tonight, especially them bouncers. They look like big gorillas in morning suits,' Jac replied, obviously completely missing the point.

Alex decided to stop speaking to his mate until the music took a breather, although he thought that Jac had made a very good observation. There was definitely a crew milling around the dance floor, that even the devil would think twice about employing.

The young man knew, that lots of people referred to the place, as the 'Star Wars' bar, because of the similarity between the creatures in the famous bar scene in the film, and the occupants who sloped about in the town's nightclub. But, he strongly believed that the people who made those comparisons were way off the mark. His own assessment was that the link went far deeper than that. He felt that it was actually more akin to the bar, that the creatures who subsequently failed the audition for being too ugly for the original film set, would drink in. Star Wars would have needed an over 35 certificate, if it had been filmed amongst these four walls. Even Chewbacca would have had his parents pick him up after the disco, in case, he was beaten up for being too much of a pretty boy.

But, even with the risk of mindless violence, which could break out at any time, or the thought of two-headed ugly people dancing around a flashing neon sign, the place still really excited Alex to death. It flowed through his veins, straight to his heart. It was part of his growing up. The quintessential lesson in the education of, real life, and ugly bug-eyed people.

He also loved the way that every time he paid to get in and approached the red carpeted stairs leading to the magical room of a million strobe lights, the record *'Celebration',* would always be playing. It didn't seem to matter what time he arrived, or if he came in disguise. As soon as his suede shoes touched the bottom step, the sound of *'Celebrate... goodtimes... come on,'* would just rise up to meet him. He had developed a serious love/hate relationship with that song down the years.

What he admired most about the sweaty nightclub, where walking on the carpet was like trying to wade through a tub of superglue, were the girls. The girls were everywhere. These were 'honest-to-God' real girls, not your pretty college types with mouths full of braces and pompoms. They were not your Saturday shopping girls, all tanked up with credit cards and tired legs. No, these girls were street girls. And, what's more, these were street girls on the pull! They would swoop down like bats in skin-tight sequined boob tubes, with white handbags and matching Woodbine accessories. He found it amusing how they all had at least one tooth missing, enabling them to talk without taking their fags out of their often-decaying mouths.

They were, 'cave-man' girls, who would end the night by dragging some poor, blind, drunk victim home, to a cold council flat out in the sticks, usually occupied by six fatherless kids and a two hundred year old grandmother. He shivered at the thought, but smiled, knowing that the chase would soon be on, and the female dogs would soon get a sniff of the male rabbit.

Alex continued with his private 'eye-spy' competition of people watching, and carefully observed the array of party goers that were packed into the club, waiting for the countdown to midnight.

He tried not to make eye contact with the reserved table positioned up next to the ladies toilets. This was the favourite resting place of a new strain of lesbian, which the town seemed to be breeding at an alarming pace. He couldn't help, but slyly glare at the tribe.

'Why?' he thought, but not too loudly, 'Were lesbian couples always made up of one nice looking piece, while the other could give Albert Steptoe a run for his money in the ugly sweep-stakes.' That, was the biggest mystery about lesbians that men couldn't understand. He had been involved in a million male conversations about the unknown hidden secrets of the 'Todger Dodgers', and he knew most men said, that if they came back in a new life as a girl, they would definitely be a lesbian. That was everyone except Kieran the postman, who was adamant that he would definitely be a straight girl.

He couldn't remember even hearing the words during those serious debates that went like; 'Yes, if I came back as a girl, of course I would be a lesbian, and I would obviously go out with somebody that looked more like a man than most East German shot putters (who had been forced fed testosterone since birth) did,' No, the scenario never went like that. He knew that eight out of ten regular male users of lesbo fantasies echoed the same sentiment. It was never envisaged that ugly lesbians existed, in this male romantic conversation that normally occurred straight after the football results. He recalled, that most men would usually end up saying; 'Yes, if I came back as a girl, of course I would be a lesbian and I would spend all day going down on Sophia Loren until I needed Wimpy to re-tarmac my tongue.'

'So, why were proper lesbians so different in real life?' he thought. 'Perhaps it was something to do, with the stereotypical misconception brought about by the one-eyed male dominated monsters who produced cock-books.'

He then saw the leader of the lesbo pack, (Hairy Mary), get up on the chair, neck a pint back in one, then flex her muscles as if she was trying to impress the judges in a 'Mr Universe' competition. Apparently, she could spit, fight, and ride a bike as good as the next man, and was the proud owner of the hairiest set of shins in the county. He noticed her lack of girly dress sense, unless someone would consider, a rolled up pair of Bill Stunt stretch jeans, a checked blue shirt, short crew-cut hair, a necklace made out of a dozen love bites, and ten earrings in one ear, to be lady-like. He watched as she then proceeded to jump off the chair, grab the hand of a girl who must have been the sexiest person in the room, and pulled her towards the female toilets. Before she disappeared, she turned to the rest of the table, and wiggled her devil shaped tongue at them.

'Fuck me... did you see that?' Jac seemed to come alive.

'I heard that she has a 15 inch rubber vibrator always strapped to her leg, and that she uses it to break in any new member of the gang,' Alex mouthed back.

'Who told you that?' Jac asked, looking for the outline of the plastic weapon on her thigh.

'The boys in the Labour club.'

'How would they know?' Jac rightfully asked.

'They know everything.'

'Yeah,' replied Jac, 'and what they don't know they make up.'

Silence followed, as Alex then realised that he hadn't had a good shag for ages. He had a couple of bad shags during that time, but nothing worth writing home about. As he watched the dancing crowd pretend to row boats while sitting on the dirty wooden floor, he thought about his life. He always imagined that he would be married by now, or at least engaged to some attractive girl. But up until this point in his short life, he was still very much single, earning some good dosh working in the Button factory, and living with his parents and little sister. He considered his predicament as he watched two gorilla-like bouncers, with arms dragging on the carpet, gladly helping a drunken punter to the nearest exit, by his hair.

He had made a conscious decision that, in the New Year, he was going to start to map his life out, step by step, and to stop wherever possible having awful bouts of bad sticky sex.

Jac got up and headed to the bog. He stepped over a young boy named Maxy, who was lying unconscious on the edge of the dance floor still holding his can of lager in his hand. He passed a table of students who were in fancy dress costumes. There was a five foot Tarzan, several furry animals, and a remarkably good Adolf Hitler in jackboots with a cardboard cut-out tank. Next to them, there were six boys dressed as The Four Musketeers. Jac stopped for a while to listen to the heated conversation between the pretend French aristocrats.

'Look,' said one of the boys angrily, 'You can't be D'Artagnan... because I bagged him yesterday.' The boy pointed directly at another student.

'Well why can't we have two D'Artagnan?' the fatter boy answered, also starting to get upset.

'Don't be such a brat,' his mate yelled, 'Look around. Can you imagine what that chubby boy on the next table, covered in shoe-polish, would think if another Idi Amin walked in? Now you knew that I was going to be D'Artagnan, and Peter was going to be Porthos, and Wayne and Neil were coming as Athos and Aramis respectively, so why the fuck you and your cousin decided to gate crash the party and copy us, is starting to spook me out a bit, if you must know.'

'What did you think this was.... a New Years Eve bash, or a Noah's ark party?' Peter the Porthos piped up.

Jac decided that he would make a suggestion before there were hat feathers flying all over the place. 'I was sure that there was another two musketeers called Jeremy and Jemimah.' He quickly entered the toilet, knowing, that he had just thrown a humorous hand-grenade amongst the students.

'Hi Jac... what happened to you? Been up to your old tricks again?' he was asked about his black eye, by a youth dressed in a grey suit with cream shoes and a red tie.

'Don't ask, it's not funny,' he replied sheepishly, but added, 'No, sorry, it is funny.'

He then went on to inform the youth how he had come home on Christmas Eve tanked up, and starving. On checking the cupboards, he decided that the tin of Fray Bentos pie was the only thing that would satisfy his ravenous hunger. He put it in the oven, and waited patiently for the processed feast to cook.

'Next thing I remember, I was waking up on the floor an hour later, with the kitchen covered in black smoke. Luckily, I was below the smoke line, which left about eight inches of fresh air at ground level to breath in.' Jac finished peeing, and tucked himself back into his trousers.

'What happened then?' The youth said, combing his Mullet hair-do.

'Well... I could see two pairs of legs rushing around in the smoke. I could hear my father shouting, 'Where is he?.... I'll kill him!' So I decided to just lie still, but my father stuck his head below the smoke and spied me. Then, he dragged me out into the garden and the fire brigade came'

'Is that how you got the shiner then?'

'No,' Jac laughed and added, 'It was the day after. I hadn't realised that the Christmas turkey was in the same oven that I put the bloody pie into. Burnt the fucking lot. Turkey, stuffing, sausages, everything.... even the spuds were ruined by the smoke. You'll never guess what we had for Christmas dinner?'

'Don't know?' the youth queried, more concerned with trying to get his hair to spike up.

'Fish fingers and spaghetti alphabet letters.'

'No fucking way... not for Christmas dinner!!' The youth said amazed, turning to face Jac.

'On my life, that was the only thing we had in the freezer. We all sat around the table with party hats on, and crackers, eating a small children's size happy meal.'

'Still, doesn't explain how you got the black eye though?'

'Well, what pissed my father off at first, was my sister made the word 'Turkey' out of the spaghetti alphabet letters, so every time he took a bite of a fish finger, he would turn around and give me a stare from hell. Then for the craic I asked him if he would like to pull a cracker with me and that's when he punched me off my chair.' Jac finished the story and asked the boy if he could borrow some of that Brut that he was splashing all over.

'Are you all set for Cherry-nose tomorrow?' Jac asked, swilling some of the Brut in his mouth.

'Yeah... I've just sold my grandmother's china to get some extra cash.... just in case it's a biggy!' the youth replied.

Jac left the toilet, just as the D.J. was about to start the count down to welcome in another year.

'10,9,8,7,6,5,4,3,2,1... Happy New Year everyone,' he bellowed down the mike. He then slapped 'Auld Lang Syne' on the twin decks. A giant circle of people joined hands, and for five minutes only, there was peace and harmony in the world. There were no car bombs on the streets of Belfast. No Street brawls in Trafalgar Square. No muggings in Notting Hill. No violent acts at all, not even in the local Gurnos housing estate, where it had been reported that a murder took place every sixty-five minutes.

Even Old man Pozzoni and his wife sang the song, merrily bringing in the New Year, and did an Apache 'Okey Cokey' with a gagged Cyril Beaverman, who was still fastened to the tree in the master bedroom.

Back on the dance floor the song finished, and everyone hugged and kissed each other. Then all the men made a mad dash for the bar, leaving all the girls crying uncontrollable in each others arms, except the lesbian clan, (who were all still French kissing each other passionately).

Jac and Alex held each other tight for a split second. They had been friends for a long time.

'I wish Lusty and Kinsey were here,' Alex said. 'We should promise that we do more things together in the New Year. You never know what's around the next bend.'

'I think that you are starting to go around the bend. Now stop being such a sentimental old drama queen, and get the beer in. We still have a drunken train to catch!' Jac turned away hiding the little tear in his eye.

Ten minutes later, all niceties that had been evident in the nightclub suddenly changed, as everyone knew it would, but just hoped, that perhaps this year, just for once, it could end peacefully. Sadly, for everyone who was out to enjoy the festivities, Mr Violence, and his dancing partner Miss Aggression, took centre stage yet again for the free-for-all communal boogie.

The first punch thrown by the skinhead was more of a slap than a full Thomas Hearne's one-punch special. But it triggered off a massive domino effect, and by the time someone had turned on the main lights, and the dickey-bowed Gorillas had realised that trouble was brewing in the far corner, pandemonium had already broken out with a capital 'P', that was growing so big, it was surrounded by a ring road, had a Cathedral, and two airports.

Jac and Alex just watched in fascination, as the entire dance floor became a fully blown battle ground. Alex was sure he saw one man with blood streaming down his face carrying a bazooka and hand grenades into the affray. Feuding gangs were trying unsuccessfully to snap the plastic trees to use as weapons, as others used tables as human battering rams. They actually saw a girl metamorphosize into a blood crazed animal, twirling on the back of another girl's boyfriend. He was snarling like a pit-bull in a fit of rage.

The disc jockey was all geared up for the vicious shenanigans that were unfolding at a rapid pace before his eyes. He turned to the records sections, marked up 'Riots and Punch ups', flipped out one of the twelve inch disc's and rotated it onto the turntable. Suddenly, the strains of Talking Head's 'Psycho Killer' accompanied the fists and boots that moved to its own destructive rhythm. He flicked on the strobe-lights, and settled down to watch the entertainment.

As soon as the bouncers seemed to put out a fire in one corner of the room, another would explode in a different part, but with a heat and violence more ferocious than before.

Malcolm 'Knuckles' McCormick, was sitting alone in the other bar of the nightclub when he heard the ruck going off on the dance floor. Malcolm had the inert ability to pick up a brawl on his inner sense radar from over a mile away. He would then consider it his duty to get involved. This was because, he had been born to fight. Stories of him travelling around the country, challenging the hardest and meanest from all areas when he was in his late teens, were often told in the many pubs throughout the town. Although these tales of false chivalry were probably greatly exaggerated, the scars that littered his face were a reminder that there must have been some truth in the stories of these skirmishes. A broken nose from the docks in Liverpool; sixteen stitches across his left eye courtesy of a gypo from Bolton. These battle scars, and many more, made up the stone boundaries of his face. But, over that time, his fists had damaged the contours of many of his opponent's features, a hell of a lot more permanently than his stone-hardened face had ever been altered.

He slowly rose from his bar stool, took off his jacket, handed it to the barman, and rolled up his sleeves. He ambled into the middle of the mayhem and stood just underneath the giant disco ball, which was designed in the shape of the world, and he took up his fighting stance. The sparkling lights from the artificial glittering globe bounced off his intimidating frame.

The bouncers all knew what this man mountain was capable of, so they collectively decided to skip out of this particular dance. The first unexpected soul to accidentally stumble into the all-action man, was knocked so far back into last week, that when he finally woke up fifty minutes later in casualty, he asked the nurses could he watch the Queens speech and the Christmas Day 'Top of the Pops.'

Two brave students, who must have thought that they were indestructible in their dashing Musketeer costumes, foolishly rushed at the street fighting man. A right hook sent D'Artagnan high into the branches of one of the plastic trees, while poor Jemimah's chin connected squarely with Malcolm's famous windmill overhead punch, projecting the student onto the table of the lipstick lesbians, where Hairy Mary took exception to a man having the audacity to join her gang on the strictly 'Penis-free' table. She bit into his groin with all her might.

On a call of four, the rest of the fancy dressed students decided to storm the Bastille that stood in the form of Malcolm, who had now turned into an Octopus with eight deadly fists. Bodies flew in all directions. A tiger smashed into the amplifier on the stage sending sparks spitting out. A boy disguised as Dracula, was hit so hard, he needed hospital treatment, and required three pints of blood. They came in waves, but were dispelled by Malcolm's speed and agility. During the massacre, he suddenly stopped himself from pummelling a boy dressed as a bird. Malcolm loved birds. He was an expert when it came to the feathered species. The bird-boy stood completely still in front of the street fighting man, who patted him on the head and told him to fly home to his nest. The boy thanked God that the sparrow costume had been the only thing left in the fancy dress shop that morning. Malcolm then proceeded to beat a racoon and a bumble bee to within an inch of their lives.

When the smoke from the disco had finally dispersed, the dance floor was awash with moaning bodies and a river of blood. Malcolm however, was only just getting warmed up. He smiled as he strolled towards the bouncers, who legged it out of the building towards the police station.

Earlier that night, Billy '2 amp' Kinsey had watched his mates Alex and Jac join the bustling queue that snaked it's way towards the heavily guarded door of the nightclub.

He had reassured them that he really didn't want to see in the New Year in that dreadful knocking shop. He told them that he'd meet them in the pub tomorrow afternoon and slowly walked down the steps into the cold concrete precinct.

'Do you wanna buy a puppy mate?' A voice came floating out of the shadows.

'What the fuck do I want a puppy for?' he snapped back.

'Best chat-up technique known to man. Once the ladies see a poor defenceless puppy in your arms…they will be all over you like a rash,' the faceless salesman replied, opening his coat to reveal a jacket full of small baby dogs.

'I don't know about all over you like a rash… most of them in there,' Kinsey said pointing back to the direction of the music, 'Will give you a rash that will be all over you!' He went to walk away. The salesman grabbed his arm.

'Last chance mate... half price to you. I've got one here with only one eye. Great for a quick sympathy shag,' the man gestured, showing him a pup with a leather eye-patch.

'Do you call him Patch?' Kinsey asked jokingly.

'No... Julius Caesar' came back the very straight reply.

'No I'm Ok... I'm banned anyway,' Kinsey said, walking quickly away from the dark door to door canine salesman.

Deep down, he wished that he could have bought one of those dogs and entered the nightclub with his friends, but he didn't have a chance of stepping over the threshold for another nine months at least. He only had himself to blame. He was the one that had lost his temper several months ago, while out celebrating at a stag night.

Perhaps it was the all day drinking binge with a twist of mild drugs that had clouded his judgement, but he was sure that the guy next to him by the bar was just asking for trouble. He was positive he was. So he did what his uncle had always told him to do in this situation. 'If in doubt... lash out'

So, as he saw the guy in the white trousers and waistcoat reaching out to surely smack him, Kinsey got his premature retaliation in first, and stuck the head in.

'It was a beaut too.' He remembered the noise as the guy's nose shattered.

As the music from the New Year's Eve disco was disappearing on the wind, he walked passed WH Smiths, hitching up his coat collars as the drizzle started to fall from the heavens.

How could he have known, that the guy in the brightly coloured clothes was the artist for the night? And not just any old artist, the man with the broken nose, minus two front teeth, was no other, than Sammy Weathership, the one time winner of the southern heats of Opportunity Knocks.

Kinsey remembered that the bouncers were quickly on the scene, but not until he had peppered the pole axed man with several firm spices of shoe leather.

A twelve month ban, from the only nightclub in town, for banging a class 'D' comedian, whose act was so bad that they actually paid him off at the interval.

'They should have made me a life member for nutting that useless twat,' he told himself.

Kinsey had seen a shrink about his behavioural problems, he was just too aggressive for words. He didn't need a doctor to tell him that! What he required off the quack, were answers to the questions about why he was so hot headed in the first place? Why couldn't he keep his cool? There were times before the shutters came down and his fists came up, that the inside of his brain felt like a blast furnace in the steel works, a combination of pure molten white anger mixed with a catalyst of hatred.

He marched on, kicking a coke can in temper. A homeless street beggar asked him for a few coppers for something warm to eat on this cold New Years Eve night.

'Fuck off…. and get yourself a job,' he replied and stormed off towards the upside of town.

'Where the hell was he going to go to celebrate the old year's demise?' he thought to himself. He played back his options. He could go home and watch the chiming of Big Ben bells on television with his parents. But, on second thoughts, he would rather nail his balls to the statue outside the town hall than spend a minute with those boring tits. He could try to sneak into Tiffany's like the last time, when he covered himself with an overcoat and had Alan the Midget to sit on his shoulders. The stares that the eight foot man with an abnormally large head pulled in the disco queue, needed to have been seen to be believed. The plan would have worked and all, if Alan, the idiot, had only ducked when they climbed the stairs inside the foyer. People screamed as the eight foot giant suddenly split in two. Kinsey could only lay there and watch, as Alan, the short yellow bellied shit, ran to the safety of the fire exit, leaving him to take a shoeing from the gorillas in monkey boots.

'Ok,' he said to the telephone box on the High Street. 'When everywhere else is slamming its door in your face, there is only one place left to go…. Hing Hongs…. the Chinese restaurant.' He found a new vitality in his footsteps as he focused in on the food sign at the top of the street.

Several moments later, he opened the door into Hing Hongs, and thankfully left the deteriorating elements firmly outside. It was as if Willy Wonka himself had prised the door to his magical chocolate kingdom ajar. The place was bouncing with activity. He waited in the small corridor for the pad-locked gates to be opened by Suzie Yoo. They had recently been erected to stop unwanted people from getting in, but more importantly to stop potential, non-paying clients from running out.

As he waited, Kinsey glanced at the photographs on the corridor walls, which showed the identity of the large amounts of individuals who had been banned from the establishment. They had been divided in three categories. Category C, was for people banned for up to three months for minor offences, like setting tablecloths on fire, or throwing curry across the room. The 'B' section was for a more serious breakdown of the strict rules, such as, stabbing the waitresses with forks (all knives had been banned since the riots of '76), or willingly disfiguring other customers by dipping their head into the extra hot curry. This brought with it a maximum penalty of up to six months. The last and final category, which was for class 'A' offenders, was strictly for murders which had been committed on the premises. This of course carried a life-long ban, unless it was an unusually quiet night. The mug-shots of three people, (two males and one female) hung their heads in shame on that section of wall.

The gates were unlocked, and Kinsey entered. It was packed that night. He could recognise most of the local people occupying the tables around the perimeter of the restaurant. It was an unwritten, but golden rule that all regulars should always sit with their backs to the wall just in case of trouble. He noticed that the tables inside the inner circle were also full.

'Must be some out-of-towners in here tonight,' he said to the man known as, "the struggling man who would always sit by the door and take four hours to eat his meal."

The man nodded back, his mouth full of sweet and sour, and a small black and white puppy (with no ears) sitting on his lap.

Kinsey was lucky that a wall table had become vacant as he strolled in. He sat down and studied the menu. On looking around he couldn't help but notice how the attitude of the restaurant owners had changed. It had worried him they had become much too serious about life over the last couple of years. He remembered how pleasant the Chinese had been when it first opened. They couldn't do enough for the customers. There was always a smile and a noble nod of the head, followed by an After Eight mint and a selection of Chinese fortune cookies. Sadly, over time, their polite mannerisms had completely eroded away, along with the free, end of meal snacks. On reflection, he could perhaps understand why their attitude had become stretched during this period with all the abuse they had to put up with. And maybe, the fact that their grandfather had been killed while trying desperately to stop someone giving a half eaten spring roll to another table, may have pissed them off a little. But, he was sure that there was no need for the barbed wire, or the observation towers with spot lights that were situated at each corner of the room. He also firmly believed that it was a tad over the top, arming the waitresses with Alsatian dogs and police truncheons.

'Hello 2 amp,' muttered Colette, the only non-Chinese waitress to hold down a permanent job in the place. She had become part of the furniture. She was a very likeable woman who unfortunately, smelt of piss and neat gin. She had more lines on her face than the London underground, and enough dirt under her fingernails to grow potatoes. She was a legend amongst a town overflowing with peculiar legends, but, to the Chinese, she was extremely cheap to keep and had a great way with most of the difficult clients.

'Going to see the Cherry-nose show in the pub tomorrow?' she added.

'Hello Colette, of course I'm going. It's going to be a good one,' Kinsey replied. He scanned the ripped menu and asked, 'What do you recommend tonight?'

She closed in so no one else could hear and answered 'A fucking pizza from across the street. These kitchens are stinking. I'd rather eat in the bus station toilets. I'll tell you what,' she continued, 'There's a cockroach living under the cooker that goes to night school.' She then added, 'And they've all had the shits this week.' She pointed towards the waiters who rushed around with their arse cheeks firmly clenched.

Her last comment had definitely helped him to narrow his selection down. There would be no special curry for him tonight.

'Just get me a Chicken Maryland and chips, please Colette.'

Colette took the order and went to the next table, which was occupied by a rather well to do gentleman and his wife, joyfully taking in the quaint carnival atmosphere.

'Hello Madam,' the man said.

'They must be from out of town if they call Colette a Madam.' Kinsey noted.

'Oh yes! Please Madam, may we have some Chinese tea for two?' The man said innocently.

There was a loud outbreak of laughter from all corners of the room, including the Chinese teenagers who were manning the watch towers.

Colette was not fazed by this unusual request, and as sharp as a knife she replied, 'This is a fucking Chinese… not a coffee shop. Now unless you start to get serious I'll get you banned for life. Chinese tea… do I look like the chimp off the fucking Typhoo advert?' She then proceeded to bound around the tables, impersonating a monkey scratching underneath her armpits.

A big hurray followed Colette words of pure wisdom.

The man looked physically confused. 'Ca… ca… can you tell me what the difference is, between a 'Special Hing Hongs' and a 'Hing Hongs Special.?' He pointed to the menu.

Colette shrugged her shoulders looking bored, and replied, 'Yep….. a Hing Hong Special comes with only two fried eggs on top.'

If looks of disgust could have been measured between the husband and wife, then it would have shaken the foundations of their middle-class lifestyle to the very core.

'A fried what?' said the woman, her ears pricking up.

'A fried egg, love,' Colette batted back, getting annoyed with old starched collar and his stuck up wife. 'You know. You get them from out of Chicken's arses.' She pretended to squat over their table, laying a golden egg while clucking at the top of her voice.

Another loud hooray from the cheap seats. Colette was on fire tonight.

'Ok!' interjected the man, knowing when he was on a loser, 'Could we have two Hing Hongs Special but without the fried eggs and two curry sauces please Miss.'

Colette looked confused. 'You don't want your fried eggs? Veggy are you?'

'I'll have their fried eggs,' said a boy dressed as Elvis, who then started to sing *'Fry me tender… .Fry me do… never crack my yoke!!'*

'You buy own fried eggs,' Suzie Yoo appeared and snapped at the young king of rock and roll. 'Only fifty pence per egg and stop that singing or you banned. This ain't no disco.' The Alsatian growled and the spot lights from the observation towers zoomed in.

Seconds later, the chef came out to plead with the odd couple to just sample his egg topping delight. He was very upset, because he had been sent over especially from China because of his egg frying skills. He went back in the kitchen still disappointed at the couple's continual insistence that they didn't want any eggs, and so he jerked off in their curry sauce. The egg-less fried rice and the bowls of curry, (with that extra dollop of Chinaman), arrived at the table where the couple sat. Kinsey stared at their reaction to the food that was dished up to them. Giant oval plates piled up to the sky with enough rice to single-handedly feed a African village for six months.

'Have you got any chop-sticks?' The woman dared to ask.

Giggles were heard at every table, as Colette, who was too tired for all this nonsense at this time of the night, stormed into the kitchen, snapped a couple of pencils in half and threw them back on the couples table.

'Enjoy,' she said, walking away to go for a fag.

The man decided to go and wash his hands before the feast. His good wife could feel eyes burning into her. In fact no one was looking at her at all. Their eyes were clearly focused on the freshly arrived plates of nosh. But, she became extremely nervous in her husbands absence, and she too decided to visit the little girl's room.

Kinsey shook his head in disbelief on seeing the couple leave an untouched, and unguarded, plate of food all alone. It often surprised him how stupid people were. Within fifteen seconds the two meals had been shared out amongst the hungry locals and devoured.

The couple came back from the toilet hand in hand.

'Where's our food?' the man screamed at Colette.

'Easy come…easy go!!!' she answered.

'What was that?... Where's the Manager?' he said sternly. 'I want to see the Manager!'

Suzie Yoo appeared stern gun uncocked. 'Whatz problem?'

'Mr Chinese tea and Mrs Chop-sticks here, have a complaint.' Colette piped up walking away smirking.

'Someone's pinched our food,' he snapped.

'That's own fault… we don't except responsibility for stolen food. You shouldn't have left food alone.'

'We only went to the toilet. I am phoning the police,' the man replied.

'You should've taken food with you.' She pointed to a well lit sign on the wall that said, 'Watch out there's always a food thief about.'

'We want our money back, and we want it back right now.' The man raised his voice. 'I have never been to such a place in all my born days.'

'Ok you banned and your wife banned. Please get out now… get out now.' Suzy was having none of that sort of tone in her establishment.

He turned to his wife and told her to get her coat. Unfortunately, this was also a place where unguarded, and expensive coats, got shared out amongst the local community.

With that, an Alsatian jumped onto the table, and a small Chinese boy came running, and took two Polaroid photographs of the shell shocked pair to display on the wall of shame. The man and woman ran out screaming, with empty stomachs, but with a pocket full of unhappy memories about the meal they never had.

After a while, the mild disturbance settled down, and the young Elvis spent the next thirty minutes serenading a table of blind drunk women, who kept asking him to sing 'Green Door'.

'Happy New Year,' Suzie Yoo shouted out, as the clock struck midnight.

Then all the staff and customers, including Kinsey, joined hands and sang a verse of 'Auld Lang Syne.' Two boys by the door saw an opportunity to do a runner. But sadly for them, Suzie activated the trap door by the exit, and the two were sent down to the basement to meet the original Chinese owners, who spent all day in the dark peeling spuds, and were suitably armed with 15lb whacking woks.

Chapter 3

'Wake me up before it blow blows (again)'

The car alarm's pitiful screams for attention, that tried desperately to inform the world that something was seriously wrong, fell flatly onto 'the morning after the night before' deaf ears. Most of the people in the street were still in bed, and had automatically decided that there must be a wiring fault with the rusty piece of metal plonked outside, so ignored its demands. In fact, if the Ford Escort could have shouted out instead of just being programmed to make an annoying siren sound, it would have screamed out, 'Come quick. Some little fucker has just smashed my rear passenger side window, and at this moment is pinching my bloody expensive sound system.'

The car waited in anticipation for people to come running to save it from being man-handled. It was convinced, that at least its owner, who had not only bought the car and the sound system, but had also installed the alarm in the first place, would soon come into view. But as Luke Pozzoni snapped the last of the electrical cables from the dashboard, and pocketed the contents of the glove compartment before disappearing into the morning gloom, no one appeared, and the car was lost for words. Now it really wished that it could say its piece, and it would be loosely based around comments like 'What's the point?' 'Are you all happy now?' and some sentence ending in, 'You're just a bunch of wankers!'

Alex could hear a whining sound enter the far corners of his dream and quickly take over. The noise became so loud that it woke him up. He could only manage to prise open one of his eyes, which closed immediately, as if operated on a very tense spring mechanism. He was lying on his side facing the wall. He tried again to enter the land of nod, but something that he had just seen during his moment of enlightenment, disturbed him. He didn't remember having a giant poster on his bedroom wall of Limahl from Kadgagoogoo, with no top on, in a bathtub of champagne. He forced himself to open his one eyelid again to double check. Yes, it was definitely Limahl. He could tell by his skunk-like features. His eyeball moved without the support of the rest of his head, and sent even more confusing images back to his sensitive brain.

The pictures relayed back to his sleepy head from his second foray into the unknown, and reported back, that there was a bundle of women's dirty clothes sprawled all over the floor. On a dressing table, a million bottles of cheap perfume fought hand to hand combat, with an army of empty packets of Player No 6 cigarettes. A disused container of baby oil lay exhausted on its side, fast asleep.

'Where was he?' he asked himself, too afraid to turn around and make the answer to the question easier to get correct.

He could feel a presence next to him. He racked his brain for a clue.

'What day was it?'

'New Year's Day,' he told himself. 'Or Cherry-nose Day, as it was known around these parts.'

'What happened after the nightclub? Who did I go home with?'

Although his sub-conscious knew exactly what the answer was, it had decided to place its hands over it eyes and just giggled wickedly.

'Why don't you turn around and see for yourself?' he taunted himself again.

'Why was he so scared to face the music, was it really that bad a tune?' he searched around in his memory bank before he was faced with the inevitable.

'Think!... nightclub... big scrap... police... blood.... ambulances...nothing unusual there then,' he thought, and then added, 'Jac disappeared with some slut in a cat-suit. What happened next?' His hangover kicked in with a vengeance.

'On no!' he said out loud, as a face jumped in front of his minds-eye that would have sent a severe shockwave through the volcanic fault in San Francisco.

He recalled how Lois 'the Swallow', had smiled at him from across the bar, just after the police had taken Malcolm 'Knuckles' out with a tranquilliser bullet. Now Lois was not called 'the Swallow' because she liked to live in a nest and fly South for the winter. No, she was christened with the unprestigious title, due to her swift technique when emptying the seedy contents of young boy's fruit machines. She was renowned for always hitting the jackpot, and leaving the poor males with buckled knees and a row of cherries in their eyes.

By the bar that night, she was standing with artificial ringlets that appeared like snakes dancing out of her hair. He remembered turning his glance away, but her power of ultimate persuasion was too strong. He caught her advances full force in the back, which turned him instantly to stone as she welcomed him into her web.

'Not Lois, please God.' He felt like crying. 'Not the bald lady with the deep husky voice and nicotine arms?'

It wasn't the fact that Lois was completely smooth all over that frightened him so much. For as long as he could remember, she had always been hairless. Some sort of alopecia disease had sentenced the poor girl, to a lifetime

49

of looking like Uncle Fester with pencilled on eyebrows. It was the little matter of her craving for kinky sex that had seen off even the most sexually advanced males in the town that had worried him more.

She could clear a room faster than the cough and drop nurse, as she would normally enter in her thick, cheap, twelve carat gold necklaces, which she displayed around her shoulders. He had been told by the boys from the Labour club, that she wore one chain for every man, who had either given her a baby, or through whom she had to have a back street abortion. That night, under the plastic palm trees of Tiffany's nightclub, she looked like Mr T in a mini-skirt.

Suddenly, it all came flooding back to a petrified Alex, as he remembered her dragging him home to her flat, and then thankfully the rest was a blur.

She cuddled in next to him and farted on his leg. A tornado of gas nearly burnt a section of hair off his thigh, as the smell floated up and punched a hole in his senses. He felt like being sick

He could feel eyes staring at him from somewhere in the room. He looked at Limahl, who he was sure was having a little chuckle at his expense.

'Fuck off skunk face... you one hit wonder.' He gestured back towards the direction of the poster.

He slowly looked towards the door, and there, standing in a giant sized cot, were four kids in vests, who must have been between the ages of one to three. He couldn't help but notice, that they all had different coloured hair and skin complexions, even the set of two year old twins.

'Why me?' he asked himself. 'Why didn't I go home by myself?' He continued to lie on his side cursing his luck and his lack of self-discipline, especially after he had indulged in a couple of beers.

Then he heard it!

'Copy Mavis!.... Copy Mavis.'

Alex sharply moved his head, expecting to see a TV set blasting out in the corner, or one of the little brats playing with some new Japanese wonder toy. But he couldn't see either object that would have made those sorts of noises.

Then the words came again loud and clear. 'Copy Mavis... Copy... Come in you stupid, lazy bitch.'

'What the hell is going on?' Alex muttered, pulling back the bedcovers.

He found no radio hiding there either, just the nakedness of her body and a half empty jar of peanut butter. A flash of last nights sex session lit up his memory circuit, as he now realised what that nutty taste was on his lips, and why his eyebrows were rock hard.

'To be fair to her, she was built well,' he thought out loud. She had a fairly decent little chassis, even though she'd had numerous reckless owners and had run up lots of hard miles on the clock. Unfortunately with Lois, her facial exterior didn't match her bodywork. In fact, her face was like a retired cement-mixer that had been put out to stud after many Irish labourers had become sick to death of whacking it with a shovel.

'I said copy Mavis.... COPYYYY.'

'What do you want Fred?' someone called Mavis finally answered. 'Don't you realise that I'm having a slash!' the sound of water trickling filled the room, and played tricks with his mind.

'Can you do a pick-up from Swansea Road to Church Street in about fifteen minutes, my petal?'

'Of course I can.... Fred my dear.' She replied flushing the chain.

Alex put his ear to Lois's stomach. He shot back in amazement as he realised, that the conversation between Fred the taxi and his wife Mavis was coming out of Lois' belly, just above her fanny.

Nausea took control of what was left of his sanity. He felt like running, but his legs had turned to jelly. He felt like screaming, but his tongue had hidden away behind his tonsils and refused to come out.

'Oh no,' his mind raced. Not only had he found himself in bed with a woman with no hair. This woman was a baldy with a talking abdomen, who had a gaggle of kids who could put the children of the Damned to shame.

Was she an alien? He jumped up and searched for his trousers. He stared at the kids, who he now noticed, were covered in Impetigo and yesterday's Ready Brek.

'Should he take them with him?' he asked himself. 'But what if they too had talking belly buttons, perhaps they would burst into song like some mini council estate barber quartet as he wheeled them into the police station.'

In panic, he frantically searched in the morning light for his trousers. He eventually found them still standing up in the corner of the room, still in obvious shock, with his underpants perfectly positioned inside. An image of Lois tearing off his Chino's with one tug of her expert hands, mouth drooling for his meat, flashed into his scrambled mind. He pulled them on, buckled up the belt and looked around for his shirt. He spied it on the floor, next to a fresh dirty nappy. He raced towards it, heart beating uncontrollably. He placed his finger to his lips to indicate to the staring kid to keep quiet.

Suddenly he let out an almighty cry, after treading on something hairy on the floor.

'Uggggrh… What the fuck is that?' He pictured a rat with fangs tucking into his exposed feet.

He kicked out at the hairy monster, but stubbed his big toe on the side of the bed. Another cry escaped out of his lips, as he fell to the floor, wishing that it would open and swallow him up whole.

He could hear Lois stirring on the bed. He lay there motionless, waiting to hear the unwelcome strains of *'Fee Fi Fo Fum…. I smell the knob of a horny man'* departing from her possessed lips. Thankfully nothing came.

He tried to squeeze under the bed, and moved a cardboard box that was blocking his path. He recoiled back in horror on seeing a big black face staring back at him, it had thick lips and an afro hair-do. On second inspection, he noticed that the face was made of rubber, and it had a bicycle repair patch on its neck. He checked the box that he had moved aside. There in large letter across the front it stated:-

. *'Jungle Jim...The best and most real inflatable man that money can buy. Twelve inches of pure black circumcised stallion pleasure'*

'Bloody hell…. I've just been to bed with an hairless alien, who's two timing me with a rubber Kunta Kinteh.' Alex would have laughed if it wasn't for the fact that this was a serious matter, and that he was in grave danger.

He turned and started to crawl across the floor. He bumped into a graveyard of discarded underpants, which seemed to have all but given up hope, of ever meeting up with their once proud owners, ever again. Alex could envisage boys physically shaking, as they ran for their lives out of that bedroom of darkness, bruised, speechless, and pants-less. Or perhaps he was wrong. Maybe Lois was some kind of underpants washing line thief. Perhaps after dark, she would sneak around backyards, nicking teenagers briefs. He really didn't think so, because most of these pants were not even clean.

He knew that most boys normally kept their best pair of briefs for the weekends, just in case of the chance of an unexpected ride. There was nothing worse than a girl going down on a boy, only to be faced with a pair of grotesque coloured underpants. So, some of these undees that were imprisoned in Lois' treasure chest, were of the highest quality cloth. He was just thinking of rifling a couple of pairs, especially the black 'Y' fronts with the Pope's head on the front, when he heard the sound he had been most dreading.

'Hey you….. what's all that noise?' she grunted.

'There's a rat the size of a cat running around the floor,' Alex said rising up on his knees from the carpet.

'That's not a rat, that's only my wig darling,' A bald Lois said casually, then broke wind again.

She reached down and repositioned the artificial head of goats hair to her head, then added 'And where the hell are you going? You still owe me an orgasm if you remember. I swallowed hard for you last night. My jaw is still aching.' She dribbled spit down her chin to emphasise the point, and to live up to her nickname.

'You're possessed... you're evil.' He stood up. 'Strange voices... stomach.... Fred... Mavis... what the hell is going on?' he spurted out the words, pointing to her lower regions.

'Oh that.' She answered so matter of fact, while grabbing his hand and leading him back to bed. 'That's just my coil, darling. It always picks up CB's or radio airwaves. Luke Pozzoni sometimes uses me to pick up police signals when he's doing a big job. It's a strange occupation, but it pays very well.'

She then told the kids to go and have some corn flakes; she threw Alex on the bed, spread the rest of the peanut butter on her undercarriage and squatted on his face. As he struggled to catch his breath, he could just make out the traffic report on the Simon Bates show, leaking out of her mid-rift.

At approximately the same time that Alex was being forced to survive by breathing out of his ears, Steve 'Lusty' James was ambling down the steps of the plane, and touching down onto British soil for the first time in nearly two years.

The extremely good looking boy in the ripped jeans and Levi jacket, had been bumming around the island of Ibiza, feasting on a diet of relaxation and casual sex. This 'no strings attached' way of life had suited Lusty down to the ground. He had never been one to conform to normality. Since leaving school, he had never owned a pair of socks or an alarm clock. He never cared much about personal possessions or how much money he had in the bank. His unwritten motto was, 'Life is for living … but slowly'.

'I'm positive that he's that pop star,' a woman mentioned to a friend as he walked past.

'Which one?' her friend quipped, her eyes already on springs at the sight of his firm buttocks and strong thighs.

'One of them out of that group Wham …. I think.'

'Andrew Rigby.'

'No. He's the bloke with the huge conk. The other one. His father works in a kebab shop, or an Indian takeaway, or something to do with food. Remember he wrote and sang that great love song. Ahhhh… what was it now? I remember…. Whispering Grass or something.'

Lusty let out an internal smile on hearing the brief extracts from the ladies' conversation, and sauntered out through the Nothing-to-Declare section. He tried to imagine how George Michael would look, performing in front of thousands at Wembley stadium dressed in Lofty's baggy shorts and pith helmet.

He mingled into the busy hustle and bustle of airport life.

Deep down inside, he was glad to be going home. He really missed his mates, Jac, Alex and Kinsey. He hadn't seen them since the day he went on his travels. He had fully intended to keep in touch by postcards, but he never got round to it. He wondered if they were still as mad as ever.

First up, he missed the way that Jac would always be the life and soul of any party. Always up for a laugh. Always looking to carry out a little piece of mischief, with a mind as overactive, as a naughty schoolboy let loose in a girls dormitory with a sack full of mice and spiders. He wondered if he had found a cure for his strange affliction by now.

Now Billy '2 amp' Kinsey was a different ball game altogether. There were times when Lusty had sat, watching the erratic Spanish families argue about every single issue under the sun, from the state of the nation, to why bread tasted better from the north? These bouts of family feuding reminded him of Kinsey, and his no-nonsense approach to situations. Now there was one person who had mastered the art of internal combustion from the inside out. Lusty loved to watch Billy's anger thermometer climb way above boiling point and then explode. He couldn't wait to get back, just to wind him up and let him go.

On the other side of the scale was probably, his best mate in the entire world, Alex. Alex was the calculated one. Always with a plan hatching in his mind. Always looking to go forward, even if the only way to do that was to go back. He trusted Alex with his life. He trusted Alex with his mother's life. He wished he had trusted Alex with his late father's life, and then perhaps his late dad wouldn't have drunk himself to an early grave. Alex could have been his family's guardian angel.

He couldn't wait to see their faces when he walked back into their life. He couldn't wait to go home and get smashed and spend the night reminiscing. When he had first arrived in Ibiza town, it had been a once in a lifetime experience. There were lots of crazy things always going on. From the all night parties, fuelled by all night drugs, to the lady boys, parading down the narrow streets with their womanly legs, and blowing provocatively on attention seeking whistles.

But his hometown on the weekends was like no show on earth. It was a mixture of Macey's parade with more than a sprinkle of the Wild Bunch. On every corner, someone would be standing up and yelling at the world to 'Walk this Way.' It was packed to the brim with tramps, clowns and bottles, full of no-bodies (all trying to be some-bodies). It was a perfect mix of madness and mayhem.

He had genuinely missed the way that people loved and hated each other in the same breath. The way that pain and the constant rain was a way of life that most people just accepted. He couldn't wait, to walk between the buildings that hid many secrets of bizarre events, that had been past down by word of mouth through the years.

Lusty had reached his decision to go home during a midnight BBQ underneath the stars on some golden sandy beach. He realised that life for him revolved around his old town, and if he wasn't careful, it maybe moving too fast for him to ever jump back on.

He also needed to go back and be strong for his mother. He had become tired of doing it in his early teens, when his old man had sadly left them. At that time he needed, and wanted, a break to go and find himself. Now his batteries were fully recharged, and his experience meter had been more than satisfied, it was time to go back and become the man of the household once again.

And there was another reason for Lusty deciding to leave the sunshine and head back into the driving rain. He had been given a Spanish Warning, which was a lot like a Gypsy Warning but in a different language, involving bigger meat cleavers. It all started when Miguel Fernando the shop keeper, and his three sons, took exception to Lusty's passionate fling with Miguel's only daughter, Francesca.

Now Lusty had never been the type to fall head over heels for anyone. Over the years, he had experienced a couple of missed heart beats, but never really felt that full force smack in the face, that only the clenched fist of love could provide. That all changed, when he visited the Fernando family shop to get some supplies for an afternoon on the beach. There, on the cheese counter, was the angel of his dreams. This was a new experience for him. He was normally the dashing prince on a white charger, sent to rescue the damsel in distress with a passionate kiss. He became tongue-tied, and started to sweat. He ordered 10lbs of extra mature cheese, it was so strong it nearly burnt a hole through the top of his mouth, and had the rest of the apartment block up in arms about the smell. He went back each day and spent all his money on blocks of the strong yellow stuff!

Then one day, while he was on another cheese pilgrimage, she actually asked him for a date. She fancied the well-built tanned boy, although she was a bit disturbed by the amounts of cheese he consumed daily.

They started to meet regularly, to the obvious disappointment of her family. Then one night, her father and her brothers came-a-visiting on his door, without an invite, and they didn't even bother to wipe their boots on the welcome mat. At first they talked at him. Then they all swore at him, cursed, and finally threatened him.

Lusty eventually saw sense, and agreed to stop seeing Francesca, after realising, how fast blood flowed into the brain whilst upside down dangling over a barrel of boiling chip fat.

When the little facade was over, and Lusty had been forced to sign a 'leaving on a jet plane' agreement, the men of the family, including Lusty, sat down for some sardines and red wine. Francesca's father later told Lusty that it was nothing personal, and the boy seemed a decent enough chap, who perhaps needed to watch his cholesterol levels with the amounts of dairy products that he ate daily, but tradition was tradition in this part of Spain. This meant that Francesca was going to marry an upstanding, and noble Spaniard, who would probably get her up the duff with four babies in four years, while still demanding that he was watered and fed, and insisting on going out every night to try to pick up English girls. It was a strange and ironic world at times.

Lusty checked his pockets as he departed from the terminal building at Gatwick. Unfortunately the cupboard was bare, except for a large packet of extra strength Gorgonzola that he had purchased for old time's sake, from the first love of his life. He pulled his rucksack onto his broad shoulders, dropped the cheese into a rubbish bin, and headed to the nearest roundabout, to thumb his way back home.

Chapter 4

'*A Pub called Malice*

There were two posters displayed in the pub window on that New Year's Day morning. The smaller, more official document, was asking anyone for information regarding the whereabouts of a TV detector officer, who had apparently been missing since Christmas Eve. Of course, there were no photographs of the missing person on the poster, because the identity of TV detector men, just like FBI agents, DHSS fraud officers, and Chemistry teachers, were shrouded in secrecy.

The other notice, which was hand-written, and took centre stage in the frosted glass window, simply told the many passers-by, that New Years Day was 'Family Fun Day' at the Buffaloes Arms pub.

Percy Norman stared at the sign with envy and longing in his eyes, just before his dominant wife pulled him away from the door by the ear, and shouted loudly so everyone could hear 'Come on lazy bones… you haven't finished hoovering the upstairs yet.'

Percy picked up the shopping bags, and with shoulders stooped, trundled after his wife

The second sign, (although written in pigeon English and littered with spelling mistakes), was adequate in its design. It was the actual content on the ten by ten laminated card that was questionable. There was no doubt that the majority of activities which took place on that afternoon in the grubby public house were very funny. The 'Over 60's, nude space hopper race', and 'Throwing Alan the Midget through a car tyre competition', were just the warm up act for the main events, which concluded with Old Cherry-nose and his magic stunt. The contentious bit of the poster was the word 'Family.' If taken to court, the pub would have been found to be in serious breach of advertising standards, because no wives or children, had ever been allowed to attend Family Fun Day. It was against the rules, and alien to the deranged moral code of the public house.

Family Fun Day, was strictly for the regulars who had spent all of their drinking time, and most of their dole money in the establishment, over the previous year.

But all in all, it was a glorious watering hole. Famous throughout the land for housing more criminals and robbers on a Monday afternoon than either Alcatraz, or Strangeways had ever locked away in their cells in their heyday. It was an exciting but scary place, where boys and men would often get beaten into submission by a well-directed comment from an old timer, or by the vicious hand that swung a revenging baseball bat. Both punishments were dished out in equal measures on a weekly basis.

Jac and Kinsey were lucky enough to grab a couple of seats in the far corner by the bar. It was only 10.30am, but already the pub was bursting at the seams. Pints of Snakebite, a lethal concoction of Stella lager and rough house cider, were displayed along the wooden bar.

Lined up by the toilets, was a queue of men. Luke Pozzoni stood blocking their path and handing out tickets, before the men were allowed inside. The reason for this was, that the toilets were being used as a fitting room for people, trying on the selection of stolen suits that Luke had acquired during the Boxing Day sales. The cheeky designer thief even had swipe tags fitted to his hot property.

'You can't trust anyone. They'll pinch the teeth out of your head,' he often told his nephew, who was actually serving a four year modern apprenticeship, in the Art of Pick Pocketing and majoring in Criminal Law.

Most of the toilet cubicles were fitted with mirrors, so that the customers could examine the fit of the cloth before they haggled with the light-fingered boy. He was even known to take a rack of suits back to Burtons, and exchange them for a bigger size or a different colour. If cheek was measured in inches, Luke would have been a giant amongst dwarfs.

But, to be fair to the council estate thief, he possessed a generous streak, that even Robin Hood would have been embarrassed about. It was allegedly rumoured that he had been solely responsible, for hand pinching, the entire wedding wardrobe for Benny Jones and his new wife Davina. The haul included, seven pageboy outfits, a ten tier wedding cake, and a new walker for the expected baby. He charged next to nothing for the stash.

Grown men openly shed a tear, the afternoon, that Davina appeared like a virginal angel from the men's toilets, in her hand-stitched white gown, with a twenty eight foot trailing veil, while Ronny Mouth-organ slowly followed behind, playing the wedding march on his tuneful organ

It was a place, where anything was available at a price, and nothing was impossible to get. Thursdays were especially busy, and were known as 'Black Market Thursdays.' The pool table at the back of the pub was moved aside, and replaced by a temporary paddock for livestock. Rustled sheep, goats, and even the odd-looking cow were paraded around, before being sold and slaughtered out in the beer garden. Poached fish and skinned rabbits hung gutted, on hooks dripping fresh blood into the men's urinals. It was definitely not a safe place to be a vegetarian, (or a sheep, cow, goat, fish, rabbit or detective). There were strong rumours, that two undercover policemen had been buried in the beer garden after the Merthyr riots of '76.

Van loads of stolen televisions and video recorders were raffled off to the old age. Drugs were shipped in under the cover of darkness from the four corners of the globe. The best grass from Africa. High quality uncut speed from Colombia. The biggest magic mushrooms from Charlie Walter's farm. Uppers and downers were dished out like Tic Tacs, and to cope with their mind-blowing effects, a chill out room was set up in the beer cellar. People, high on the happy side, ventured in, and didn't come out for several days. Apparently, it was like visiting the Psychiatric ward in the film 'One flew over the Cuckoo's nest.' There was even talk of a seven foot Indian that no one saw, but who apparently would sweep up and practice throwing cabbages into a basketball hoop, by the old worn out dart board.

Jac and Kinsey were halfway through their second snakebite when Alex joined them, wearing a suspicious looking black polo-neck jumper.

'Ended up with Lois then did you?' Jac said grinning from cheek to cheek. 'I could see her reeling you in.' He made fisherman actions towards his mate.

'No,' Alex replied quickly. Perhaps a little too quickly for his reply to sound convincing. 'Why do you say that?' He looked nervous.

'I just thought that the polo neck was hiding Lois' famous lovebite trade mark. A red ring of hickies that are always in the shape of a heart.' said Jac still sure that he was on the right track.

Alex had a growing suspicion that he had been rumbled, and then sheepishly replied, 'Ok I did sleep with Lois!' at the same time flashing the red marks that circled his raw looking skin.

'Correction Alex,' Kinsey was more than happy to jump in. 'No one ever sleeps with the bald vampire. One fucks all night with Lois until one's knob drops off.'

At this point, they all laughed and each of them thought back to their first time with the sex crazed fiend, who would go drifting into some sort of orgasmic trance, while riding them with all her might.

'She should come with a serious health warning attached,' he commented to his mates, after turning around and seeing at least another half dozen males with polo neck jumpers and a nervous look in their eye. Alex wondered if they were nervous because their mates might catch them out, or for the safety of their favourite underpants. He noticed one poor man with lumps of peanut butter encrusted in his beard.

He then remembered the rubber doll under the bed, and only then realised what had probably caused it to have a bike repair patch on its neck. 'Even the great Jungle Jim couldn't escape the clutches of the Swallow,' he joked to himself, and imagined her puncturing the blow-up Zulu while sucking his neck, sending him flying around the room like a burst balloon in a kids party.

His thought pattern was disturbed when the landlady informed the masses that the buffet was now open. But this was no ordinary running buffet. This was a feast, that would sit quite comfortably on an inflatable bean-bag, in any hippy tent, at Knebworth, or the Reading festival. There were plates of space cakes, mushroom cookies, Acid covered ice gems, paracetamol and pineapples on a stick. Of course there were some nibbles as well, like bowls of Hula Hoops, Bazooka chewing gums, traffic light lollipops, large Brazil nuts, and a year's supply of Rennies.

The boys tucked into a £10 sherbet speed dip, with three liquorice tube straws to feed their need.

'So what did you get up to last night anyway…. smart arse?' Alex directed his question at Jac.

'Don't ask,' he said, but added 'That piece in the cat suit took me for a ride in her car. I didn't realise that she was married, so we ended up in the lane by the golf club.' Jac dipped his black tube into the white powder.

'When we parked up, she told me to strip off completely, and she jumped on me in the passenger seat. Her husband must have a real small dick, because she howled like a banshee when I entered her. Anyway, when we were done, she said she needed to go pee.'

Kinsey interrupted 'Go pee?... no one talks like that.'

'Look, her words not mine. So, she goes for a slash and I'm there, bollocks naked in the passenger's seat trying to get some wind in it for round two.' Jac shakes his head before continuing. 'Then there was a tap on the window, and when I wound it down, there were two coppers shining a fucking torch the size of Porthcawl lighthouse in my eyes. They ask me what the hell I'm doing sitting in a car by myself, naked, overlooking a field full of sheep, playing with my old boy.'

'What happened?' Alex laughed realising by his friends expression that it wasn't a word of a lie.

'They were two right pig twats. I could tell they were really taking the piss by the way they joked about everything. I told them that my girlfriend was in the bushes. They shone the torch and shouted out. But the stupid married bitch didn't answer. She must have panicked, and I could hear her trying to climb over the cemetery wall.'

He continued his fable. 'She kept quiet. I'm freezing my nuts off, and these two blockheads are really playing the role of PC fucking Plod. One of them pretended to radio in to the station, to tell them that they had caught the hillside sheep shagger, and that my little dick fitted the artist's description of the perpetrator.'

Now it was his mates turn to giggle.

'I knew you lot would find it funny. It was bloody cold, alright.' He muttered and went back to the story. 'Suddenly, there was an almighty scream as she fell backwards off the wall and landed in some stingy nettles. The two coppers went running to help, so I put my clothes on and legged it home.'

'Have you spoken to her since?' said Kinsey smirking.

'Nope. Last I saw of her she was in the back of the police car covered in a very large doc leaf!'

The compare for the day tapped on the microphone and announced, the penultimate event before the main attraction. This activity was not to every taste, but it accounted for a hell of a lot of money changing hands during the day.

The 'Chamber Pot Donkey Derby', had started after someone had rolled a fresh turd underneath a cubicle in the men's toilet, when it was being used by someone trying on a stolen designer three-toned shell suit. To the immense pleasure of the regulars, the person on the receiving end of the sick joke, ran straight through the door and vomited all over the floor. Now from that day on, the regulars would roll logs in like hand grenades on unexpected users. To commemorate this sick and childish event, a turd race was arranged every New Year's Day. The winner for the last three contests, was a big man known as Big Ken, who was an immaculately dressed ex-teddy boy in a previous life.

For today's competition, two similar thirty-five metre tracks, were erected out of down pipe that snaked its way throughout the bar, and finished by the space invader machines. For genuine effect, they were filled up to the top with piss and fag nips. Big Ken was really in for a tough challenge today, because his opponent was no other than Tony, a 26 stone burger van owner, who was coming with a perfect played 24, won 24 record. He had one 'brown mark' to his name, when he was disqualified from the regional finals, after it was discovered that he had ball bearings strategically placed in his mix.

Tony entered the pub with his faeces, which was the size of a large chicken tikka baguette, transported in a shopping trolley. He was eagerly followed, by his large posse of hangers-on, with 'Tony the Turd King' tee-shirts on. Alex was amazed to see the lengths that people would go to win this coveted trophy. He saw that Tony's prize offering had the corners chamfered off it, for a more aerodynamic effect, and had been sprayed with some kind of lacquer.

'That will take some beating,' Jac said to Kinsey, as they watched four men pick it carefully out of the mesh trolley and place it on the start line.

'Bet Big Ken will win,' said Kinsey 'I heard that the rats use his logs as small bridges, or scoop them out to use as eight man-rat canoes and go white water rafting down the Taff.'

'Who the fuck told you that nonsense?' asked Jac.

'The boys from the Labour club.'

But unknown to everyone, Big Ken knew he was in for a tough race, and had prepared for his greatest battle well. He had been on a strict diet of high protein for three weeks, and had stored the four day old log in the freezer. That was an old conker trick that he had developed as a boy. He entered Buffaloes to a great ovation, dressed in a glittering costume, with his prize in a large action man box.

The race commenced with a shot from a pellet gun. It was neck and neck for the opening fifteen feet. The smell didn't prevent the flood of great excitement in the now packed arena. Unfortunately for Tony, he hadn't compensated for the sharp bend in the track by the bandit, and his pride and joy, which he had only been able to deliver with the aid of gas, oxygen, and a midwife, got stuck. Big Ken's smaller, and more compact jobby, cruised in over the last eight feet and passed the chequered toilet paper at the finish line.

Big Ken completed his customary lap of honour carrying the trophy, and did his usual joke of pretending to throw the turd into the crowd. He then went home, but not before he dropped it in the river for the rats to play with.

After the excitement had subsided, Jac went to the bar to collect his winnings. Alex looked across at the gambling tables in the opposite corner. Every table was fully occupied. He noticed that, (for whatever reason), all the card players on the 'Very serious, lots at stake, don't play unless you can pay' poker table, were made up, of a collection of men in very dirty builder's clothes, or were coal delivery merchants with black soot faces. He wondered if people needed to dress in stinking gear to gain access to take part in the proceedings. His question was answered, when he observed a man in a smart suit and a duffel bag, go into the toilets, reappear dressed as Ben Gun off Treasure Island, and immediately be given a seat on the £200 a hand crib game.

Jac came back carrying three pints of something that was green and red and plonked them on the table. Just before he could explain, Lusty, who had entered the bar, put his hands over his eyes and said messing about, 'I've got you now boy'

Jac hesitated, and before he looked around, nervously protested 'Look small dick, she asked me to take her home, and I couldn't help that she fell in the stingys.'

Everyone except Jac and Lusty burst out laughing.

'Lusty... fucking hell... Lusty... it's Lusty.' Kinsey screamed out, informally informing most of the pub, that the last member of their gang was back amongst them.

'How's it going sexy?' Alex asked a little calmer than his other electrically charged friend. 'Welcome home.'

Several people looked up from the gambling tables to see what all the commotion was all about. Lusty had this effect when he entered a room. He sizzled like a well cooked steak on a hot plate. Even the pack of Lesbos looked across admiring the tanned stranger, but were all knocked back into shape with one clout of the 15" dildo that was swung around by Hairy Mary.

The compare for the day interrupted the various conversations, again, to declare that it was time for the main event.

'Cherry-nose is still not doing his prediction bit... is he?' Lusty asked, while savouring the taste of his pint.

'Yes... and there's not long to go!' replied Kinsey sharpening his pencil with a glint in his eye.

Now, 'Arthur Cherry-nose's Prediction Special', was one of the reasons why New Year's Day was so popular at Buffaloes. It had all started four years ago to the day, when one of the contestants in the final of the 'Prettiest Horse' competition kicked out wildly, after somebody kept smoothing the horse's back legs, which were covered in black seamless stockings. The farmer responsible for dressing up the animal, had been desperate to get some silver wear on his mantle-piece.

Unfortunately, at the time that Slaughterhouse Bill's hooves shot back, they connected firmly with Arthur Cherry-nose, who was balancing on his cane waiting to get served by the bar. The impact, sent poor Arthur sailing through the pub window, where he landed unconscious in the High Street. There was an unusual stunned silence, as the regulars dragged the man back into the pub and laid him out on the pool table. It was approximately ten minutes later when Arthur regained whatever senses he had in the first place. He shook his head, and finally said that he knew the correct eight score draws for Saturday's football pools. He then blurted out eight random numbers.

Of course, no one took him serious. No one took Arthur serious, even when he told everyone that he had something extremely serious to tell everyone. And since a horse that was suffering from hay fever had just booted the little man out of a pane glass window, it was a wonder that anyone took time out to listen to him at all. It wasn't Arthur's fault. It wasn't the pub folk's fault. It was just that sometimes, there are people in the world, who can't get away with telling anyone anything serious. Arthur fell savagely into that category. So, when the eight numbers escaped out of his mouth and floated around the room for anybody to catch, they were largely ignored, except for John McReady, a very sharp cookie, who happily wrote them down and stored them up in his calculated brain.

The following Saturday, as if by magic, the eight score draws came up. The entire pub watched in amazement as John, 'razor sharp cookie' McReady, jumped up and danced around, flicking the V-signs to everyone, and telling them how his luck had changed. He rushed off to phone Littlewoods and plan his new life after becoming an instant millionaire. Everyone, including Arthur, (who had forgotten the numbers), cursed their luck and stupidity on having no faith in fate.

They had an emergency meeting the following week after watching John, 'McLucky-Rich Bastard', move out of the cold town and not even leave a tenner for a drink for the boys. In that meeting, they came to the conclusion, that Arthur was either a 'Little Diamond' who could help them all solve their financial difficulties, or, he was a 'Demon Witch' who needed to be destroyed. After they were stopped by the police from burning him at the stake in a bonfire of car tyres, they finally decided to see if they could set up the same scenario the coming year.

Cherry-nose was wrapped up in cotton wool until New Year's Day in 1984. The scene was set, and the same hand groped the same horse's leg, which kicked out, and for the second time, sent Arthur and his new cane, (which the regulars had bought for him for luck), flying to a tarmac bed. To be fair, they had allowed him to have a crash helmet on, and a cushion for support. A pin could be heard dropping from across the street, as they crowded around the man flat out on the table. It took fifteen minutes this time for him to come around, then, as he sprang to his feet, he announced:-

'Blue Murder will win this afternoon's three thirty at Chepstow.' There was a mad dash for the betting office, as runners sprinted to get a bet on the 28/1 outsider.

But Arthur had another tip to share with them. 'And ten minutes after the race, everyone in the pub will lose their voice for four hours.'

'What the fuck is the mad Demon Witch on about? I wish we had burned the big nosed idiot last year,' everyone thought and carried on placing bets on the horse.

The race was delayed for several minutes, which seemed like a lifetime to the masses that had crowded around the small TV screen. Even the dirty clothed card players stopped. When the commentator finally stated that the winner by a whisker was the rank outsider Blue Murder, the cheers dislodged several tiles off the roof of the old building.

They were all rich. Ok, not rich beyond their wildest dreams. Not even rich beyond the end of the week, but the money felt good as it bungled out of their normally empty pockets. Men were dancing with each other. Arthur was placed on a chair on top of the pool table and saluted by the jubilant men.

Suddenly, a large figure blocked the doorway, swaying from too much alcohol. One by one they saw him. One by one they could tell by his eyes that something was up. Malcolm Knuckles slammed the door closed and bolted it shut from the inside.

'Alright Mal... everything Ok?' the owner said, but deep down dreading what the reply was going to be.

'No, everything is not OK.' He placed his massive hands over the door frame. 'Someone, has nicked my wallet... and no one, is leaving until I find it.'

The room went silent for the second time that day. No one looked up. They all felt guilty even though they all knew that they hadn't seen the wallet, and if they had accidentally come across the old brown leather purse with the initials MKM in large red letters, they would have left well alone.

Malcolm stared at each and every one of them in turn. They all died inside for a split second, as his eyes pierced their skin, and ripped at their souls. Then the doubt started to creep in.

Little devils appeared on all of their shoulders and whispered in their ears. 'You have seen it. You picked it up. It's in your pocket, remember? and the psychopath with hands made of granite is going to punish you, badly.'

The phone rang, which made the entire room jump as if a balloon had been burst in Sunday mass.

Malcolm told the man by the door to empty his pockets. They all watched in terror as the shaking man placed his car keys, a spinhaler, and some money, onto the beer stained table. Malcolm growled, and told the next in line to do the same. This continued right around the room. The phone continued to ring and ring. Disappointed about not finding his belongings, he made them all strip off to their underpants, again, one by one. This still didn't uncover the lost property, which made Malcolm more inconsolable. He stood in front of the pub, clenched his massive muscles, and growled loudly. He closed his eyes deep in thought. No one said a word. Alex was amazed to see the collection of items that sat piled on the tables. There were Stanley knives, small wraps of white powder, and one old man had produced a dead mouse in a matchbox coffin from deep in his pockets.

Four hours later, the big man still with his eyes shut, guarded the door. No one had said a word for all that time. Arthur Cherry-nose smiled to himself. Kinsey, who was feeling brave, if also a little foolish, decided to answer the phone before it drove them all insane. It was like the Japanese water torture, but without the water, and minus the slanty eyed Japs. He picked up the receiver and the guy on the other end said 'Hello, about bloody time. Is that Buffaloes?' The brave muted Kinsey nodded, which was of course no use to the man on the other end, but the man continued anyway. 'Can you do us a favour?' the mystery voice added, 'If you see Malcolm Knuckles, can you tell him that we found his wallet behind one of the chairs. It must have fallen out of his pocket when he had the Cockle-man in a half-nelson stranglehold. I wouldn't wanna bump into the big beast if he's looking for it.' He put the phone down.

Kinsey coughed lightly before telling Malcolm, that his belongings had been found in the Kings.

Malcolm didn't apologise, he didn't really know how to. He just turned around and stormed out of the door.

A minute after the silent siege had ended, two language students from Italy, in search of some refreshments, walked into the bar. They ordered two diet cokes, and turned around to be greeted by a room full of semi-naked beer bellied men all in white ankle socks and even whiter faces. Some of the captives who were of a more nervous disposition, queued up to see what damage the last four hours had caused on their underpants.

The year after that, Arthur dislodged his shoulder blade for the cause, but had won everyone a stack of money, when he informed them of the winner of the Eurovision song contest, and the exact day that the dog off Blue Peter would get mysteriously poisoned.

Everyone was hoping, that this year was going to be a extra bumper prediction year. Lusty joined his mates, just as Arthur entered the room through a screen of artificial smoke accompanied by the deafening strains of, 'The Eye of the Tiger.' He was met by an avalanche of cheering, as people dripped from every convenient position to see the great magic man. They stood on the bar, hung from the light shades, and chanted his name. 'Arthur..... Arthur.... Arthur.'

Some youth who didn't know the importance of the event, shouted out 'Cherry-nose.... Cherry-nose.'

He was pulled sharply to one side and told that today, (of all days), Arthur Cherry-nose, would only be referred to, as 'Arthur or The Holy One.' The youth sat down obviously very upset, and supped his beer dejectedly.

The event had become so well known amongst the community, that the local radio station broadcasted every second of the activity into thousands of households in the town. Phil Haddock, a cheesy bit actor who nearly had a famous walk on part in Crossroads, had been asked to present the running commentary on the proceedings. Even Ladbrokes were represented, and had set up betting booths at the end of the bar for the avalanche of calls that were going to come. Homing pigeons were lined up on the back fence to deliver titbits of information quickly across town, and a Morse code machine stood revving its engines in the corner.

Outside the pub, loud speakers had been erected on the walls to inform the gathering excitable crowd of all the action. The police had good control and had cordoned off a section in front of the window where Arthur normally landed. As usual at these events, the obligatory token street protestor in a body placard, with the words 'The end of the world is nigh,' was roaming around with a megaphone, telling everyone that it was morally wrong to use horses and old drunken idiots in this way. Luckily, nobody took any notice: They either prayed to their gods, or clutched rabbit's feet for luck, for King Arthur to come up with the goods that would change their lives forever.

They were even taking bets on what would be Arthur's first words when he woke up?

'Fuck me.... where am I?', or, 'I need a double Whiskey and quick', were the two favourites at odds of 3/1.

Everyone was in position, and everything was ready to go. Slaughterhouse Bill was again dressed up in the farmers wife stockings and a Rah-rah skirt, while Arthur made a quick sign of the cross behind the animal, holding tightly onto his cane. On a communal countdown from ten, the horse's legs were fondled until he kicked out in anger. Slaughterhouse Bill didn't hold back, and he connected full on with Arthur's chest sending him sailing through the smokey atmosphere, with the grace of a blind drunken giraffe on a water trampoline. He bounced onto the tarmac, out cold, legs twitching.

The crowd again cheered, until the master of ceremonies hushed them all down with two bangs of his baton. The only sounds that could be heard, were the distant noise of a cabbage being thrown through a hoop in the cellar, by the seven foot Indian, (who no one could see), and who didn't believe in gambling, and the monotonous voice of Phil Haddock, who set about describing every little detail of what was happening in his very own, adjectively full, colourful way.

'Arthur is being placed gently onto the illuminated green pool table,' he said, with all the feeling of a Sir John Gielgud. 'I can hear hearts beating, I can see fingers crossed. The tension is climbing the walls. Come on Arthur, wake up... wake from your future forming sleep, and tell the world what the future holds.'

Thirty anguishing minutes later, and still there was no movement or sign of life. Many thought that perhaps it had been one kick too many for the old man.

'This doesn't look good everyone,' Phil informed the worried crowd. 'He hasn't moved a muscle. I should know, I once played the main role in a fabulous production about a dead pit pony. I was amazing. I didn't move or say anything for three hours. I should have been nominated... you know!' Phil had drifted off somewhere off the coast of, 'I should have been a star' island.

Then suddenly Arthur's little finger moved. Phil was back on dry land in an instant, and informed the worried crowd in a low throaty voice that there were signs of life.

'Ahhhh... Oooohh,' came back the reply from nervous lips.

Arthur rose upright. A resurrected Frankenstein in a dented crash helmet. A thousand eyes and hearts held their breath, willing him on. Waiting, for him to utter his first words.

'Is my beak still huge?' Arthur said feeling his fruit shaped conk.

'Yes…. come to daddy,' cried Jac, who had been the only one to put £10 at odds of 25/1 on Arthur muttering those immortal words.

'How the fucking hell did you know he was going to come out with that??' Kinsey looked bemused. Jac shrugged his shoulders.

'We should have the fucking horse kick you out of the fucking window next year.' The jealousy came flooding out of Billy's mouth.

'Quiet down by the bar please,' Phil asked and then pushed the microphone up close to Arthur's face.

'Give him some air folks,' the actor pleaded, he then continued. 'Arthur, can you tell me and the millions that are waiting with bated breath by old transistor radios, drinking warm…. '

'Get on with it you ponced up old tart,' came a voice from the back of the room.

'Sorry Arthur… the world is full of amateurs. What did you see old chap? What did you see?'

Arthur motioned for his usual double whiskey, which he downed in one without it touching the sides.

'Are you ready,' he asked, just as the horse started to sneeze uncontrollably.

'Lock that stupid animal in the cellar,' the landlady instructed the bar man. There was a short delay.

'Ok…firstly…I predict that Ipswich will beat Liverpool at Anfield today…... by seven goals to one.'

'Ooohhhh, that's a bold call,' Alex whispered to Lusty. 'Liverpool haven't lost a game all season, and Ipswich haven't scored a single goal.'

'Arthur are you sure?' Haddock asked the question that everyone was thinking.

'Positive, and their centre-forward will bag five of the goals.' Arthur's response caused a hive of activity, pigeons flew up in the air, phones lines were red hot, and six year olds were despatched on push bikes to place bets on the unlikely scoreline.

Phil was back in with the microphone. 'Is there more, Arthur old boy? Is there more?'

'Yes, by nine tomorrow morning, twelve inches of snow will have fallen across the land.' He motioned his glass for another top up.

Again there was a massive groan, because the last couple of days had been wet and windy, with the weather men predicting that it was to continue well into the New Year.

'How can you be so sure it was exactly twelve inches Arthur? That's a lot of snow.'

Arthur took the microphone off the actor, and slowly told them that he had seen the mountains, and the streets covered in a thick white blanket, and Alan the Midget was wading through it up to his waist.

'Then you must be right.' Phil looked shocked. 'If it's up to Alan the Midget's waist, then it is exactly twelve inches.'

'It's twelve and a half inches if you must know… you bunch of tall cunts,' Alan the Midget, who had clambered up onto the bar, shouted at the top of his voice, just before the landlady sent the deranged dwarf abseiling back into the crowd without mercy, by whacking him with half a pool cue.

Again there was a second wave of betting, as six year old soldiers were sent out amongst the afternoon skies with all the precision of an artillery division.

'Thank you Arthur dear man,' Phil announced, 'Lets give our hero a big round of applause, and fill his glass with his favourite tipple all afternoon. He's again done us all proud, and hopefully, put a couple of shillings in our impoverished pockets. Three cheers …. hip hip'

But, before the actor could finish his speech, Arthur had some more news to add. 'There's one last thing that I saw.' His voice was shaking enough for everyone to feel the shivers. No one dared to utter a sound, as they all breathed in trying to pull the words out of his mouth.

'He's got another,' Jac said.

'He's never had three before,' Alex stuttered.

'And... and... where do I start?' Arthur searched for the right words. There was a look of genuine fear in his eyes, and his voice dropped a couple of notches. 'And the world will end in five days!'

There were one or two gasps, but mainly this potentially devastating piece of news was greeted with shocked silence.

'What did he say?.... the girls will bend over and play!' muttered Jac.

'The world's going to end in five days... you fucking deaf sex crazed twat,' came the reply from a restrained Kinsey.

'Can you repeat that last bit there Arthur dear...I thought you said that the world will end in five days,' Phil tried to make a joke.

'Yes... I've seen it end... there will be a big bang... there will be panic..... then complete darkness.'

Feet started to shuffle uncomfortably. Hands were rubbed together, while many closed their eyes to try and imagine what darkness would feel like. It didn't feel nice, and it didn't look good.

A man with an angry face pushed through the crowd in the bar, and closed in on Arthur. 'How can you say that? Frightening everybody with your mad ranting,' he questioned in a loud voice. 'Who are you to tell us that news? You must be some kind of evil witch!'

The return of an old word like 'witch' seemed to bring out the worst in people. Birds flew from the trees and dogs started howling. Blood ran cold in people's veins.

'Yeah, he must be some kind of witch or demon,' a youth with a red football shirt on screamed, pointing towards the man on the pool table. He quickly added, 'There's no way that fucking Ipswich could beat the best team in the land. You must be one sick bastard, scaring me like that.' He then spat in Arthur's face.

'Arthur's a witch,' came the shout from another man in the corner. The fact that the man had been hired by the local betting offices, and instructed to do whatever necessary to stop these yearly predictions, hadn't been considered by the feverish crowd.

'Burn Cherrrrrry-nose... kill... Cherrrrry-nose.' He started a mass chant. Within seconds the town was filled with cat calls for his head. He was roughly man handled off the table, and thrown into the cellar with the horse and the seven foot Indian that everyone had forgot lived there.

Phil Haddock tried to restore calm by telling everyone that Arthur was not feeling too well, and that he had just announced his retirement from New Year's Day predictions.

Depression landed with the rain drops on slumped shoulders, as people headed home not sure what to think. Back in the pub, no one said a thing for the entire afternoon. Arthur's posters were either ripped from the walls, or large deformed noses were drawn over the top of his already rather bulbous nose.

5:15 pm, and Bobby Wilson sat upright in make-up in the Grandstand studios. He couldn't wait to tell the football public the brilliant news. Bobby hated Liverpool, and days like these, although few and far between, were always well worth the wait. And he was in the mood, to milk it dry.

Even before, the last note of the introduction music had finished, with a smile that was as long as it was wide, Bobby happily informed the audience of the amazing result from Anfield, where Ipswich were leading the mighty Liverpool, six goals to one. He added with glee, that there was still thirty seconds remaining, and Ipswich had just been awarded a penalty.

'Unbelievable,' Jac said to his open mouthed friends. 'No one scores six ...sorry seven,' the cheers from the jubilant away fans in the blue and white, informed them all, that the scoreboard had clicked over another notch. 'goals against the Reds.'

Bobby Wilson asked the camera man for a close up. 'Did you get that Britain? I said, Liverpool 1 Ipswich 7' He turned to camera two and said, 'Hi, Gerry and the Pacemakers.' He taunted, mockingly, 'your ferry has just sunk in the stinking condom polluted Mersey. Hi, Beatles, you need more than love to put a smile back onto the faces of all of you robbing scouse gits.' Bobby was really enjoying this. He jumped up on the desk. 'Shankly, Parsley, Fagan… your team are Shite. That's Shite with a capital Shite. Boot room boys, you are nothing but a big bunch of benders.'

The guy in the control booth screamed at Bobby Wilson to cut to Stamford Bridge, where Chelsea had drawn two all with Norwich.

'Bollocks to that, Jeremy,' Wilson barked back. He threw the papers in the air and then started to dance around the room shouting '7-1…7-1…7-1…. 7-1 .7-1 7-1111111.'

Sanity seemed to have returned to the front man as he took his seat back behind the desk, he straightened his tie and looked into the camera lens, and added, 'I'm so sorry about that. I do apologise for my behaviour, but I must just tell you one last time, for all those people who have just joined us, let me tell you the wonderful score line. The champions of England 1 goal…the worst team in the land, who are actually bottom of the league with nil points until today, and were soundly thrashed by the Arsenal one nil last week… SEVEN. That's not six or five of four but SEVEN. Just like the seven dwarfs, or the seven deadly sins.'

The sound crew, were actually pissing themselves at this point, and the camera man found it impossible to hold the camera still. Jeremy the floor manager, had switched the focus to the classified results. The faceless man started his usual round up.

'Now for today's classified results starting with Division one,' the man's voice took over.

'Arsenal 2, Manchester City 1'

But big bad Bobby wasn't finished yet, he cried out at the top of his voice, which could be heard in every front room in the land, 'Well done the gunners.'

'Aston Villa 0, Tottenham Hotspurs 3.'

'Seven brides for seven brothers,' Wilson sang out loudly.

'Chelsea 2, Norwich 2.'

'The Seven Wonders of the World.' The security guards tried unsuccessfully to shut him up.

'Everton 5, Newcastle 4.'

'Seven members of Showwaddywaddy, not including the drummer. Bridge over the River Seven.'

'Leeds 2, Wolves 3' For the first time ever, even the classified results man appeared to get flustered.

'Seven men on the moon, Goldilocks and the seven bears, and before I go… seven exceedingly good cakes made by Mr Kipling… and his seven sons… goodnight.' He finished, just as Jeremy from the control tower knocked the ex-goalkeeper out cold with one swing of a boom mike.

'Bloody hell, I think Bobby liked that,' Lusty squawked, just before the youth with the Liverpool shirt on launched a missile at the TV screen, smashing it to bits.

All eyes looked at each other but were too afraid to see. In the distance, from out of the cellar, the following chilling message came pouring out from under the locked door… 'I told you so… I told you that they would lose seven goals to one. You better get your snow boots out and say your prayers.'

Someone tried to shout for Cherry-nose to shut up but no actual words would escape out of the person's dry throat.

Chapter 5

'We could be Zeros ... just in five days'

Jac rolled over in his warm bed switching on the radio that helped to bring the bedroom to life. He felt behind his left ear, and touched the little electrical impulse device that his parents must have fitted on him while he slept.

'Bloody hell,' he said to himself. 'That was a quick month.' But, by now, he was very much used to trying to cope with the unfortunate bouts of attacks, that normally took place at least once a month. The doctor had originally told his parents that he would grow out of his strange illness by now, but annoyingly for him, (and his parents), there was no change.

He stretched out, underneath the fresh cotton sheets that felt so soft next to his skin. He liked the feel of fresh bed linen. There was nothing worse than bed clothes that were a month old. Not only did they usually smell to high heaven, but because Jac was a healthy teenager with an unhealthy supply of porno mags, they normally ended up as stiff as a board. Jac embarrassingly remembered the time, after he spent the entire weekend studying the delights of a rather X-rated stash of imported Hustler magazines, the sheets actually broke in two as his mother pulled them off the bed. But unknown to Jac, his mother had started to sell his stiff, yellow stained bed sheets, to the local Indian restaurant as a substitute for poppadoms, that were served up to their delighted customers with small jars of chutney and onion.

Jac's morning thought pattern was finding it hard to make headway in his lazy mind, until it came quickly to a junction that was clearly sign posted. It was decision time. The one sign pointed North, and was all about getting up to face a new day. The other arrow headed downwards in a southerly direction, and motioned for him to stay in bed and discover the pleasure that lurked in his underpants. He considered the two options for about five seconds, before he remembered that his mother had a new edition of the Gratton catalogue, which had sixteen undiscovered pages dedicated to the wonders of women's underwear. He decided to take that well worn road to Wanksville, as he reached down for the tube of lubrication that would help to kick start the journey.

Now Jac Morgan had developed sexually very much the same as the next teenage boy growing up. When he was twelve, he was asked by his mate Lusty, during PE lesson, 'Had it came to life yet?' Jac dismissed the question because he didn't understand what his mate was on about. But that all changed three weeks later, when he awoke on a Sunday morning, to feel a strange sensation between his legs. He pulled back the sheets and there, glaring back at him, where his little worm (as his Aunty used to call it) normally hung harmlessly down, was this angry looking cobra snake staring up at him. It seemed to be demanding him to touch it, to stroke it, and to man-handle it, roughly.

He touched it and stroked it, until the snake spat right in his eye nearly blinding him. He swore he wouldn't touch it again, but ten minutes later, he was playing snake charmers with the two handed vice grip as if there was no tomorrow.

He told Lusty as soon as he got to school. He was then informed that he had just become a man, (which confused the young boy even more). Alex mentioned to him that he had heard from some mates, that a boy in the upper form had tugged it so much it had dropped off.

This piece of earth shattering news still didn't deter Jac. He couldn't wait to play with his new best friend whenever he had a spare minute. He turned into an abnormal, sex driven, teenager. He locked himself away for hours in the bathroom, devising exciting ways of gaining more pleasure from using fruit or common household objects. His favourite was the toilet roller holder, which he covered with the fur from the hood of an old parka. But he was also partial to cutting the middle out of a Granny Smith apple, and using the fruit as a pleasure device. He developed dark circles under his eyes, and went into cold turkey if he went for longer than three hours without playing a tune on his flute. He had the DTs and had terrifying attacks of hallucinations, seizures and palpitations.

But, as most boys' urges climbed to their sexual peak then plateau out peacefully, Jac's quest for sex continued to rise and rise.

Even his parents, who were quite liberal about things like that, started to get concerned, when they noticed that he had an erection while watching the animated rabbit off the Cadbury's Cream Caramel adverts. He nearly got expelled from school when he asked the resident nun, (who had all the sex appeal of a duffel coat), what colour knickers she had on?

It got worse later on that same night, when his mother woke up and pulled back the bed covers, to find her demonic son, in some sort of trance, suckling on her right breast. His father went absolutely berserk, because he had been sucking away on the left one at the time.

The weeks that followed witnessed a steady decline in their son's behaviour. The final act that caused his distraught parents to think their only son needed serious help, was when they had a call from Farmer Charlie Walters, who had found Jac sleep-walking, and trying to have a 69 with his prized cow called Lady Dale. The terrible sight as they entered the stable, of their beloved son in the nude, with his legs and arms wrapped around the underbelly of the cow, caused his parents to immediately seek medical advice.

He was taken to see a procession of doctors, then priests, and more doctors, but disappointingly, no one knew what caused the gentle boy to change into the devil with a wicked pair of love-lips. Then a travelling medicine man called Doctor Ernie, diagnosed that Jac was suffering from Tourettes Syndrome. Unusually, he didn't have the normal swearing and spitting tic, but had an advanced case of Tourettesex Syndrome. The doctor proved this theory, by putting the boy through some basic Tourettesex sex test, using a carrot, a large fluffy pillow, and a bag of ox's blood. Within forty seconds, Doctor Ernie was covered in a river of saliva and semen. On further examination, he prescribed a new wonder cure that sent electric pulses to the brain, to slow down the effects of this unusual affliction.

Back in his bedroom, on that cold January morning, Jac quickly finished his pleasure boat ride through the pages of the catalogue, wiped himself in the bed clothes, and listened to the radio, as the sports reporter was interviewing, the very happy Ipswich manager, about the game that had surprisingly propelled them into the media spotlight.

'What were the chances of that happening?' Jac thought, 'Ipswich winning seven one at the home of football. Bloody hell… what next?'

The reporter asked, what the manager had made of the outburst of the famous ex-Arsenal goalkeeper, Bobby Wilson, who had apparently flipped his lid in the studio because of the score line, and had consequentially been sacked by the Beeb.

The weatherman's words, which closed the morning's radio show, caused a shiver the size of a jagged light bulb to run down Jac's spine.

'Overnight, across the entire country, exactly twelve inches of pure white snow fell.' The weatherman added, 'this is the first time since records began that the whole island had been covered by a white blanket at exactly the same time.'

'Fucking hell,' Jac switched off the radio alarm clock and clambered across the bed to the window.

There it was, in all its Winter glory. A thick shaggy carpet of pure white driven snow, exactly a foot deep, that had worked its way into every nook and cranny.

He observed how children were already enjoying the wonderland surprise, and snowmen appeared in nearly every garden. In several doorways, he saw many adults shaking their heads in disbelief, and talking to each other in quiet whispers. He wondered what the significance of all this meant. This was all moving too fast for him to take in. He wondered what Alex thought? He needed to sense check this with his mate, and quickly.

Jac could normally make a joke out of any strange situation, but this was starting to get a little too spooky for words, and his sense of humour had deserted him. But, as if by magic, it returned with a bang, when he witnessed Alan the Midget prancing through the snow in a cap-sleeved tee-shirt and eight inch platform shoes. He knew that the little man was sensitive about his lack of height, but even by his low standards, he had really hit rock bottom. He laughed from his belly when a snowball toppled the dwarf over, resulting in him being completely immersed under a sea of snow, and rolling around trying to get back up on his little feet.

A soft knock on his bedroom door spun Jac around. His mother waited a few moments, before sticking her head in to inform her son that Lusty and Alex were downstairs.

The formal knock system before entering, had been decided upon by the whole family after the mishap in the kitchen. On that morning several months earlier, Jac, who was going for a kick around in the park with his mates, had accidentally walked in on his mother giving his father a blow job in the kitchen.

Jac stood in amazements at the oral lesson being given for free by his parents. His father had his back to him, while his mother was on her knees facing him. His dad had hold of his mother's head tightly, so although she could see the horror of the situation unfolding before her very eyes, she couldn't do anything about it. She tried to mutter, but was told by his father 'Not to talk with her mouth full.'

To save his embarrassment, he looked away immediately, but his eyes were dragged kicking and screaming towards the kitchen table, where staring back at him he saw his mother's false teeth, with a piece of freshly cooked toast still in between her dentures. Next to them was a carrot covered in pubic hair. As he rushed out, he heard his father reaching the point of no return.

'Oh no,' Jac thought, 'I thought that only dirty girls like Lois swallowed.' He later told his best mates about the whole earth shattering episode, that had been played out in slow motion before his very eyes. His mates were helpless when he mentioned the part the vegetable had played in the scene.

No one could believe it. Jac was in shock for weeks. He couldn't look his surprisingly calm parents in the eye and stopped having milk in his tea and helping his father on his allotment.

What Jac didn't know, was that it was part of a set up by his parents, who had been told by Doctor Ernie, that they could try and shock their son out of his ailment. It was a new technique from Sweden, that was built on a bit of reverse psychology.

Alex and Lusty were told by Jac's mother to go on up to her son's room. They entered and they all sat facing each other for the first time that morning.

'Weird shit or what?' Lusty spoke first.

'Fucking hell…. I don't know what to think!' Jac replied. 'It's just getting out too of control for my liking.'

He pointed out of the window where Alan the Midget was still trying to get up. He had started to go blue from the forehead down.

'Oh no... It's not that time of the month again... is it?' Alex asked on noticing the battery operated ear device positioned behind Jac's ear.

'Yeah it is... it must have come on me during the night. Help me get it off!' Jac struggled to displace the thing that his parents had secured on him.

'Fuck off Jac, if your parents have put that on you, your hormones must be right out of control,' Alex threw his reply back at his mate's innocent looking face.

'Come on Mate.... quick untie me. This buzzing noise is driving me mad!' Jac reached behind his head and tried to pull the straps apart.

'No way! Remember the last time? The spiteful Mrs Griffiths went into a coma for three months because of you,' Alex reminded him.

'She was asking for it,' Jac retorted trying to prove his innocence.

'She only bent over to pick up a lump of coal in the street,' Alex continued. 'You were on her like a limpet... and she was bloody seventy four!'

'She looked younger.'

'Oh yeah,' agreed Alex, 'Fuckin seventy three and a half then, and she's got a beard like an old Billy goat.'

'Not.... from... where... I was... standing,' Jac slowly smiled to himself. 'Come on. I'll promise to behave.'

Alex looked at Jac, before reluctantly releasing the well-secured straps.

'But one wrong movement, or if you start licking my ear like the last time, and it goes back on,' Alex added.

This was music to Lusty's ears. Where else in the world would conversations like this be classed as normal?

'What are we going to do?' Jac said, hiding the device in the drawer.

'You don't believe it is going to happen, do you?' Alex asked. 'The world can't end in five days time because some big nosed tramp performing some circus stunt had a premonition.'

'Well, the first two things have happened.' Lusty replied.

'Yeah, but those things happen every day.'

'They don't,' snapped Jac. 'The mighty Reds getting thrashed at home…. no way. Twelve inches of snow falling over all the country. That's not normal.'

Lusty pulled an old book from out of his coat and told the other two to sit down. 'Listen to this then.' He spoke in a clear tone, but with just a twist of a Spanish accent. 'Have you heard of Nostredamus?' His eyes lit up his face.

'Yeah. Wasn't he some kind of mad monk who looked like Christopher Lee?' Jac answered, looking towards Alex.

'No, that's Rasputin. Nostredamus was a guy from the 16th century, who predicted nasty things that were going to happen in history.'

'Like what?' Alex entered the debate.

'He predicted lots of things, like Hitler, and Napoleon. Even the atomic bomb.'

'Was he booted out of the window by a transsexual horse as well?' Jac interrupted.

Again, Lusty had to let out a smile. He knew that there were tribes, in the darkest rain forests, in the darkest parts of the world, that actually survived on drinking their own grandmother's urine, who would find this discussion between two of his best mates bizarre, in the most extremely bizarre sort of way. He was so glad to be home.

'Look, when I was away, I studied all this stuff, and this morning I read this in Nostredamus' book.' He turned to the chapter entitled 'In the Year of the Dragon.'

'Listen to this,' he slowly enlightened them.

The birds will sit on castle high,
He will come and fly in circle grand,
And the wind will blow in darken sky,
A long silence with cover the land.

'You see it's all there.' Lusty said. 'The Year of the Dragon. Did you know that it is the Chinese year of the dragonfly this year? It's just uncanny.'

'Are you sure Lust?' Alex asked diplomatically, looking around the room for support.

'It sounds like the lyrics to a Depeche Mode song to me.' Jac jumped in, again using humour to cover his self doubt.

Lusty started the process of breaking down each line of the warning.

'The birds will sit on castle high' he said. 'That is definitely reference to the pigeons that were sitting on the wall yesterday, at the pub,' He watched them chew over the words of his explanation. He realised that if they hadn't spat them out by now, there was hope.

'He will come and fly in circle grand,' that must be relating to Arthur being kicked through the window.' He continued, his explanation gaining momentum.

Before Lusty could go on, Jac excitably jumped in, *'and the wind blows in darken sky,'* must be the time before he made the prediction.' He stood up and paced around.

'Of course… it's all making sense now.' Even Alex added his bit. The both boys, were now suddenly completely enthralled by the power of Lusty, and his 16th century friend.

'A long silence will cover the land.' Lusty continued and they all joined in and slowly mouthed 'The world will end in five days.' Everyone in the room let out a deep breath.

'Bloody hell Lust… you are right.' Alex said while observing Alan the Midget finally getting to his feet, but instantly falling backwards, landing in another snow drift.

'I told you boys. The book of Nostredamus is never wrong.'

There was a long but comfortable silence in the bedroom, as the three boys contemplated life without life. No one could explain why it felt so comfortable, it just did.

Billy '2 amp' Kinsey had slept in and hadn't realised that the world outside of his window was slowly starting to question itself. On seeing the snow, he knew where his friends would be. They would all be around Jac's house. Over the years, Jac's house had always been the place to head if there was a crisis in their midst. The day the news came of Sid Vicious dying saw them all heading there, and crying the night away. It was also the top place to go if they just bunked off school and needed somewhere to crash for a couple of hours.

He dressed quickly, and half way out of his cul-de-sac he saw the Graham family filling their saloon car up with their belongings. It was laden down with suitcases full of clothes, the television set, a tent and supplies of food.

'Where are you going Mr Graham... on holidays?' he asked the father.

'Haven't you heard the awful news my boy? Cherry-nose said the world's going to end in five days. It's not safe around here,' the father replied, whilst still trying to squeeze an electronic weighing scale into the boot.

'So what?' Kinsey asked confused. 'So where are you going to go to?' The frown on his forehead became prominent. This was always an early warning sign that things in Kinsey's mind were on collision course.

'Anywhere. Don't you understand kid? The world's going to end next Wednesday!'

Patronising comments made by an ignorant old man, were like a red rag to a bull as far as Billy '2 amp' was concerned. He looked the man straight in the eyes, and launched into a one of his famous verbal attacks. 'But where the fuck are you going to go to? The fucking moon?' He simply added. 'You and your family, are going to hop on a star ship and go to Venus are you? Arthur said, that the WORLD IS GOING TO END,' Billy screamed the last five words as if Mr Graham had only the tiniest grain of his hearing left. 'Not the world in fucking Merthyr, the fucking world like in the whole wide fucking world. You know that big round ball full to the brim with layabouts, scroungers, and stupid fucking people like you.'

But the old man was oblivious to the ranting of Billy, he was staring up towards the sky, and nodding his head as if he'd seen the light. He ushered his three children, wife, two dogs, a cat, and a goldfish into the car. 'Sorry Billy old boy. We can't hang about. We've got to get to safety, and you and your parents should do the same!'

The car drove off in a puff of smoke, leaving Billy flabbergasted to the point, that he felt like phoning the people responsible for laying landmines, and pleading with them to set a trap for a red saloon occupied by a bunch of idiots, who would probably be trying to read a map which was upside down.

As he approached Jac's house, he bent down to help Alan the Midget out of the snow. He carefully put the dwarf, who was stiff as a board, onto a dustbin to thaw out.

He entered Jac's room about two minutes later, shaking his head, as if he had the weight of the world on his shoulders.

'The world's gone mad!' he announced, while sitting on the bed. 'I'll rephrase that. The world's gone fucking mad with big fuck off spots on. We must be the only ones that don't believe old Cherry-nose and his stupid forecast,'

Unbeknown to him at the time, his outburst was met with coy expressions. The other three looked at the new arrival with pity in their eyes. Their stares were that of car sales men, who needed just one last sale to complete their quotas for the month, and win a holiday for two in Jamaica.

'What?' Kinsey's confused demeanour had been unaware of the growing cloud of doom that was also sitting in the bedroom, chewing a gob-stopper. 'Don't fucking tell me that you believe in all that nonsense?'

'Tell him about that Nostredamus guy Lust,' Jac said anxiously.

Kinsey turned to Alex, 'Tell me you don't believe this nonsense.... please.'

'Just listen to what Lusty has to say.' Alex answered back.

Lusty slowly went through the entire scenario explaining in minute detail the prophet's words and the exact linkage to events over the past few days. All three mouthed the last words. *'A long silence will cover the land.'* Which was followed by the now familiar... *'And the world will end in five days.'*

Kinsey sat on the bed, a look of anxiety on his face that belonged to the shocked expression, of a hard working man, who had come home early to find his wife in bed with his father. The others nodded knowingly in his direction. They had all been converted, or, brainwashed. If Kinsey had read body language, he would have noticed, that his mates were so far converted to Nostredamus' beliefs, that another word from Lusty, and they would have been at a major airport, heads shaven, giving leaflets out to busy passengers.

Kinsey was not about to be taken without a fight. He had barricaded his negative thoughts in his mind, and had put a 'Do not disturb' sign out for them to read. He smiled uneasily, which eventually broke the thin ice. 'Have you all gone fucking insane? Winds, birds, end of the world. I thought you were a bunch of normal individuals, especially you,' pointing towards Alex. 'But I now realise that you are just as bonkers as the rest of the nutcases that live in this fucking hellhole.' He stood up and glanced out of the window, to see Alan the Midget who was still frozen stiff, being used by some kids as a bobsleigh, as they rode him down the street.

Kinsey couldn't believe his ears. To make a point, he gave them a squeeze to ensure that they were still functioning. He then smashed his head against the wall.

He was not quite finished yet. He refuelled and flew back in for a second blue air raid. 'Have you all been on the fucking glue? Lost prophets. Are you seriously telling me that some guy who was probably a complete lunatic from the 16th century, predicted that some homeless tramp getting booted out of a pub window in Merthyr Tydfil in 1986, would signal the end of the world? Fuck you... I'm going home.'

At that moment, Jac's mother shouted up that there was someone at the door to see him. Jac told Kinsey to hang on a moment, and raced down stairs to see who was calling.

'Yeah, it's probably the men in the fucking white coats coming to take you lot away.' Kinsey was to the point, as always.

Downstairs, Jac was met at the door by the young and extremely beautiful Tanya, the girl next door. He could see her mother and aunt hovering in the background on her doorstep.

'Hello Tanya,' Jac said 'can I help you?' he knew exactly how he'd really like to help the young seventeen year old, whose body must have been designed by an angel with a chequered past and a colourful future. He wished he hadn't had Alex remove his sex free safety device. He didn't know if he could control himself in the present company.

'Yes,' she muttered, trying to look beyond him into the hallway. 'It's a bit awkward, and I don't know how to say this.'

'She's going to ask me for a date,' Jac thought to himself. Before he had time to consider that statement, his imagination had already dashed off to see what he should wear on their night out, and was selecting the appropriate underwear, when the next words that came out of her mouth shattered his dirty dream.

'Is that Lusty boy here?' She knew he was. She had seen him walk past her window, and had been on guard waiting for him to reappear ever since.

'YES.' Jac snapped. 'He's upstairs.' 'I bet she's going to ask him for a date,' he thought. He felt like crying. His imagination had already slowly and regretfully closed the pants drawer, and was lying on his bed with a migraine.

She seemed to come over all tongue-tied. 'I was going to ask him for a… a…. a…' she found the words hard to let go of. The words bounced around the inside of her mouth too embarrassed to pop out, in case the daylight turned them blue.

Jac jumped in to save her from the misery that she was going through, 'Do you want me to ask him if he will take you out on a date?'

She replied quickly 'Hell no! There's no time for all that dating malarkey. The world's going to end in five day!'

'No four days, twelve hours and ten minutes exactly.' He interrupted.

'OK four days and whatever… I wondered if the sexy bastard would be up for a shag?'

To hear the heavenly word 'Shag' coming from the lips of someone as lovely as Tanya, was too good an opportunity to miss.

'What did you say?' he asked again.

'I would like Lusty to shag me this afternoon, before all the girls in the town start to demand a piece of him.' She looked around and saw her mother and aunt waiting on the door step. 'Oh yeah…. and my mother would like a go after me, and my aunt, who is unfortunately in the middle of the change, would just like him to take a shower while she watches.' She smiled and added 'Do you think you can fix that up for us?' She looked like an angel.

'I'll tell him, and I can't see a problem,' Jac commented knowing Lusty would have no complaints about doing his duty, for King, Queen or whoever else wanted a piece of the action.

He closed the door, waited for the lump in his trousers to subside a little, and he went to tell his mates that something strange was happening around them. It had nothing to do with Tanya's request for sex with Lusty, which was par for the course. Girls always used the good-looking boy for acts of pleasure. But more worryingly he had just seen Percy Norman in his best suit, without his wife, heading towards the pub.

Back in the bedroom, and still no one was sure what to make of the situation. Jac walked back into the eye of the storm and joined in on the fierce debate, which was still raging.

'Ok Kinsey, perhaps the link with Nostredamus is a bit weak!' Alex conceded, 'But what about the other things? Liverpool losing, and the snow falling. How can you explain that?'

'Fucking weak! I bet your explanation wouldn't beat a feather in an arm wrestling contest,' Kinsey said standing his ground.

'Who was it Jac?' Lusty asked.

'I'll tell you after.' He looked at Lusty, who was just happy to be back amongst his friends. Jac cursed his own parents for being born on the wrong side of Ugly Street.

'That prediction was a lucky coincidence, or, a good guess,' Kinsey answered back unconvincingly.

'Yeah, but what if it's not? What if it's true? What if the world really is going to end in five days?' Alex mused.

'Four days, twelve hours and five minutes exactly,' Jac jumped in to correct the ticking clock.

'Oh yeah.... four days and counting fast? What if Wednesday night at 12 'O' clock, there is an almighty bang and we are all sitting here like lemons pretending that everything is peachy?' Alex remarked impatiently.

'Right then, let's get a video in and miss the last day on earth,' Lusty snapped back, still slightly aggrieved at their lack of trust in the words of wisdom of his hero Nostredamus. 'Perhaps we could watch 'Carry on up your Khyber Pass.' I bet it will be a scream watching Sid James talk about Barbara Windsor's tits, just before the end of civilisation.'

Kinsey knew he had all the answers to all their questions, but he decided he would save them all up for a better time.

A hush fell over the room, that would have put a library full of deaf mutes to shame. The four life long friends sat on the small bed, thinking of what the next couple of days would bring. Jac was so pleased that his mother had changed the sheets, because otherwise they would have snapped into tiny pieces.

Alex decided to take hold of the situation by the throat. 'I have an idea!'

They all sat and listened.

'What if we all pick something we're always wanted to do in our lives, and see if we can do it in our last couple of days.'

'Like what?' said Jac

'Anything! Walk up a mountain, or swim across the Channel. I don't know exactly. Use your imagination.'

Sadly for Jac, his overactive imagination was already in bed with an erection and a cold flannel on its forehead.

'So, we each decide on something each and we all try and carry it out.' Lusty asked.

'That's the general idea.'

'I'd like to shag that girl next door. That Tanya. She's gorgeous,' said Kinsey entering the debate, and finally peeling off the shackles that were holding him back during their earlier conversation.

'She's already spoken for,' Jac motioned. 'Lusty, I need to talk to you after.'

'She doesn't want to shag him,' Kinsey looked angry.

'Not just her… her mother and her aunty would like a go as well,' Jac informed them.

'Bloody hell Lust, go back to Spain for four days and give us all a fair chance,' Kinsey asked nicely, but with a serious message playing in the background.

Alex coughed loudly, trying to bring them back to face reality.

'What if the idea is stupid? Can we veto it?' Jac asked.

'Like what?' Alex replied.

'Ah like…. ahhhh…. robbing a bank.'

'I was thinking of suggesting that,' Kinsey leaped in quickly.

'What's the point? Where would we spend the dosh?' Alex pointed out.

'In the pub,' Kinsey gestured.

'And what happens if the world doesn't end and our mug shots are all over the news, and we get banged up for twenty years?' Jac said.

'Ok, I didn't think of that. But I bet some fucker is digging a tunnel as we speak.'

So, they all formally agreed that anything that they suggested couldn't be too dangerous, or, too outside the law.

'I bet that shagging Tanya, and her mother, and her fucking aunty, must be against some sort of moral law or code of the jungle,' Kinsey savagely commented turning his back on the good looking boy.

'No, sorry,' Jac apologised. 'The aunty doesn't want to shag him… no, she just wants to watch him having a shower. She's apparently going through a change thing.'

'Oh, that's OK then. It's only the mother and daughter who would like to fuck him. How silly of me.' Kinsey tucked his knees up under his chin and sulked.

There was a knock on the door, and after a count to thirty his mother entered carrying a tray with four steaming mugs of tea and four slices of cake.

'Hello boys. Thought that you would like something to eat.' She placed the tray on the sideboard and picked up her son's dirty washing from the floor, (that for some reason refused to live in the washing baskets).

They piled into the snack.

'Just like the old days Mrs Morgan,' said Lusty.

'Lovely cake. What is it? Kinsey asked.

As she closed the door behind her, she said mischievously, 'Carrot cake boys. A nice big slice of carrot cake.' She could hear the muffled laughter from the hallway. But unknown to them, it had been her intention. Her husband and herself, had just come back from the advanced lessons by Doctor Ernie, concerning, 'How to shock his friends and cure him at the same time?'

Chapter 6

'Ta.. Ta.. Talking ....about a chain reaction?'

Malcolm Knuckles looked around his sparse one bedroom flat. The poor light from the single hanging light bulb, made the room appear a lot smaller than it actually was. The air of depression, hung heavily in the darkness. On first inspection, it was easy to spot that the contents in the room lacked that womanly touch. In fact, it balanced on the wrong side of drabness, and was similar in design to the layout of a prison cell.

He had spent all his life being called meaningless titles like, 'The Champ', or 'The Hardest', and other such worthless names. These meant so much to the hangers-on that wrapped themselves around him, but very little to the majority of upstanding and decent people. This was confirmed by the lack of medals, or trophies, to confirm the misplaced adulation of his fans. There were no photographs of him with his muscular arms around celebrities at the opening night of some fancy gala dinner. There were no, superstar lifestyle or expensive suits in the wardrobe. There was no, flash car on the driveway.

There was the odd letter pinned to the wall, from some fanatical fan who had written to thank the street fighter for changing his sad world for him. One nut had perversely written, how he had experienced immense pleasure when witnessing how Malcolm helped someone, to lose the chunk of skin that once covered their nose after he had sunk his teeth into the flesh. Or the fabulous occasion, when his hero had sent the jagged side of a bottle into someone's flesh, which left scars that ran deeper than the tramlines on the poor man's face.

'Sad bastard,' he said about the writer of the distressing correspondence. What he had completely forgotten, was, that the letter was hanging with pride on his wall.

He stripped his white shirt off his shoulders, and examined his ageing but still intimidating frame. Several fresh bruises, reminded him of a recent fracas with a battalion of soldiers on manoeuvres in the Brecon Beacons. He recalled how the street battle, had balanced precariously on the edge of a rarely experienced defeat for the self proclaimed 'Hardest Man Ever', when his grip, on a stray, but welcome iron bar turned the tables back in his favour.

'Four days left to go.' His deep voice echoed around the room. 'Four bloody days left… and what have I done in my life? He dipped a wet towel on his ribs and winced in pain Even his budgie screwed his little green patchy face up into a ball, when it saw Malcolm pour pure salt into the gaping cut on his eye. It was an old boxing trick that had probably been invented, by a person who had never boxed in their lives, let alone applied it to a wound above their eye.

He walked back and fore the small basement like a leopard waiting outside a delivery room for his leopard wife to have their first leopard baby. The budgie watched his owner pace the floorboards and became hypnotized with spots in front of his tiny eyes, consequently falling off his perch.

'Do I really wanna be remembered just for these?' He flashed his bare knuckles to the cracked mirror over the empty fireplace.

He knew there was more to him than a fighting machine. There was a brain locked away far in a place that he never let anyone in to see. He bent down to reach something from under the bed. His knees were feeling their age. His reflexes, which had shocked lots of opponents during savage scuffles, were quickly disappearing, along with his eye sight. This worried him more than anything else in the world. He had seen the animal documentaries, about how 'Age' had fair and squarely beaten old lions who had once ruled the pack. He had seen, how 'Age' didn't have a system to distinguish between royalty and peasant, and had not used a knuckle dusters, or a broken bottle, on that once feared 'King of the Jungle'. It had used the hidden strength of Old Father Time as a weapon. 'Age' had merely jabbed away at the lion, until he was sick of fighting back, then the younger ones stepped up for the crown. The once indestructible King of the pride was isolated, and left to die. There was no state funeral, just a corpse for the vultures to feast on. He wondered how many of his so-called friends would abandon him as yesterday's news, when he turned into Clarence, the one eyed crippled clown lion.

He punched out at the wall.

He stared long and hard at his reflection, until he made a decision. A decision, that he knew would change his life (all four days of it and counting) forever.

He continued to rummage under his bed, until he found what he had been looking for. He held the small shoebox in his misshapen fists, and opened the lid into a different world.

He searched about amongst the papers. His face broke into a faint grin on pulling out a crumbled sheet. It hadn't seen daylight for many a year. He plonked his frame down onto the single bed which instantly groaned and buckled under his weight.

He held the paper up towards the natural light that flooded in from the small window, silently he mouthed the words on the page, written in a different time.

'Not bad... perhaps not Keats or that other one... but quite respectable for an old street fighter, with a won five hundred lost three record. I may be slightly punch-drunk, but I can still write a mean verse,' he told the budgie, (who was still feeling groggy), referring to the poem that he had written called, *'When ships sail away towards Lovetown bay.'*

He remembered that it had been brought to life, during a short sharp stretch of incarceration in Swansea nick, for a run in with some blacks in an alleyway. Even the screws had commented to him, while they were fitting him with a straight jacket for the emergency court hearing, that he had a real talent, not only for destruction, (the blacks had all been hospitalised during the affray), but also for the pen.

'You have talent.' Those magical words had picked away at his brain. No one had ever said that to him before. There were many who had said, 'Mal... you are one tough mother fucker,' or, 'Mr McCormick, can you do me a little favour? I'll pay you well.' This normally meant that he had to visit some drug or gambling addict's house, and take whatever was not really theirs to give. The work was easy pickings, as his massive frame outside the soon-to-be victims door, always ensured that somehow they found the exact amount required. But as he pushed the money into his pocket, he left them with his complimentary calling card, of a broken jaw for the men, or a bloody nose for the women, for the sheer inconvenience of the situation.

He remembered, with regret, the incident when he had accidentally mixed up house numbers during one of his visits. He had terrorised a retired schoolteacher and his wife for up to six hours, until they finally decided, that although completely innocent of money borrowing, the only way to get this beast out of their detached house, was to stump up the cash that he was demanding, for the drugs and handgun that his employer had supposedly supplied them with. He felt so bad when he realised his mistake, that he went to the hospital the next day to apologise, in person, with a bunch of flowers.

He read another poem. Then it hit him like a flash. It hit him harder than any opponent had ever done.

'That's it' he told his budgie. 'People are going to remember Malcolm McCormick, not for his knuckles, but for the sensitivity of his verse and the way of the pen.'

Malcolm felt like a young boy again. He felt rejuvenated and invigorated. He spent the rest of the afternoon, in between his daily fitness session of a thousand push-ups and a quick eight rounds on the punch-bag that hung in the corner, trawling through the shoebox, picking out the best ones, reworking some others, and sadly trashing the ones that didn't make the mark.

He finally ended up with twenty-five ditties, that were going to change everyone's perception of him. He fed the budgie, put on a fresh white shirt, combed his hair, and with the box under his arm, he opened the door and walked out into his brand new world.

Percy Norman stopped shovelling the snow from the drive, closed his eyes, and imagined what life could have been like if he had taken another route. He saw himself walking hand in hand on a beach, with the girl from the Bounty advert. In his mind's eye, he obviously re-scaled the scene a little, he was a handsome dark haired six footer, and not a five foot four Bobby Charlton look-a-like. His lips turned up into a smile, that was so rare these days, they had almost forgotten how to do it. Small cobwebs were washed away from the corners of his mouth.

'Oy… lazy… after you finished messing about doing that,' his wife bellowed out from the upstairs bedroom window, 'Don't forget to clean out the fridge, make me a bacon sandwich with tomato sauce, and then go and get the shopping from the corner shop.' She slammed the window closed and padded back to bed. A bed that had only been employed during the last five years, for sound sleep and eating bacon sandwiches.

'You don't have a dog and bark yourself,' she told her mother on the phone as she polished her nails.

Percy put his dream back inside its box, and locked it tight. He continued to clear the pathway to the front door.

'Why me?' he whispered to himself. 'With all the nasty people in the world, why did he end up with the worst life, bar none? What did he do in a past life to deserve this sentence of endless punishment? Perhaps he had been Jack the Ripper, or Albert the Axe Murderer who had cut up his family and made a soup out of them. But even those desperate men hadn't had to suffer the constant nagging that took place in his life, morning, noon, and night. Complaint followed complaint. Moans followed moans. Over thirty six years of marriage, she had finally sucked his will to live. She had taken the once carefree spirit that circled over him, and turned him into a shell of his former self. It had left him with no friends, no hobbies, and stooped shoulders from the weight of her selfish expectations.

Suddenly, Percy stiffened. Every muscle in his body tensed up, as he saw Malcolm Knuckles swaggering menacingly towards his direction, carrying a small shoebox.

'Do I owe him money?' His mind raced and his heart beat so loud it hurt. 'I hope her upstairs haven't gone into debt.' He started to inwardly panic. He had heard of all the terrible things this man could do with a toffee hammer.

'Hello Percy.' Malcolm grunted.

Percy was extremely surprised that this feared man knew his name. He thought that perhaps it was all part of a dream, and he looked around to see if he could catch a quick glimpse of the Bounty girl.

'This is a fine morning. I was wondering if you would like to come for a pint with me, Perc.' Malcolm flashed a set of teeth that a racing horse whose father was a dentist, would have been proud to own.

This confused Percy even more. Had Malcolm been taking drugs? Or perhaps he'd had his brains beaten to pulp in a recent fight. 'I can't Malcolm... I got chores to do.' He lowered his voice to be on the safe side.

The comment sailed over the big man's head. 'Do you like poetry?' Malcolm asked Percy. He was itching to try out his new theory of everlasting friendship on someone.

Percy didn't know what to say. He had come to expect many strange things from living in this town, but every day seemed to get stranger than the last. It was as if Lucifer himself was asking him to put his hand into a lucky, or maybe, unlucky dip bag.

'I've never heard any really, except in school'

'Would you like to hear some?'

Of course, Percy said, 'Yes.'

Malcolm reached into the box, produced a piece of paper, and proceeded to enlighten Percy with a five minute poem about bird's eggs.

'That was really good Malcolm, I didn't realised that you were a poet. Why don't you put them into a book and get them published?' he asked the big man.

'No time. Haven't you heard the news?' Inside, Malcolm was chuffed to bits at Percy's reaction to his first attempt. He felt better than the night he settled an old score with Charlie Gold, the East End hard nut.

'No,' Percy innocently replied. 'What news?'

Malcolm then went on to explain to him all about Arthur's prediction about the end of the world. A shiver ran straight through Percy in a pair of Adidas trainers and matching headband.

'Are you serious Malcolm?' Percy lost control and aggressively grabbed the street fighter by the collars.

'Look over there Percy. Why do you think all those people are crying?'

Percy looked cross the street, and sure enough he saw people walking aimlessly around, eyes full of tears.

'Sorry Malcolm.' Percy realised that he had hold of the man's jacket. He straightened out the man's lapels. 'I've got to go. There's something I've got to do.'

Percy walked slowly into the kitchen. There was a distant far away look in his eyes. He put the kettle on the gas ring, and placed three rashers of bacon into the frying pan. He took off his boots, and headed upstairs. He heard the sound of the sizzle of the Danish as he reached the top step. He took a deep breath.

He could hear his beloved still nattering with his mother-in-law, who he pictured still laying in her coffin waiting for nightfall to appear, when she would start her job, of sucking the world dry.

He half grinned at his surprised wife as he took the phone out of her hand and placed it back on the receiver. She stared at him in amazement, and yelled, angrily, 'What do you think you are doin….'

The shovel bounced off the side of her head with a sickening thud. The first blow caused maximum confusion in her mind and knocked her clean off her feet to the floor. The second, third and fourth strikes, switched her lights off temporarily, but with the intention of being a permanent fix. The rest of the blows that rained down on her exposed skull were just Percy's extreme way of extracting revenge, for the years of pain and heartache.

Percy washed the blood off his hands, just as the whistle on the kettle announced that it had done its job of purifying the water. He made a mug of very strong tea, and sat down to eat his very own bacon butty, without interruptions.

Later on, he put on his favourite clothes that he hadn't worn for many a day, and then prepared to go for a long overdue pint with his best mate…… Malcolm the Poet.

Cyril innocently witnessed the savage demise of Percy's wife through the bedroom window opposite. He was still fastened to the tree, which was starting to wilt. Brown leaves lay dead at his feet. He looked on in horror at first, as he saw the flash of Percy's spade pierce the air. But his shocked reaction turned to sheer respect for the once downtrodden man, on seeing the smile suddenly replace the frown on the fresh murderer's face.

'Good on you my son,' he mouthed, as the edge of the spade chopped her to bits.

Cyril laughed to himself when he remembered the old joke about the man who killed his wife, and buried her in the garden with her large arse sticking out of the earth. 'Need somewhere to park the bike,' the guy in the timeless joke, had apparently told the judge.

'Go on Percy…. be a devil and plant the old bitch with her crack pointing to the sky,' he laughed, thinking that Percy could probably have parked a minibus between the cheeks of that arse.

A serious thought then crossed his mind. He wondered if he would report the incident when he finally got out of this mess. That thought was quickly followed by a more urgent appointment concerning, why the hell no one had come to rescue him?

He knew, that he had been tied up for at least six or seven days since the loony Red Indian had captured him. He was slightly unsure, because the days had quickly blended into one another. To be fair to the wild banshee and his family, they had fed him well, if you considered fish and chips three times a day as a staple diet. He had even been allowed to watch TV with the old man, after 9pm. He didn't know if this was Pablo being kind, or the old man's way of rubbing salt into the wounds, because Pablo had lined up all twelve televisions in the front room, and continually smirked at his captive during the programmes. One of the TVs actually had a 48" screen with dual surround sound and Ceefax, his son had borrowed this from a late night visit to the social club. In the kitchen were two bandits and a pool table, (which was used on the weekends to skin deer on), that he had also acquired.

Cyril was starting to get concerned as to why no one had come for him. He had envisaged by now, the SAS, smashing their way through the bedroom window, armed to the teeth with guns and chiselled chins. But no one came, except for the regular supply of greasy food wrapped in newspaper, and mugs of boiling hot tea, which burnt his mouth.

During this time, he had got to know the room quite well. The green striped wallpaper that had been hung badly, the yellow glossed doors, and the smell of poverty, which somehow had been locked in the room with him, with little, or no chance of escape. They had all become his closest allies.

There were lots of questions spinning around in his mind: Where was his wife? Where were his work colleagues? What he didn't know, was that his wife had eloped with his work colleague, and was currently sitting at a beach bar in Malaga.

Romana tapped on the door. She entered in full squaw dress, a bowl of home made rabbit broth in her hand.

After two painfully bad mouthfuls, he turned and quietly asked, 'Please untie me. Please let me go!' I have a girl your age back at home,' he lied.

'You have fork tongue… my pop said.'

'Why are you talking like that?' he sniggered.

She looked away, and fed him another spoonful, which contained a chunk of rabbit's ear.

Cyril continued with his plea, 'Look, this is not a film. This is not some kind of Indian reservation. This is the Gurnos, and you and your family are all in deep trouble. I work for the government you know.' He then considered his outburst. He satisfied himself with the content of what he had just said. One place, was indeed full of wild animals and savages, the other, was somewhere in North America.

'Your father is a real bad man. Did you know that he hasn't paid his TV licence since 1967?'

She knew that he hadn't paid any bills in his life, and relied on the social security to carry out that aspect, of self-imposed duty to mankind.

'We don't have a television set.' Now it was her time to lie.

'I've seen them... I watched Jaws with your father last night. He even pretended that I was Hopper from the film and drew a little beard on me.' Deep down, Cyril had enjoyed the experience, and the thrill of the chase. 'I have seen all of your twelve televisions my girl.' He smugly smirked at her.

'Fifteen,' she quickly replied.

'What?' he choked. The piece of the rabbit's ear shot out of his mouth.

'We have fifteen Teles. We have another two in the coal shed, and a brand new one still in the box in the attic, which Luke stole from Tesco.'

Cyril cringed and his body went limp.

'Fifteen, fifteen... the electric chair would be too good for that bastard,' he cried.

It took him several moments to calm down and get the picture out of his mind, of how this arsehole was treading on the very moral fabric of modern society. He decided to try a different approach on the daughter. 'Don't you ever go to school?'

'White man school... with old white man rules.' She grunted back.

'But you are white!'

'Only in colour.' She banged her chest. 'I am Romana White Wolf Pozzoni, daughter of the Great Chief Giro-cheque.'

'You're a 14 year old teenager who needs to get out more.'

She hit him square on the nose with the solid metal spoon, and said, 'I'm not the one tied to a conker tree, Mister.'

At that moment, the evil Luke entered carrying a Bowie knife. From the landing, Cyril could hear the radio blasting out a Kid Creole song.

'If I was in your blood... you wouldn't be so ugly.' Luke sang along with the words.

The boy threw the dagger across the room. It landed in the tree just above Cyril's head.

'Is he bothering you Sis?' he asked. Glee shone out of his eyes. 'Because if he is, I'll cut him from ear to ear.' He motioned the deadly steel blade against the petrified throat of Cyril. A drop of blood fell, onto the detector man's once fresh, white, shirt.

Romana, who knew how uncontrollable her bigger brother could be, interrupted 'No.... he's OK Bro.' She continued to feed him with the soup.

A loud knock on the door rescued Cyril from the stare of the young buck brave, and the revolting taste of the broth.

'Yes at last... it's the police,' he shouted triumphantly.

Both the youngsters ran to take up their positions. Romana turned on the chip fat, which stood already prepared on the gas cooker, Luke got the petrol bombs out of the sock drawer.

Old man Pozzoni reached for the double barrelled shot gun that lived behind the settee, and he sniped along the hallway to the front door. He placed the head of the gun through the letter box, and aimed it at the groin of whoever dared to knock the door, just as the credits to Jaws were rolling.

'Can I help you?' he squeezed the words through the door opening.

Kieran the postman, remained unaware at first, that there were twelve inches of life-threatening steel positioned precariously at his manhood.

'Fucking hell.... Pablo.... It's me, Kieran the postman. I've got a parcel for you... but you need to sign for it. It's recorded delivery.' The postman jumped back as if bitten by a cobra.

'Me not signing for nothing,' came the sharp reply from the letterbox.

'If you don't sign…. I can't leave it for you.'

The click of both barrels suddenly persuaded the postman that risking life and limb, for the minimal wage he received, was not in the call of duty. 'Ok, I'll sign for it for you.' He scribbled a signature, dropped the parcel, and ran for cover.

As Old man Pozzoni opened the door, he saw Kieran the postman scampering away in a long blonde wig, six inch stiletto heeled shoes, and a tight fitting pencil skirt. The strangely dressed delivery man, then proceeded to empty his mail sack and clip board into a dust bin, put some dark red lipstick on his lips, and sauntered off down the street.

'Every man to his own.' Pablo said to himself, picking up the big parcel in the plain brown wrapping.

Chapter 7

'Under a Bloodshot eye'

The pace of frightened expectation was slowly taking a firm grip on the excitable town, and was starting to gain momentum. It was as though all four seasons had suddenly arrived without warning, on back-to-back council buses. Within a couple of hours, the people of the town, had taken a back seat ride on the change curve roller coaster. To begin with, when they had heard the football score and seen the snow fall, there was shock, followed quickly by denial. The resistance part of the journey had been the hardest, and during this stage they had again tried to burn Cherry-nose at the stake. But now, in the cold light of day, it seemed that everyone had accepted their fate and were quite looking forward to melt down.

Of course no one liked the idea of their world coming to an abrupt end in four days time, but they had collectively agreed, that if it was going to end 'What the fuck… Let's party like it's Wednesday Midnight January 6th 1987,' one happy go lucky youth had shouted out into the night sky.

An emergency meeting, to discuss the plan of attack for the coming days was organised at the town hall. The place was jam packed. Alex took a seat next to his mates.

He noticed the Mayor on the stage, with his ever present poodle sitting on the back of the chair. Every time the Mayor spoke, the little dog would move its tail, which appeared like a movable quiff on the man's forehead.

'How the fuck can you take someone like that prick seriously?' Kinsey said, taking a swig of lager.

'They only gave him the pointless role, to stop him from writing angry letters to the paper, about the proposed refuge tip that is planned for Dowlais,' Jac replied, then added 'Ain't it a bit early to start drinking, Kins?'

'What the hell? It's not going to kill me, is it?' he answered back.

The Mayor stood up. The poodle rolled down the front of the vacated chair. 'You all know why I called this meeting today.' He addressed the masses.

'Is it about the smelly tip?' someone shouted out.

'No, No. That's yesterday's news, which I've got a meeting about tomorrow, and we already have a plan for the future. No, this is more serious. This is about Arthur.'

Loud boos filled up the room on hearing the name of the newly proclaimed evil witch of the town.

The Mayor continued 'It's not just about Arthur, it's about his prediction. I think it would be a good idea, if we collectively decide what we all should do.'

'String the no good hobo witch up from the nearest lamp post.' Someone screamed from the back of the hall.

'No... not with Arthur. What should we do about the world ending in a couple of days?'

'The world is not going to end,' a reply came from the obligatory street protestor, who only two days previously, had been walking around with a placard informing everyone that the world was going to end soon. Now the turn coat had changed the words to say, 'The world is not going to end!'

'I wish he'd make his fucking mind up,' Kinsey spat the words out. 'He only does it for the attention. If we said grass was green… he'd contradict it. Remind me to smash his fucking protesting teeth in next week.'

The Mayor felt he was getting nowhere. 'Any suggestions,' he pleaded, trying to move it on a bit. Since his time in office, he was well aware that this town had always been content to leave issues revolve around the tumble dryer of life, until they became scorched.

'On what?' an old lady asked.

'On what we should bloody well do before the world ends.' The way the Mayor felt at this moment, Wednesday couldn't come quick enough.

'How about robbing the bank?' the youth with the Liverpool football shirt grunted.

'What's the point in robbing the bank?' came the reply from the masses, who had all said it to one another, over the last a day. 'What are you going to do with the money?'

The youth went the same colour as his tee-shirt and cursed himself for opening his mouth, yet again.

A small boy put his hand up. The Mayor hushed the crowd and asked the boy to speak. 'We could just ignore it and hope that it just goes away.' He said in a quiet voice.

Everyone was thinking what a good idea that was, if only it was as simple as that.

'Yeah…. and perhaps we could put a, 'Gone to Lunch' sign on the front door, and hope that the grim reaper reads it and tip-toes right past.' A nun gestured sarcastically towards the boy. 'Haven't you got homework to do? Now either sit there quiet like a good little boy, or get out.'

The Mayor tried again to address the crowd but had the same sort of meaningless response, until someone asked him 'Well you're the Mayor, what do you think we should do?'

'I bet he says to write a letter of complaint to someone,' Jac whispered to his mates.

The Mayor's face lit up. He was a very clever manipulator of people. He knew exactly how they would all react, and he just waited his turn, until the bottle of opportunity popped its cork in his direction.

'I was thinking of having a Big Grand Town,' He paused for a few seconds… 'Raffle.'

Kinsey was on his feet faster than anyone else. 'A fucking raffle… the world's going to end, and that's the best you can come up with… a fucking raffle. What about a game of Bingo, and Five Card Brag to follow…. you prat!' He sat down, happy that he had made his point.

'Just listen a second.' The Mayor hesitated before continuing. 'I was thinking, that whoever won it, could do whatever he, or even she, would like, for the remaining days. It's a bit like that TV show, 'We can make your dreams come true.' But sadly, we can't base it in Cape Town.' He sat back in his chair, and the poodle's tail moved feverishly.

There were a few mutterings, but mostly the audience agreed, that on the surface, it was not a bad idea. Some even thought, that this may have been the best suggestion that any Mayor of the town had ever come up with.

'Can anyone enter?' a voice boomed from the corner of the room.

'Everyone except Arthur.' The Mayor suggested.

Again, loud boos followed Arthur's name wherever it went. Arthur's name, had now evolved, into the hatred thrown at the ugly sisters in the Christmas panto

'What about the seven foot Indian?' Another sensible question was asked, from a normally, not-so-sensible source.

'Of course…. as long as we can find him.'

Now the ball of excitement was rolling downhill at an unstoppable pace. 'What about children?' said another.

'What do you think?' The Mayor threw the question back to the people. An old politician's trick.

The nun piped up 'As long as they can talk and are potty trained. We wouldn't want to spend all our time wiping their behinds.' There was a mass consensus agreement with the nun's statement.

'Can I have Cyril Beaverman's ticket, since he's still missing?' someone else added.

'We'll have to give it to his poor wife' the Mayor drawled.

'You'll have a job. She's fucked off to Spain with the guy from Radio Rentals.' The nun shrieked, to the great amusement of the hall full of people.

The laughter that filled the room eventually escaped out of the ventilation ducts. When the hall cooled down a little, the Mayor informed them all of the rules of the competition. He stated, that everyone except Arthur, Cyril and unpotty trained sprogs, would be given a ticket, and they would all meet back at 6pm to draw the lucky numbers, and make somebody's last few days very enjoyable. They all stood up and clapped the Mayor, as he slowly disappeared from the stage, holding his dog and trying to figure out how he was going to fix it so his number would come up.

It took four hours to distribute the large amount of tickets to all who were eligible to receive one. The time dragged out, because as usual, no one could find the seven foot Indian. So, in the end, they pinned it to a cabbage that they found on a barstool at the back of the pub.

A big oil drum had been positioned on the stage, attached with a bigger handle to rotate it. All the coloured tickets had been placed carefully inside. The Mayor had put two of his own tickets, to one of everyone else's. Phil Haddock had personally volunteered to comment on proceedings, and in his very own words, 'bring a little bit of class and decorum' to the event.

Everything was set. The lights were lowered, until someone screamed out to turn the bloody things back up because their coat and handbag had been pinched.

'The mesmerising roll of the drum,' said Phil in anticipation. 'Round and round it goes…. where it will stop…. no one does know.'

'Remind me to smash that fucker's teeth in and all.' Kinsey trilled, pointing to the has-never been actor.

'Hush,' came a thousand concentrated voices.

Phil picked a ticket out of the drum. Heart's were beating loudly like a little drummer boy leading a jazz parade. He unfolded the blue coloured ticket. 'The winning number is….' He dropped it on the floor.

'He's fucking done that on purpose.' Kinsey had to be physically restrained by his mates from jumping up on stage and clonking the actor.

'Sorry folks,' Phil said. In fact, he had done it on purpose. He was on stage, and he was going to play the crowd even if they killed him. 'The winning number is a pink ticket …. number one.'

'YES… YES.' The Mayor screamed out. 'I'm the winner. Bollocks to you all. I going to close the tip immediately, I want all the council money and I want you to send young Tanya to my caravan tonight.'

'Oh sorry Mayor, I've made a dreadful mistake. It's not number one at all. It's number thirty six thousand and twenty two.' Phil smirked at the annoyed mayor and flashed the pink coloured ticket so the crowd could see. He had accidentally seen the sly man behind stage trying to fiddle the result of the draw. Phil hated cheats.

'Cross that Phil off my hit list,' Kinsey smiled at the cunning old actor fox. 'He's alright in my book.'

Suddenly, from the back of the hall a woman's voice pierced the air. 'I'll have a number fourteen with half fucking rice and half fucking chips.' Colette, from Hing Hongs, appeared through the large crowd, holding up the winning number. She then leapt onto the stage, pulled up her skirt and mooned at the stunned faces.

Phil sat the ecstatic woman on a chair. His microphone already in hand.

'Well Colette… good on you girl.' Phil looked across at the shell shocked Mayor, who had kicked his poodle off into the wings.

'Bloody hell…. I've never won anything before, except when I had the most nits in the school…. but that's different, ain't it?' She giggled to herself.

'Just a little,' Phil interrupted. 'Well, what would you like?'

He was stopped by the Mayor, who had composed himself enough to butt in. 'I came up with this idea, and I will ask Colleen what she would like to do.' There was no love lost between the two gentleman on the stage.

'It's Colette… not Colleen,' said Colette.

'Ok Colleen,' the ignorant Mayor continued. 'What would you like to do for the last couple of days? Don't forget, you can do anything that you want.'

'Anything?' She double-checked with him, speaking clearly into the mike.

'Anything. Your wish is our command.'

Colette looked around at the faces staring enviously back in her direction. She found this a hard situation to take in. No one had ever looked at her before with jealousy etched in their eyes. It was normally a look of pity, and a stare of hatred as they shouted at her to, 'hurry up you dopey slag and get our order.'

But this was her time. She was the Belle of the Ball. The Princess trying on the diamond glass slipper. It was her, sitting on the throne with the peasants walking behind her trail.

'I bet she asks for a couple of flagons of Strongbow and twenty Embassy regal' Alex said.

The silence was deafening.

She finally snapped out of her trance and slowly said, 'I would like… I would like to be….'

'Come on girl, spit it out,' Lusty muttered quietly.

Colette stared straight ahead towards the crowd.

'Come on Colleen, don't be shy now!' the Mayor suggested. 'Would you like a front seat at the bingo, or free scallop and fish cakes for the rest of the week?'

She turned to face the patronising little man in front of her and said, in a clear concise voice, 'What I would really like to do…. what I would really like to do… is to be the Mayor for the next three days.'

The cheers rang around the town in waves. People cried with laughter, the perplexed Mayor's face becaming frozen in time.

'You can't be the Mayor,' yelled the Mayor.

'You said that I can do anything that I wanted. And I wanna be the Mayor in the big black car, with the fancy number plate, and the shiny gold chain thing, and I want that poodle,' said Colette, pointing at the terrified dog.

The place was in uproar. People banged on the tables and shouted her name. They all knew that Colette was one sharp metal object when it came to taking the piss out of people, but this not only took the biscuit, this had the cheek to break into the biscuit company, start up all the machines, produce the biggest Digestive in history and then dunk it in a giant mug of tea.

'Well you can't be the Mayor.' The Mayor picked up his dog and headed for the exit. Unfortunately for the soon to be defrocked councillor, Malcolm Knuckles was blocking his path in his normal threatening manner. He picked him up with one hand and marched him back onto the stage, where he proceeded to strip him of his car keys and chain, and then detached the confused poodle from his tight grip. Malcolm put him on a coat hanger, to dry for a while. The big man placed the gold chain gently around Colette's neck, and put the dog on her lap.

'Speech,' Lusty shouted from out of the mists.

'Speech,' everyone joined in.

Phil and Malcolm motioned for her to step up to the microphone.

'Hello everyone.' She was nervous. 'I'm not used to speaking, unless it's asking someone for their order or telling someone that they are banned.'

Her new servants laughed on key.

'There are only two things I would like to say for now. First is, I think we should all have a big piss up.... sorry.... party on Wednesday in Tiffany's.'

Another loud cheer escaped and hit the ceiling.

She was enjoying this. She added 'All paid for by the council.'

This time the cheers burst through the roof tiles and hit the moon, toppling the cow, and sending it floating out of control for several light years. The ex-Mayor went to complain, but a stare from Malcolm made him swallow his words hard, before they had a chance to surface.

'And the second thing is I would like my hero, Malcolm Knuckles, to do whatever he wants to do.'

This was not greeted with a cheer. In fact, chairs moved sharply and feet were ready to run with all their might. They all envisaged Malcolm lining them up, for an attempt on the world record of, 'Knocking the most people out in one seating.' Malcolm stepped up to the mike, and thanked the new Mayor from the bottom of his heart. He then turned and informed everyone that he would like to read them one of his poems.

'Is this a joke?' Alex nudged Lusty. 'Has the world already ended?'

But Phil, like a true professional, was in like a shot from a colt 45 revolver. 'Ladies and Gentlemen, I would like you all to give, the utmost respect and a little silence, to our very own street fighting man, who, by the way, still has his very own teeth, (which can't be said for some of his victims, Phil thought but not too loud), who is going to recite some poetry that he has penned with his own hands.

'What is it called Mal?' Phil asked nervously.

'I killed you with my bare hands for crossing the street,' Jac quietly whispered to his mates. Lines of brave shoulders shook with hidden laughter.

'It is called 'Farewell to the Old Year,' Malcolm proudly announced.

'Ladies and Gentleman, put your hands together, for Malcolm Knuckles …'

Before he finished his introduction, Malcolm pulled on his sleeve and whispered something in his ear.

'Sorry Malcolm. OK, ladies and gentlemen, please put your hands together, this time for Mister Malcolm McCormick, and his poem entitled, 'Farewell to the Old Year.' Phil left the stage and lit a fag. Malcolm winked at Colette.

No one said a thing. Everyone stared at the stage. Malcolm was nervous. Colette, who was positioned behind the big man, was suitably impressed with his broad shoulders and well-trimmed butt. She hadn't noticed these things before. Perhaps now that she was Mayor, she would notice a lot more pleasant things.

'Hello everyone… this is called 'Farewell to the Old Year.' Malcolm's words escaped from his mouth and he nervously started.

> *All join hands and sing, to what a New Year will bring,*
> *But don't forget a farewell for the Old,*
> *Only Mother Nature knows the reasons for the ever circling seasons,*
> *Full of memories to cherish and hold.*

His voice was shaking. His giant hands were shaking. He focused his eyes on one poor soul, who, unfortunately found himself in the front row. The man didn't know if he should look away, or just nod his head and fake a smile. Malcolm pushed on with the next verses.

January had its day, but danced swiftly away,
For the 'Rest of the Years' waltz to begin,
February sneezed and the snow covered the trees
As sly old March sneaked in.

It caused rivers to freeze with its cold wind and
breeze,
And other misdemeanours it brings,
But there's a saviour at hand, April enriches the
land,
Whistling a song called 'The Spring.'

He started to relax. His voice gained in confidence, and thankfully for the man in the front row, who had pissed himself, Malcolm looked around as he continued to the end.

May, the identical twin, full of flowers blooming,
Sets its alarm for the first,
As June opens one eye, there's not a cloud in the
sky,
And the streams are dying of thirst.

Lazy July's in a daze, just relaxes and plays,
Tanning itself in the sun,
August shakes its head; there are mouths to be
fed,
And harvesting to be done.

The Belle at the Ball, September stands tall,
Painted in colours of gold,
October shakes the trees, collects up the leaves,
For a coat to protect from the cold.

November does not lift its head, from out of its
bed,
In fact it is strictly a bore,
But the hand of December turns the last page

over,
And asks January to accompany him on the dance
floor.

When he finished, people cried. Malcolm cried. Colette cried. Even Kinsey who hadn't cried since his uncle had twisted his arm in a snakebite grip when he was seven, shed a sly tear. They all wept at the sensitivity of the piece. Ok, in the cold light of another day, it was no masterpiece, and would probably get a slating off the literary critic of The Sunday Times. But what the hell, this was a man, who rumour had it, had killed an Irish navvy with a six inch nail, who was now spilling his heart out on the stage in front of the people he had terrorised since he was fifteen. Not even Keats could boast of doing that.

He walked across, bent down on one knee and kissed Colette's hand.

'More... more,' they all roared.

Phil Haddock turned to a faceless person by his side and said, 'It weren't that bloody good.' His words were for personal consumption only, and not for the general public. But sadly for Phil, the words carried more weight than he had anticipated, and they floated over to where Malcolm was standing. The old street fighter sprung around, his fists already clenched, with his knuckles protruding out like a switchblade. He stormed over to the bit-part actor and said 'Where do you think I could improve it Phillip?'

Kinsey had seen enough. He now knew that the world had already ended, and they were all part of some candid camera programme that was being run by the devil.

A smile walked onto Malcolm's face as he strolled back to his imaginary spotlight, he then spent the next three hours going through his repertoire of twenty-five poems, six times. By the end of it, he was so confident, that he had his jacket off, his sleeves rolled up, and was prancing around like Freddie Mercury on stage at the

Live-aid concert. He even added a couple of 'Dayo's….
Dayo's' between verses, and a make-up artist touched
him up during his costume changes.

Malcolm completed his final curtain call, reached out
for Colette's hand, and they strolled off the stage like Mr
and Mrs Prom King and Queen. Colette was in love. She
turned before she left the building with her new man, and
ordered someone to take the ex-Mayor, who was still
dangling from the coat hook, and lock him up in the beer
cellar. She then ordered her chauffeur, to drive them the
two hundred yards to Hing Hongs, where a special table
was set up in her honour. The chef made a romantic
double egg surprise for the new odd couple.

'We'll do it,' Alex volunteered his gang's services
about taking the ex-Mayor back to the cell.

'Who will?' Kinsey asked.

'Look if we take him back to the pub, we'll have a
chance to speak to Old Cherry-nose and find out a little
more on what he saw?'

'Ah… good plan…. Batman,' Jac said, spit dribbling
down his chin on seeing the young Tanya walk past.

They unhooked the ex-Mayor and frog marched him
towards the cold room at the back of the pub.

Chapter 8

'Save a Prayer
(for the bloke with the big nose)'

Arthur Cherry-nose sat in a corner of the damp cellar and wondered where it had all gone wrong. One minute he was the toast of the town, being treated like a King. He ate in all the best chip shops, with extra fish tails being dished out to him without him even asking for them. He shopped at the exclusive Oxfam store; it was none of that old charity RSPCA shop in the High Street for him. He was even given his own room under the stairs in a terraced house, courtesy of the Housing Association. There he lived in relative comfort, with thirty-two other hobo's, who each owned a dog called Bob. It was small and cramped, but it was home, and life tasted sweet.

Almost over night, he soon found out how quickly sweet can turn sour. It only took one wrong prediction. A few misguided words that people didn't like, and they all turned against him. If he had kept his mouth shut, perhaps he wouldn't have been thrown in a dark pub cellar with a seven foot Indian, who never said a word and got upset if he was beaten at basketball, and a horse with hay fever that went through a box of tissues a day.

Arthur felt that all this was unfair. He had been told that the Housing Association had given his room under the stairs away to a family with four kids, and Oxfam had taken back all of his third hand clothes.

'I didn't ask to be the magic man,' he told the horse. 'I didn't want you to boot me out of that window. In fact it bloody hurt.' The horse sneezed all over him.

He remembered way back to the first day he had hobbled into that pub, face covered by the fur hood of his parka. He could feel the silence, and the eyes burning into his back. He heard their snide comments closing in around him. He had heard similar comments all of his life.

'What is it? Is it a man?' the same questions had followed him around like a bad smell.

On that fateful day, he ordered a pint of ale and sat alone in the poorly lit back room, along with people of similar dispositions. They were all curious, but too afraid to ask any direct questions. Rumours spread like wild fire, ignited by a thousand sparks on a patch of dry grass. Where had this thing come from? Was it man, woman, or half-beast? There were no clues, and nobody ventured to uncover the truth. People had heard, that the thing was actually a man, who had been badly burnt in a terrible fire on the other side of the valley. But no one was sure of this. Others said that it was a ghost, and stories of it never leaving footprints in the mud, were told on cold winter nights around the oil drum street fires.

Then one day the inevitable happened. A youth with an appetite for devilry, who was tanked up on barley wine and black bombers, sneaked up on poor Arthur and yanked his hood back to reveal his face.

Scream and gasps of horror circled around the town, like vultures around a fresh dead Zebra carcass. Even the barmaid jumped onto the table, resembling a woman who had seen a mouse carrying a machete in one paw, and the head of a ginger-haired tom cat in his other.

'What a hooter!' the youth cried out, commenting on the size of Arthur's nose. 'There's enough skin on that thing to wallpaper my hallway.'

'It can't be real…. it must be fake.' A policeman, who had come running in to investigate the screams, added.

The Environmental Health Officers were summoned immediately. They analysed it, and sent for the Mayor. He wiped his eyes in disbelief and sent for the Zoo Keeper, who turned up in gorilla slippers, Rupert Bear pyjamas telling all that he only dealt with real animals and didn't do people, especially ones with big noses.

Several emergency council meetings were called, which carried on long into the night. A question was finally asked, that really threw a spanner into the works. 'How long has he been here?' someone asked innocently.

'I think he was born here,' replied one council officer.

'Don't be so stupid. If he was born here… he would have had a nickname by now, and all the kids would throw clodges of earth at him every day.' The Mayor shot the council officer's theory down in flames.

The disgruntled council officer picked up the Town's book, and searched for the chapter on 'Tramps and Hobos'. He finally found what he wanted between the large sections on, 'Unmarried Fifteen Year Old Mothers' and, 'Psychopathic Woodwork Teachers'.

He quickly flicked through the pages. There were hundred of nicknames of tramps, thieves, and hobos from down the years, but none with reference to the man they had before them.

Everyone in the room was aware that this was a very serious matter. It was law in the country, that all weird people, had to have a suitable nickname within fifteen days of residence of the town, village, or household that the unnamed thing resided in. If not, the council could face a possible heavy fine, or have it's financial support for housing all these types of individuals removed. They all knew that that would be a disaster for the town, as nearly half of it's population were claiming for some kind of deformity benefit.

The council decreed that if he was staying, a nickname was required for the mystery guest urgently.

So, for a short while he was known as the Bulbous Beak. This seemed quite acceptable, and the small kids found it easy to shout abuse at him while pelting him with clodges. Everything was rosy, until the original Bulbous Beak from two valleys over, put in a complaint to the Name Sanctioning Committee, for a copyright infringement of trade. A writ was served on the town, preventing them from using the name again.

An emergency poll was organised to decide on a suitable name quickly. There was a shortlist of four names for the town's folk to choose from. They were:-

1. Plain Big beak
2. Cherry-nose
3. Lightbulb snout
4. The Ant-eater (suggested by the Zoo Keeper)

Everyone in the village voted and it had been a very tight race between 'the Lightbulb snout', and 'Cherry-nose'. It appeared to be neck and neck, until the latter just poked its conk out in front at the last hurdle.

Soon after, a name declaration form plus certificate were produced and ceremoniously hand delivered by a select committee, to the newly named Arthur Cherry-nose. The women of the town had also crocheted a new black parka with the words, 'Cherry-nose', displayed on the back. When they left, Arthur was well chuffed. He decided that he'd like to stay here for quite a while. This had not only been the first town to give him an official nickname, but had not tried to burn him at the stake. He was, in hobo heaven.

The four boys and the ex-Mayor opened the door to the cellar. The smell of hops climbed the walls. Someone was crying uncontrollably, in the dark corner, of the damp room.

'Who's that,' a voice meowed. 'Look I'm sorry…. I didn't mean it…. you can't blame me!'

'Sorry about what Cherry-nose?' Kinsey said, switching on the light. 'Sorry about making up that stupid bloody story about the world ending, and frightening everyone to death.'

'Oh no! I thought that you were him coming back for another game.'

'Who's coming back? You've been locked in here by yourself with that horse since Friday,' Alex queried, wondering if the horse's kick and the lack of proper food, had started to takes its toll.

'I thought you were the seven foot Indian. You see, I played one-on-one basketball with him today, and just because I sunk a cabbage from over by the old beer crates, he sulked and stormed off, and took Slaughterhouse Bill with him.'

The boys looked around, and were amazed that the horse, had in fact disappeared. Fresh horse dung in the corner made the situation more mysterious.

'Hey Arthur…. that's a fair shot from that distance,' Lusty commented, throwing the cabbage himself. It fell way short.

'What's he doing here?' Arthur asked, pointing towards the ex-Mayor.

'It's a long story. Let's just say, that not since Goliath told his mother that he wouldn't be long, and could she put his tea in the oven, while he went and squashed some little upstart called David, has a plan backfired with such dramatic effect. Colette from Hing Hongs is the new Mayor,' Alex informed the man.

'Oh good…. she's a lovely woman. It's about time we had someone with a bit of sense running this town.' Arthur's eyes burnt into the ex-Mayor's face.

'Look Arthur, I don't know if you realise how much mayhem your prediction as caused. The town's gone mad.'

'The town's always been mad. They bloody call it the mad town.' He replied unmoved.

'Ok it's gone madder than abnormal. Just think back to the maddest you have ever remembered it.'

Arthur thought back, the boys waited.

'The maddest, was the time last year when someone shot Santa as he was about to switch the Christmas decorations on.' He recalled. All except Lusty nodded in agreement.

'Who got shot?' Lusty thought he had heard wrong.

'It's a long story Lust,' explained Alex. 'But basically, last year, someone fatally wounded the man who was dressed up in the Santa costume.'

'Who would do that?' again Lusty asked, wondering if he shouldn't have fought it out in Spain against the Fernando family, instead of coming home.

'There were lots of conspiracy theories. Some were adamant that the bullet was fired from the old library, by a hitman who had been paid to rub him out because of his gambling debts. But many believed, that the shot rung out from the grassy knoll, where the winos hung out by the bus station. Many eyewitnesses swore they saw a Santa-like figure carrying a rifle, getting into a car and driving away.'

'I thought you were going to say that he made his gateway on a reindeer.' Lusty laughed.

'No, that was his accomplice,' Alex was quite serious with his reply.

Lusty was street wise enough to know when not to delve deeper in this debate.

'Well take that madness that occurred after the shooting of Santa, times it by fifty, and you are still not even close. Even Percy Norman has been seen drinking, without his wife.'

'Fucking hell,' Arthur grunted miserably. 'If Percy Norman is out by himself.... it must be bad. I'm sorry boys, I didn't mean anything, honest.' Those words were enough to cause the tramp to place his head in his hands, and weep like a baby. 'What have I done? What have I done?'

The boys pulled up some beer barrels and tried to comfort the poor man. They realised that they had all taken a part in causing this. The town had bloody well forced him to get kicked out of that window, and for what? A couple of extra coins to waste on alcohol and chips.

Alex took over the lead. 'Arthur.... we need to try to understand what you saw, then perhaps we can help you.'

Arthur wiped his bloodshot eyes, turned, and said that he wasn't telling them, with him, pointing at the ex-Mayor, listening. Without a second thought, Kinsey spun around and knocked the uninvited councillor spark out.

'I was thinking more of locking him outside... or putting ear protectors on him.... but what the hell.... that will do.' Arthur forced a smile back on his face. 'I'll tell you exactly what happened. I remember waiting for the kick to come. I wish someone would kick that bloody Phil Haddock, his voice gets on my nerves. Anyway, next thing I entered the darkness. There was bright light, and I woke up on the terraces at Anfield, watching that guy from Ipswich sink that last minute penalty. Then I saw somebody on TV dancing around ecstatically.' The boys knew he was referring to the antics of Bobby Wilson.

'He's not dancing now,' interrupted Jac. 'Apparently, seven Liverpool fans tracked him down, broke his legs and tattooed Ian Rush's name on his arse, seven times. They're mad bastards them scousers. Good sense of humour mind.'

Arthur continued, 'Next thing... I was freezing. I was sitting on a tin roof, watching the world become white. I saw Alan the Midget prancing around in eight inch boots, and you picking him up.' His finger stretched out towards Kinsey.

'Bloody hell…. can I have your autograph?' Lusty asked. He was talking to the new Nostredamus.

'Ok… Ok… what happened next?' Jac said, leaning forward and falling off the beer barrel.

'I was in some big room. Everyone was standing there staring. There was music, but no one was dancing. There were bright lights. I could see all of your faces. There was sadness, then the lights went out…. And it all ended. It ended, just like that.' He snapped his fingers, causing them all to jump.

'I'm tired, and he'll have me up at dawn.' He muttered.

'Who will?' Alex asked.

'The seven foot Indian. He's a competitive so and so.' Arthur turned over and fell fast asleep.

The boys put a blanket around his shoulders and left the cellar quietly, locking the door behind them.

'What do you think?' Lusty asked, ordering four pints from the bar.

'He seems genuine enough.' Alex answered.

'So did bloody Doctor Crippin.' Kinsey jumped in, with both barrels firing.

'How would he have known about Bobby Wilson, and Alan the Midget in platform boots then, smart arse?' Jac said, sticking up for the defenceless tramp.

'Right, tomorrow we will start to carry out our last wishes,' Alex told them.

Their silence meant that they all agreed, even the unbelieving Kinsey.

Alex then added, 'Look I'll go first. I promised my granddad before all this, that I would make his final wish come true before he died. So, if he's going to snuff it in three days, I need to honour my commitment to him, but I need your help.'

They all nodded their heads.

'So, the rest of you had better start thinking fast or I'll have all your go's.'

'I already know mine,' Lusty said, surprising them all, by being the first to jump on the bandwagon. He was normally the silent type, who would never let his guard down. He then went on to explain to them, how he had fallen for Francesca back in Spain, and for the first time in his life, had sampled the pleasure of love. This seemed strange to his listening mates, because Lusty had girls dropping on him like leaves from trees in Autumn.

'So you wanna go back to Spain?' Kinsey hurried his question, thinking that there would be space for him with the new love of his life… Tanya.

'No… I would like ... to… to' he struggled to explain. 'To take a girl out for once, make her a nice meal, talk to her, find out about her hopes and dreams, then walk her home… kiss her on the cheek and float back to my house.'

They were completely confused by his strange request. It was lost at sea on a shipwreck of male emotion. 'Well what's so special about that?' Jac asked. The other two were also thinking the same thing.

'For some reason, I never get the chance to just walk a girl home. I normally end up in bed with her, or end up giving her one in a doorway.' Lusty looked a little depressed.

'Listen to Mister Rent-a-Shag here,' Kinsey cried out. 'We're all looking for a girl to lay, and you want the opposite. Poor boy, I feel so sorry for you. If you were a charity, I would offer you money.'

Even Alex and Jac, who rarely agreed with anything their mad short fused mate said, agreed this time.

Lusty interrupted 'Look there's more to life than sex.'

'Not to me.' Jac said, his hormones had started to surface with all this talk that included the magic sex word.

'So let me play this back to you.' Alex said to Lusty. 'You want to take a girl out for a meal, get to know her, kiss her cheek, take her home, and then wait for the world to end, without copping a feel.'

'Yeah.'

'Fair… enough. I think that one man's poison is just another man's medicine.'

'Who would you like?' Jac asked.

'That Tanya probably,' Kinsey grunted jealously.

'No… she's too hot, and her mother's even hotter.' Lusty answered. 'I don't care…. you can pick.'

'I'll sort a girl for you Lust,' Jac offered, to help his mate.

The Friends said their goodbyes. Jac and Kinsey went home, to contemplate, what wish they would be telling Alex and the genie in the bottle, the following morning

Meanwhile, back in the cellar, the ex-Mayor had woken up, and had already started to write hundreds of letters of protest on the back of beer mats.

'What you writing about?' Arthur would ask each time he saw the ex-Mayor pick up another beer mat and peel the paper off one side.

'Never you mind… you tramp son of Satan,' the ex-Mayor would reply, climbing up on top of the largest barrel and continue to scribble madly.

Suddenly, Arthur Cherry-nose turned to see who was slowly opening the beer cellar door. Tears rolled down his face on seeing, the seven foot Indian standing in the light. The Apache had come back looking for revenge. He was kitted out in a shiny shell suit, (purchased off Luke Pozzoni), a pair of air cushioned Magic Johnson sneakers, and was bouncing a brand new Iceberg lettuce.

Chapter 9

'Just like w- - king the detectives'

While the citizens of the doomed town just drank themselves into oblivion, and then slept themselves back sober, the rest of the outside world started to wake up to find something stirring from the little town in the valley. There was even a strong rumour that tunnelling had begun, underneath the bank. Even though everyone had agreed that it was stupid to try to rob the bank, with only three days to go. This hadn't deterred Luke Pozzoni, who hadn't even heard the end of world hot gossip news, but had decided a long time ago, to pull off, one last big job. He was sick of being known as a big minded thief in a small minded town. His tunnel was on schedule, even though he had a little mishap, when his hole crossed paths with an escape attempt,t being made by the Struggling man from Hing Hongs. Apparently, the reason the Struggling man had always taken so long to eat his food, was a massive ploy. Most of the time, the person that everyone could see merrily chewing away, was in fact a decoy, while the real struggling man was under the tablecloth, digging his way to freedom. To hide the dirt, he actually started to eat it, along with his sweet and sour sauce.

137

But, outside the confines of the town, suspicion was slowly starting to arrive, in a black limousine, with a sweaty overweight driver in dark shades. The ripples caused by the initial premonition, were beginning to spread their hands far and wide throughout the rest of the country.

One of the first incidents, was the discovery that the town's, Anorexics Anonymous Society, (that consisted of 16 individuals) had collectively gone on an eating rampage in the city centre. They had been on their annual pilgrimage, to view the remains of the burnt out chocolate cake factory. Their master plan ,was for them all to assembly at the 'Speak your Weight' scales in the Marks and Spencers department store, and have a giant weigh on, before attempting the last part of their daring day trip. Their combined weight, including rucksacks and raincoats, came to ninety-eight stone exactly. Their final objective was, for them all to eat at the exclusive, 'Kill and Fry' steakhouse restaurant, and then all do a mass runner.

As the thin line of fugitives, struggled to scarper out of the restaurant, they hadn't considered the massive amount of energy that this illegal activity would take up, while being followed in hot pursuit by two Greek waiters. Many of them were physically sick, before they reached the pavement. Most of the vomiting was self induced, by sticking their fingers down their throats. Two of them, actually got caught in the reflection of a confectionery shop window, like two rabbits mesmerised by the glare of a car's headlights.

The detective, who interviewed the unusually thin criminals, thought that he had been set up by his work colleagues, because it was his birthday. He had already let six of them go, before his colleagues informed him, that they didn't know or care that it was his birthday, and did he realise that he had just let loose some very dangerous eating disorder lunatics, who were probably on their way to kidnap a school kid for his lunch box, eat the contents, then spew it all back up all over the kid's shoes.

When the shamed faced detective had finally started to take the arrests seriously, he interviewed three sisters, who looked like a set of cricket wicket stumps, which had been left out on the crease all summer long.

'What did you think you were doing?' he yelled at the insipid looking girls. 'You can't just come to this city, have a meal, and then just decide not to pay. What if I came to your town and did that?'

The three girls shrugged their shoulders, concerned only, about the huge amount of calories that they had taken in.

'Where are you from anyway?' he asked, noticing that he could actually see their shinbones showing through their skin.

'Merthyr,' came back the reply in treble-phonic sound.

'Hey.... don't piss on my chips and tell me it's raining,' he demanded. 'Now where are you really from?'

'Merthyr,' their reply was a photocopy of their first.

He realised that this was the first time that he had come across anybody from that dysfunctional place. He knew, that no one, who was anyone, went to Merthyr, unless sentenced to a lifetime of being a tramp, or having been sent there by some missionary charity. He was sure that he once read that they didn't use money in that part of the world. They paid for everything, by giving each other, either red berries, or hand jobs.

'Well, why did you do it?' he tried to focused them back to his original line of questioning.

The fatter one of the sisters, who still came into the ring at under five stones, said, 'Why not? The world's going to end in three days anyway! Who wants to be thin? Come on Mister, give us some cake and we'll give you some.... berries.' She added frantically.

'Typical,' he thought. 'Berries he could live without.' Now if they had mentioned a hand-job, he would have been straight around to Howfields, and brought back the biggest puffed-up cream filled meringue in the bloody shop.

'I don't like berries,' he protested slyly. 'Anything else, you got to offer?' He was edging his way hopefully towards a quick Arthur Hank on the wrist off the triplets.

They shook their heads in unison. They knew exactly what he was referring to, but they knew that they didn't have the strength to carry out his hidden request, even if their life depended on it.

He looked at their faces and whispered to himself, 'Why me? Why do I always end up with the kooks?' He threw the sisters into a cell and had it covered with chicken mesh.

During his shift that day, he interrogated the rest of the skinny fugitives and they all told the same story about some tramp getting booted into the future. He phoned up the local nuthouses, to see if a group of their inmates had shimmied through the bars after breakfast. He called the local police station, but he had no reply. He didn't think that anything was wrong, because, the station was often getting petrol bombed. His last hope was the local churches or religious sects, to see if this was the end of Lent, or some other bible-bashing event, just like student rag week. His enquires turned up nothing concrete, so he let them all go with a severe warning, and went about his everyday business.

Later on that day, a mini-bus full of OAPs, were also led into the station, after they were apprehended down by the docks, whilst soliciting for prostitutes. The detective laughed out loud when he saw them all being frog marched into the station, handcuffed together. But his blood soon ran cold when he found out, that the randy old men were from the same place, as the thin eating criminals that he had interviewed earlier. The OAPs were insisting on 'diplomatic' immunity due to the world ending soon.

More incidents of peculiar disturbances and other major misdemeanours being carried out, from the people of the same town, were being reported all over the country, like bullets being fired from a gattling gun. The detective started to put two and two together (but he did need to use his fingers)

There was even a story from Cape Canaveral in the USA, where a family with a thick Welsh accent and a posse of animals, had disguised themselves in astronaut's suits and had stolen a space shuttle. The first indication from NASA was that at that moment, they were circling around the globe with a Russian chimpanzee, called Darren.

The most disturbing report came from an uptown café in the Latin quarter of the city, where apparently, a well-known street fighter from the valleys, dressed in smoking jacket and cravat, was terrorising the diners, by exposing them to some basic working class poems. He had an accomplice with him, who was a woman with an extensive underground knowledge of swear words, a thick, gold chain, and a pet poodle. These incidents, had Detective Roberts, starting to wonder if there was something really suspicious going-on.

He put on his raincoat, (even though it wasn't raining), filled his pockets up with red berries, and went to investigate for himself.

Chapter 10

'The bogey road to nowhere!'

Cyril could hear Doris Pozzoni snoring, as if it was going out of fashion, in the bed, next to his tree. He knew from living in this house for the last ten days, that Pablo would be doing the same sort of sleep dance, downstairs, in front of the TV.

He had decided, that this was the night that he would try to escape. He had given up on anyone coming to rescue him, so he found himself all alone, playing mind games with the entire Indian nation. He assumed that Pablo would have already sampled his usual gallon of strong cider, and his wife would have worked her way through half a bottle of sherry. He had heard Luke leaving about two hours earlier, probably up to no good, and little Romana was tucked up in bed.

He had had the first bit of luck earlier that day, when he had been allowed to go to the bathroom. There in the medicine chest, he found a pair of scissors, which he carefully hid when returning back to the bedroom. All afternoon, he had somehow used the sharp instrument to cut through the rope, that snaked around his now bloody and bruised hands.

It had been tough going, but he finally broke through the cord at about eight 'o' clock. For the rest of the night, he pretended to be still firmly secured to the branches of the tree. He even refused a scallop and mushroom pie in gravy supper, in case he got rumbled.

He coughed, to see if the sudden noise would arouse any suspicion. Happily, the snoring couple continued with their rhythm. He slowly unravelled the rope, and reached down trying to untie the dressing gown belt that shackled his legs. One minute later he was free. But, he was still in a lot of danger.

He tiptoed to the bedroom door, and although it squeaked when he opened it, thankfully nobody in the household stirred.

Cyril felt like running out, as fast as his legs could carry him. But he suspected, that the closet Red Indian had probably set up booby traps along the veranda. He decided to try and keep his cool. He stepped lightly across the floorboards. He nearly shit himself when he bumped into the two shop window mannequin dummies, which were hanging by the neck, dangling down the stairwell.

'Will this madness ever stop?' He started to cry. If it hadn't been for his strict TV detector man survival training boot camp, that he had attended in the summer, he was sure he would have cracked up by now.

He pushed himself on, the taste of freedom filling his senses. Quietly he made his way down the stairs. He could hear the buzzing of the redundant TV set, and he could see the flickering of its light escaping from the screen, making the shadows dance on the wall.

He couldn't help himself, he had to have a quick look round the front room door. His mouth fell open and hit the floor. In the middle of the living room, covering every inch of the floor space, was an enormous Indian tepee, which must have been delivered early in the week. It was so big, it wouldn't have looked out of place in Billy Smarts circus. He noticed that Pablo had cut a circular hole in the bedroom floor above the lounge area, just so the top bit of the tent could be erected properly.

'So that's what all the banging and sawing was about,' he said unbelievably to himself.

From inside this extraordinary tent, Cyril could make out the 48' TV set, and Old Man Pozzoni lying fast asleep on the settee.

He finally dragged himself away from the bizarre sight, and headed for the front door. Suddenly he heard a noise, as a shadowy figure outside was trying to get it. He darted back up the stairs, banging his head on the legs of the dummies, just as Luke came clambering through the door, carrying a dead deer on his back. Cyril was rooted to the spot halfway up the stairwell. He was aware that he was in great danger. One mistake and he would be caught. He heard the deranged teenager enter the kitchen and slap the carcass onto the pool table.

Cyril's heart was pumping. A cold sweat covered his body. He was caught in two minds about what to do next.

'Should he chance the front door, or was it too risky?' he thought, then remembered that there was a porch that jutted out over the front bedroom window. 'I could jump onto the out building and shimmy down the drainpipe,' he confirmed to himself.

He cautiously moved back towards the landing. He opened the door to the spare room. It was dark, but he was given enough light by the street lamp across the way. He noticed that it was full up with what appeared to be stolen items.

Halfway across the room he was stopped dead in his tracks by a sudden noise, coming from the corner beside the stash of microwave boxes.

Cyril had to look twice, until the sight registered with his now tired and mentally, 'shot to pieces' brain. There, tied to the radiator, with his head shaved in Mohican style, was a man in his early thirties. Cyril rushed over. The man motioned for him to remove the gag of a sock and duct tape, that had been placed over his mouth.

Cyril ripped the tape painfully off the man's face.

'Who the hell are you?' Cyril asked.

'Have you come to rescue me?…. Please say you're here to rescue me.' The man's eyes registered fear.

'No, I'm trying to escape myself.' Cyril put his finger to his mouth to warn him to talk more quietly. 'Who are you?'

'I'm Nick Parsons. I work for the Education Welfare Department.'

Cyril shrugged his shoulders, needing a bit more information.

'I'm the School Children Liaison Officer!'

Cyril still didn't understand what he was getting at.

'I'm the bunking officer.' The man finally admitted.

'Oh… the bunking officer. Then why didn't you say that in the first place. What are you doing here?'

'I only called here to see Mr and Mrs Pozzoni, about a month ago…. I think it was.' He looked vacant. 'I'm starting to lose my mind. I can't stick any more fish and chip suppers… they're rotting me from the inside. Please get me out of here!'

'So what happened?' the mention of the greasy food also made Cyril feel a little woozy.

'I came to see why their daughter hadn't been to school since last year. I only said to him that I was going to have to report it to the authorities, and then he pulled his gun on me. He forced me up here, shaved my head, dressed me in this gear, and now he keeps calling me Magwar. I've been here ever since.' Tears filled up in the man's eyes.

'Amazing,' Cyril commented shaking his head. 'The old man has kidnapped the both of us.'

'There are more than just us,' the bunking replied. 'There's a woman locked in the cupboard who works for Avon. She's been there since last Christmas.'

Cyril walked towards the tall boy to see for himself.

'Don't release her.' Nick cried. 'She's gone mad. She thinks she's Colonel Gaddifi. When they leave her out at the weekends, she wanders around the room shouting out 'Gaddifi calling' and pretends to spray cyanide perfume at everyone.' Cyril immediately let go of the door handle and slowly backed away from the closet.

'And there's more!' The bunking officer started to cry.

'More!' Cyril was starting to wonder if Pablo was some sort of serial kidnapper.

Nick went on to explain, that apparently there was a family of Mormons imprisoned in the attic. Cyril had wondered what that strange praying noise had been, coming from the little room above the master bedroom every Tuesday. Originally, he thought it was the perverts from number 31, having some sort of free for all, station of the cross, orgy.

'Ain't you the TV detector man?' Nick asked. 'I once attended a lecture you presented at the college. Didn't you win the best TV detector man of the Century award?'

Cyril looked embarrassed, but nodded, and flashed him a photo of him receiving the award, which he kept in his wallet.

'Are you going to escape?' the man continued.

'Hopefully,' Cyril was thinking it was about time he got out of this place.

'Can I come with you?'

'It maybe easier for me to go alone, but I promise to send the police back as soon as possible.'

'That's what the last one said.' He grabbed Cyril's arm tightly. 'He worked for the Mobile Library Unit and I haven't seen him since.'

Cyril shivered as he remembered reading the headline in the local paper, of how they had found the body of the Mobile Library guy, hanging from a tree with a out-of-date library card pinned to his jacket, and a 'Spot the Dog' book rammed in his mouth.

'Ok…. Ok…. we'll both go, but stick close to me.'

The cupboard started to rock back and fore.

'Quick before that mad bitch wakes them all up.' Nick said.

The newly formed escape team opened up the secondary glazed window and jumped out onto the porch.

The bunking officer went first and lowered himself down onto the pavement. Cyril followed quickly, but when he reached the stony ground, the bunking officer was nowhere to be seen.

'Nick…. Nick,' He whispered. There was no reply. 'How ungrateful can you get?' he said, but perhaps he shouldn't have been that shocked by the actions of a bunking officer. He knew that the people who worked in the education system had no scruples or values.

Suddenly he felt a tap on his shoulder. He turned around sharply expecting to see his escaped colleague, smiling. Unfortunately, he came face to face with a seven foot Indian in a shell suit and white trainers, who had the unconscious bunking officer over his shoulders.

Cyril let out a whimpered scream, before fainting.

Chapter 11

<u>'Alive and Licking'</u>

Alex and Jac sat on one of the headstones,in the over populated cemetery on the brow of the hill. The sunlight had just appeared over the mountain top, and for a change, was not being chased by the thunder and the rain. Instead, it was merrily playing hide and seek with its mate, the wickedly cold north wind.

Alex's granddad was over amongst the graves, saying his weekly hellos to his deceased wife, who had passed away during the winter of '79.

Jac was reading the local paper, which had been rushed through the presses for a special one off 'End of the World' edition. Alex was preoccupied with throwing small stones at some dead flowers that sat in a rusty urn, while watching the town of his birth come alive.

His relatively young eyes, focused on the lines of small terraced houses, that appeared like a row of rotten teeth in the mouth of a Dutch sailor who was more concerned with gutting fish, than in his own unkempt appearance. An invisible shiver ran down his spine on spying the overpowering church building, with its large steeple which illuminated the skyline and poked fun at the inferior decaying smaller houses, encircling its boundaries.

He watched as a gang of teenagers indulged themselves in a new game of stolen stock cars racing through the power-charged streets. This was not a new game to them, but the rules had now changed. The offending boys, had obviously realised, that even if caught by the police, there wouldn't be time left to charge them anyway. They sped around, with a self-confidence made up of pure arrogance and disrespect. Alex could feel the powder keg of expectation, slowly fusing towards anarchy, even from where he was sitting.

He looked at his old granddad, who was positioned by the side of the grave. He was talking and crying at the same time. Alex couldn't really appreciate how his Gramp must have felt. Forty years of marriage is a long time to be suddenly left all alone. He watched as the old man, who was confined to a wheelchair, lovingly placed a bunch of freshly cut flowers across the exact spot where his grandma's heart would be, six feet below. Alex felt like crying himself. This was made worse, when he turned and started to read the engraving on the headstone next to him, that told the sad story of little Mary James, who had struggled with her life for just over four years, before the evilness known as cancer had invaded her, set up camp inside, and then suddenly switched her body off. He just couldn't make out, that if life was so precious, why did God take it so cheaply? It just didn't make sense to him at all.

'Look at this nonsense,' Jac's words cut off Alex's vehicle of depression that was slowly chugging down the road of despair.

Jac flashed the front page of the local rag in his face. The headline that was splashed across the page in large letters simply said:-

'Nostredamus... the mad Russian monk
Agrees with our own prophet... Arthur Cherry-nose.
It's official... The world will end in three days.'

Next to the heading, the paper had imported a photograph of Christopher Lee from some vampire film. It went on to say, that there was more information, and reaction about this once in a lifetime event, on pages three to forty seven.

At the bottom of the page, the paper was still running its summer holiday competition. It proudly announced:-

'Win a trip for two. Two weeks in the sun. Entries must be in by January 26th.'

'Unbelievable.' Jac said, peering over his newspaper. 'Talk about the one hand not knowing what the other hand is doing.' He referred to the contrasting stories on the front page.

'So, if they have printed that heading, does that mean that they have left poor Arthur go?' Alex chipped in.

'No way... He's still in the cellar with the ex-Mayor, and the horse, and the seven foot Indian. Apparently, he can now throw a watermelon into the basket from over near the backdoor,' Jac commented, 'with his eyes shut.'

Alex read the back page, which again was split into two separate sections. The first showed a photograph of the local postman, who had mysteriously disappeared while doing his rounds yesterday. The initial thought of the police, was that the Postman had been kidnapped, because his empty post-bag had been handed in. But sadly, no request for a ransom had been received from the kidnappers yet. The Post Office had put up a handsome reward, of a twenty pound set of commemorative stamps, and a pack of jiffy bags, in return for any information concerning the disappearance of their man.

Below that, was an invitation to a giant 'Knees-up' at Tiffany's on Wednesday to celebrate the last days on earth. In small print, it informed the people that snacks would be provided, and that dress was informal, but trainers (and cute puppies) were not allowed.

'I wonder if there's a link between the disappearance of the Postman and that TV detector guy that went missing just before Christmas.' Alex said.

'The boys from the Labour club told me that the TV detector man has been sucked into the tele, just like that girl off that film Poltergeist,' Jac mentioned. 'TV detector man…. step into the light.'

'Yeah, I heard that too.' Alex moved off his cold seat and asked, 'Where's Kinsey?'

'His parents are making him go to confession, just in case Cherry-nose's premonition comes true and their son will be seeing his maker in a couple of days.'

'I hope God doesn't upset him, or he'll be eating soup through a straw for a month.' Jac's words made them both laugh.

Alex's granddad broke up the conversation between the two, by shouting to them that he had finished his widower duty. Alex wheeled the obviously upset man to the car and gently manhandled him into the back seat.

Alex drove out of the grey surroundings of the burial ground and back towards town.

'Thanks for that boys,' The old man smiled wearily, and added with a clap of his hands, 'now, are you finally taking me to see the second love of my life?'

Jac assumed that the old man was talking about going for a pint, or to see some racing pigeons.

But, Alex turned to Jac and explained, that he had promised to help his Gramps, find a girl that he had had a passionate fling with over forty years ago.'

'Aaaaah!' Jac made a noise that resembled confusion, while he turned around to leer at the back seat passenger.

'Look, it won't take us long. I've tracked her down, she lives by the docks in the city.' Alex winked at his grandfather in the rear view mirror. 'I told Lusty and Kinsey we'll pick them up by the park gates, in about forty minutes.' Alex parked the car opposite the Italian café, and he went inside to get some breakfast rolls.

The church was packed and restless on a bitterly cold morning. It was made more uncomfortable, by the fact that the heating in the building had been purposely switched off by the priest, and all the windows left open.

Kinsey sat stoned faced in the pew opposite the confessional boxes. He couldn't believe that his parents had forced him to accompany them to bare his soul to a man, who may have had the ear of the Lord, but was as loopy as a March hare on a sunny July evening.

Next to Kinsey, was an even stonier faced Lusty, who had been tricked into tagging along by his supposed mate, who had mentioned, that he was off to a place where all his prayers would come true. Lusty, knowing that Kinsey was a bit of a pervert, hadn't for one minute realised that the place that he told him about, would be a bloody church.

'I'll get you back,' Lusty indicated.

'Shuuush,' came back a solemn response from the other sinners that sat on the bench of shame. All the faces that had stepped inside the house of God knew, that they would soon have their souls exposed, stripped bare, and beaten to pulp by Father Clancy.

Although an imposing figure, who must have stood six foot six inches tall in the pulpit, Father Theophilus Clancy appeared much bigger, with sharp pointed features on a well-worn face. His eyes were sunk way back into his cheekbones, and he carried himself in a stoop, mainly for the overpowering effect, especially when he stood over his poor parishioners, ranting and raving. Father Clancy considered himself a fair and just man. He was tough and some would say ruthless, but his quest combined with God's will, had required him to lean on the side of discipline.

The door at the back of the large church shot open, and in floated his Holiness, flanked by his trustee lieutenant, who was a sixty-year-old alter boy, (who was still failing his basic priest entry exams).

All movement and coughing, (and in some cases breathing) were put on hold, until the procession had snaked its way to the safety of the confessional boxes.

Just before the priest went to enter the dark cupboard, he noticed a young boy chewing bubblegum. He marched over to where the boy was now trying to hide under the wooden pews. The boy shook as the religious shadow loomed over him.

Father Clancy hit him over the head with the incense holder, and led him over to where the candles of lost souls were burning bright. He proceeded to extinguish the lit wax with the back of the boy's hand.

'Get to the back of the queue.' The words from the priest shook the dust off the rafters, and everyone in the place wished that they could go and disappear at the back of some, long and slow moving line.

'Is he always like that?' Lusty asked astonished.

'No. He must be in a good mood, he can get very evil sometimes.' Kinsey cursed his parents again.

The priest entered the box of shame, and the light came on outside, informing the first person to hurry up and get their sinning backside moving. Alan the Midget was the first in line. As he walked towards the box he looked like a slug, that had been refused a blindfold just before it had been ordered to slide belly first down a razorblade. He drew back the curtains and wandered in.

Kinsey could hear the faint whisper of the dwarf, which was in complete contrast to the booming voice of the priest.

'Are you going to tell him about young Tanya and her mother and that aunty?' Kinsey suggested to the good looking boy.

'Yeah, of course.... why not?' came back Lusty's casual reply.

'What about the other one you pegged last night?'

'The other two last night.' Lusty corrected him. 'She insisted that she brought her twin sister with her for company.' He didn't say it as a boast; he was too honest and naïve for that.

'I don't believe it,' Kinsey said, then continued. 'He'll have your knob guillotined off, mark my words,' nodding towards the box of doom.

Suddenly everyone waiting in the church stood to attention as they heard Father Clancy cry out, 'You've done what? That's impossible, you are only two foot nothing tall,' the Father quipped.

'Oh Clancy!' The midget barked back, 'I was wearing a pair of platform boots, and just for the record, I'm fucking two foot two and a fucking half inch... if you must know.' The dwarf was sick to death of people taking the piss out of him because of his height. He had decided to make a stand, and he didn't care who he upset.

The curtain whooshed back in temper, and the big man bounded out. He put his hand straight through the curtains, grabbed Alan by the throat, and pulled him over to the holy water fountain. Alan started to cry, but little midget tears never cut any ice with His Holiness.

'You are a cheap and nasty short attention seeker, who needs to be purified by the holy waters of the Lord Almighty.'

The priest told him to stand on the bench, and made him eat a two pound bar of soap, then he had him winched up by one foot, and his head continually dipped into the eternal fountain of holy water.

Kinsey had forgotten how insane the man of the cloth was. How he seemed to extract pleasure from inflicting punishment on his fellow human beings, supposedly in the name of God.

It was now Lusty's turn to enter the bullring. The boy went in, but came out three minutes later, smiling. He walked over to the altar, lit a candle, knelt down and said one Hail Mary and was purified. He relaxed, gave his mate the thumbs up, settled back, and started to glance over the local paper.

'What did you tell him?' Kinsey enquired, as the light above the box went off, indicating that he was next.

'Everything,' Lusty lied. 'I showed him my soul and he licked it clean.' He lied a lot. He had actually pretended to be Spanish and made out that he had only gone in there to have his photo taken. He added 'He's Ok. Bit of a softy really. He has a real heart of gold…. a heart of pure gold.'

Kinsey entered the small dark space that was the size of a storage cupboard in a doll's house. He could feel eyes burrowing into him, as he knelt down on the wooden ledge.

'Good morning Father,' Kinsey said. But deep down he had been dying to actually say, 'Good morning Vietnam!' and spin around on his chair.

'That will be two Hail Marys…. for thinking that,' Father Clancy hissed.

'Holy Fuc..' He stopped his thought patterns just in time, when realising that the priest could hear everything that he was thinking. 'Sorry Father. It's been two months since my last confession.'

'Two months… tut… tut.' Kinsey could already hear the Priest chalking up the redemption totals on a black board.

'That will be another three Hail Marys and two Our Fathers….carry on my son.'

'In that time, I've done the usual normal teenage boy stuff. Nothing worth talking about!' Kinsey knew he wouldn't get away with that lack of detail.

'I'll be the judge and jury of that. Now explain my boy…. don't be shy. I won't harm you.'

Kinsey thought; 'He has changed. He's a little pussy cat.' He was even tempted to put his hand through the thin curtain and stroke the priest's fur.

What Kinsey couldn't see, was Father Clancy indicating for the altar boy to dunk Alan the Midget's head longer into the fountain. Alan was covered, in froth and bubbles from the mixture of soap and holy water.

Kinsey continued, 'I've swore a little bit. Again, nothing too rude, just a couple of bloody hells, and a few..... what the hecks.'

There was silence, as the priest mentally calculated the penance in his head.

'I've smoked a little weed, but only a puff or two.'

'Weeeeeeed,' Father Clancy sounded more like one of the flower pot men.

'You know.... dope.... ganja... Marijuana.'

'Marijuana,' he bellowed.

'Shuuush... please Father Clancy, my parents are out there,' Kinsey said quietly.

'Don't shuush me boy. It's not your parents you need to worry about. They won't be there when it's your turn to stand in front of those pearly gates,' The priest shuffled his feet in anger. 'It's God who can hear everything.'

Kinsey pictured a man in a white robe sitting on the edge of a cloud, with Dumbo ears and a little mouse in his hat.

'You better get that image out of your head now, or you'll be serving out the rest of your time on this earth with some incurable disease.' He pointed out, before adding, 'Anything else you want to confess?'

There was plenty, but the boy decided to quit while he still had a tongue in his head, and hadn't been covered in boils. 'No. Nothing else.' Kinsey was already worried, because the priest was using a calculator to add up his penance.

'What about masturbation?' The priest asked.

Outside Kinsey's mother put her hands over her ears.

'What?' Kinsey knew this question was on its way.

'Masturbation boy. Partaking in the pleasures of the flesh.'

'Yeah, I have your Honour.... sorry Father... but only once or twice.'

'That's not bad,' Father Clancy returned gruffly. 'That's only one per month.' A smile covered the priest's hard face.

'Oh no... that's once or twice a day, sometimes more at the weekends. I've reached five once, but I found that the skin on my nuts was as tight as a box of figs, and I couldn't stand up straight for an hour.'

The priest was nearly lost for words. 'Five.... you've had five?.... in one day?'

'That's nothing,' Kinsey interjected proudly. 'My mate Jac set a new school record once, with eighteen in one afternoon.' Kinsey didn't know why he had just confessed to that, perhaps it was the devil inside him, shovelling buckets of evil information out.

Father Clancy had left the box, even before the full stop had caused the abrupt end of the sentence. He was standing as large as life in front of the boy, who had no place to hide. At first, Kinsey had considered chinning him, but thought twice about hitting a man with glasses on, and whose job it was to parade around in a skirt, speaking Latin.

Imaginary thunder and lightening bolts shot down from the rooftops, as the hand of God reached in and yanked Kinsey out.

'Billy Kinsey of 17 Herman Close, you are charged with wilfully performing unnatural and disgusting acts.' The charges were fired at him with great accuracy.

'Unnatural and disgusting acts. With who?' Kinsey's mother screamed out.

'With himself.' The priest thundered. 'With himself and that thing!' Pointing at his groin.

'Well, that's all right then,' she thought to herself. For a moment, she had envisaged another family scandal like the time they found her uncle, dressed up in a long fur coat, in the Koala bear's cage at Bristol Zoo.

'But that's not an unnatural act,' Kinsey replied.

'What's not an unnatural act?' screamed Father Clancy, as his whole body stiffened.

'A teenager having a wan... A teenager having a wan... thingy, Sir, you know!... It's not unnatural... it's just an act of God.' Billy put a faint smile across his face. He tried to add some humour into the proceedings, and said, 'Its not like I leaped over the fence and poked the spiteful Old Misses Griffiths now is it?'

What Kinsey forgot, was that humour and religion don't mix, especially in a church run by the Father of Dryness himself.

'It's only an act of God,' Father Clancy was breathing fireballs. 'Is it an act of God that so many fatherless bastards are born into this lousy world each day?... I don't think so, Mr Kinsey!.... Is it an act of God ... that young innocent girls are being driven to sell their bodies on the streets of stinking cities?.... I don't think so, Mr Kinsey.'

The congregation had heard Father Clancy rant and rave a thousand times, and they were all silently mouthing the priest's catch-phrase of 'I don't think so, Mr Kinsey!'

He continued, 'Is it an act of God... that the town's builders spend all day eating fried breakfasts with extra rations of bread in the cafes of Merthyr, instead of doing a decent days work?... I don't think so, Mr Kinsey.' He walked over and stood three inches away from Billy.

'So it is definitely not an act of God... It is a sinful act of Satan. It is definitely Satan's way of telling us that you are the devil himself, and your shameful organ is the man-beast, that you keep by your side to deflower young virgins with.'

People were dying to laugh. Lusty had to bite hard into his coat sleeve. Even Alan the Midget thought it was funny and tried to laugh, but ended up swallowing nearly half of the water in the fountain.

'Billy Kinsey, you are guilty as charged,' the holy man warned. 'You will be castrated today after the service.'

The entire congregation let out an enormous 'OOOHHH.' All the males in the audience gently touched their jewels. Billy's parents fainted.

As everyone looked at poor Billy standing there the colour of chalk, the old altar boy sided up to Father Clancy, pulled on his sleeve and said, 'Father, I'm sorry to interrupt but you can't do that to Billy.'

'Why not, I am Father Theophilus Clancy of Merthyr, Master Green Belt…. I can do what I like!'

'But it says in the black book… that you can't carry out castrations unless it's been sanctioned by Archbishop Joyce of Windsor, and don't forget there's an assessor in the audience today, grading you for Brown Belt status,' the old altar boy indicated.

With that revealing news, both of Kinsey's parents came around and breathed a sigh of relief.

Father Clancy's face gave away his emotions. 'These damn left-wing Baptists who write these books are turning soft.' He thought. 'What can we do then?' he snapped back, very obviously upset. 'Can we cut off a finger…. his ears maybe…. or extract his teeth?' Father Clancy was adamant that he was going to get something out of this session.

'No…. sorry, none of those,' the reply came back.

The priest looked over and saw the church assessor, madly scribbling away on his clipboard.

'I am not happy with that!' Father Clancy said, but then reluctantly added 'Ok…. I've had a rethink, and for your sins, you have to say four hundred Hail Marys, two hundred Our Fathers, wear a rosary for two months, and put in an application form to become an altar boy.'

He turned to eye up the crowd, and then stormed back into the small booth, which he had also converted into a port-a-loo. He pulled up his skirt, and sat on the pan.

Lusty smiled at his mate.

'You bastard,' Kinsey whispered.

'That will be another twenty-five Hail Marys, Mr Kinsey,' the priest shouted over the top of the wooden partition, while reaching for the bog roll.

Kinsey sat down, got through half of the first Hail Mary, decided to multiply it by 424 and did the same with the rest of his penance. He couldn't remember the bloody words anyway, but put an IOU in the collection box, just in case the world didn't end in three days, and Old Big Ears was watching from his cloud.

'Let's get out of here…. before he appears again and banishes all of us to the pits of everlasting fire, for having skid marks on our pants on a Monday.' Kinsey and Lusty legged it out of the cold atmosphere into the daylight.

Alex picked up his mates, fresh out of church, and they all headed off to hopefully complete the first stage of their tour de happiness.

Alex's granddad sat quietly in the back seat with his fingers crossed, while thinking, what his dream girl would look like now? Forty plus years was a long time in anyone's book, and around these parts time had an uncanny knack, of making those years look even longer. He was really excited to be going. He was so grateful to his grandson and his mates for doing this for him, especially with such a short time left in all of their lives.

'Would she remember him?' he thought. 'Would she remember the young man who she had said had shown her great consideration, when the two of them had interlocked their bodies and souls that summer just after the war.'

He sat bolt upright holding a shovel and a bucket, that he had insisted on bringing.

'I'm so grateful boys,' he repeated for the thousandth time since they embarked on their journey to the city.

'It's Ok Mr Davies… just make sure that you give her one for us,' Jac made jerking motions in the back.

'Can I ask you something Mr Davies?' Lusty spoke.

'Of course lad. What is it?'

161

'What is the spade for?' It was such a simple question that just had to have a complicated answer attached to it.

Alex's granddad explained, to the great amusement of the boys, that although Rita was a beautiful looking girl with bright blue eyes and a smile that could sink a battle ship, she had the slight misfortune of being born with a Charlie on her back.

'A fucking hunch back,' Kinsey was first in. 'You were shagging Quasimodo.' He laughed, but a dig in his ribs from Lusty stopped him from going on.

'But why the shovel Gramps?'

'It simple boys. Every time I gave her one, I couldn't stop her from rocking back and fore. I fell off her more times than I was on. So one day, I came up with a brainwave after being at my old uncle's funeral. I decided to dig a hole in the ground that she could rest her hump into. It was the steadiest shag I ever had.'

Alex smiled as he recalled the excitement that was evident on his old granddad's face when he told him that he would finally take him to find Rita Flood. There were lots of things that Alex would have liked to have done with his last wish on earth, but as he watched the old man grow more nervous with every mile that was clocked up, he was glad that he had chosen to make his dream come true.

It had been far from easy to find her. The girl of his Gramps desire had been hard to track down, but an old school mate who was working for a debt collecting agency had informed him that there was a Rita Flood living down by the docks.

Alex had finally found her selling her body outside the Custom House. Apparently, she had become a woman of the night not long after his granddad had married his gran. Alex came face to face with her and was shocked. Not only was she as old as the hills, with a face so weather beaten it was at the point of storm damage, but she was all but blind from the various bouts of syphilis and other diseases, that at one time or another, had squatted in her ravaged and deformed body.

She was the type of prostitute that he imaged Jack the Ripper to have slaughtered, back in the days of foggy nights and taverns selling jugs of rum. At first he thought of telling his old gramps that she had died, but he couldn't lie to the old man, so he had mentioned the fact that perhaps she had fallen on hard times.

Their car arrived at the windy dock-side, just as a massive ship carrying a cargo of cars engines left, heading towards a warmer climate and a better class of life. The boys struggled to get the crippled old man out of the seat, and popped him into his fold-up wheelchair. They all looked around at the grim surroundings, which were populated with unfriendly faces peering through the windows of red bricked houses.

'Are you sure about this Gramps?' asked Alex.

But the warning was lost on the old man, who had been taken over by his younger former self. The wheels on his chair were on fire, as he raced into the alley behind the pub. The boys waited in the car, with the door locks activated and the keys in the engine.

'Are you sure he'll be Ok in there,' muttered Jac.

'I bet Malcolm Knuckles wouldn't go down there by himself.' Kinsey double-checked that the lock was down.

Alex's granddad held his breath. He whispered her name. A cat knocked a can over by a rubbish bin. Finally, someone stepped out from behind a skip, in holey black stockings with matching black teeth.

Alex's granddad put his little round spectacles on to check out his vision. 'Rita is that you?'

'Who is dat?' she tried to work it out through an uneducated mouth and poor eyes.

'It's me…. Marty… Marty Davies. We met forty years ago. You said I was the love of your life.' He wheeled his chair up closer. He had the bucket and spade in his hand.

'Forty years is a long time. Lost your way did you?' she joked. A deep gaggle echoed around the narrow alleyway. 'I've had a thousand Martys.... and a hundred Marty Davies's since then. What makes you so special?'

'I dug a hole for you.' He flashed his spade. 'Remember, we kissed all night long?'

'I don't kiss anyone anymore. I only do it for money.' She was battle hardened by her circumstances, and by her perceived lack of opportunities that had entered her life. 'Now what do you want, I have people to do, and mouths to feed?'

'What have you got?' he said a bit despondent. He knew that their reunion wasn't going to be a romantic scene from Wuthering Heights, but he thought that she would be offering a little more than a quick red light on the wrist.

'It's a fiver for a hand-job, ten for oral, and for fifteen you can do what you like.' Her words cut his heart in two. He turned the chair around and headed back to the car.

Suddenly something inside of him changed his mind.

He reached into his pocket, pulled out three fivers, and told her that he wanted the full works. He placed his pension money in the dirty palm of her hand. She politely asked him if he wouldn't mind if she continued smoking, and peeling the potatoes for her grandchildren's supper whilst he did his business. He felt like crying, but he shrugged his shoulders, letting out a scream inside.

She hitched up the rag that she called her skirt, to reveal knickers, so stained, that they looked like they had been used to clean up the table after a food fight at a boarding school. He could smell her. It wasn't pleasant.

His heart raced as he dropped his trousers. She was already on her third spud, as she climbed uncomfortably onto his wheelchair.

He entered her, with over forty years of vengeance and memories. It took her breath away, and the cigarette she had positioned firmly between her lips, shot out and hit the floor. He pumped away, by moving the wheel chair back and fore without mercy. She actually dropped the potato peeler that she had been clutching, (that was a new one on her).

She held him tight, and started to savagely kiss his neck, (she hadn't done that for many a year). He continued to motion the iron horse back and fore.

He started to really enjoy it. Rita was enjoying it so much; she actually broke the golden rule of the ladies of the street and had a real orgasm. Not fake, not pretend, not one out of a packet of cereal, but an honest to God earth shattering, come. A flood of green coloured liquid, mixed with the odd maggot or two squirted out from between her legs, (she couldn't remember the last time she done that). The old man quickly followed her, filling her up with gallons of hot sticky love. He cried. She cried. The tyres on his wheelchair smelt of burning rubber. She collapsed on the metal horse.

Back out in the main street, a black man who must have been the size of a coconut tree, tapped on the isolated car window.

'Drive away, Alex,' Jac quietly gestured.

'Don't be stupid, I can't leave my Gramps.' He replied, and casually wound down the window.

The black man sniffed the inside of the interior of the vehicle and stared at each of them. He could smell dope in the air. 'Ok, so you're not the pigs. So what do you want?' He relaxed, but still refused a smile.

'Nothing. My granddad is just visiting a friend.' Alex nodded towards the alleyway.

The man didn't spare a sideward glance. He knew that many men visited friends down that alleyway. He opened up his jacket. 'Do you want to buy some pills, some dope, maybe some women. I could organise some pieces of 100% pure black ass for you white pretty boys.'

Jac's hormones, that had been dormant for the majority of the day, suddenly sprang out of bed like two six year olds on Christmas morning. 'Let's go for that. Come on boys. I've never had a bit of black. You know what they say about black women.' He rubbed his hands in glee. 'Once you've had black, you will never go back.'

His companions looked at each other. Alex shrugged his shoulders in a 'I'm game' sort of way. Kinsey indicated that he would go along for the ride. Lusty nodded. The black man let go of a smile, that was so wide, an elephant who had just won the best tusks on the African plains award, would have been jealous of the amount of ivory that the big man displayed in his mouth.

'I'll be ten minutes.' He conveniently hid his smile again and added 'It will cost twenty-five each, and you pay before you lay.'

'I'm sure I've seen him hiding underneath Lois' bed.' Alex drawled, as their personal pimp walked away. Alex went on to explain the night when he nearly had three under the bed, with Lois and the blow-up doll.

A scream from the alleyway, not only made them jump, but made the car automatically start the engine and put itself into second gear. The vehicle had been designed by German engineers, to glide smoothly over any surface and out perform many of the cars in its class, but sadly, when it came to bravery, the machine turned into a pussy cat who had accidentally wandered into the rowdy stag night, of Big Butch the bull mastiff, and his big butch mastiff friends.

The boys raced up the alley. Alex cursed himself for letting his granddad, the man who had not only fathered his father, but also fought in the war; go down that alleyway by himself. When they reached the bottom of the cul-de-sac, they saw a woman who must have been at least four hundred and fifty years old, with what they assumed was her knickers around her ankles, stuck firmly between the wheels of Alex's granddad's chair. She was straddled aside him, and trying to kiss him passionately. Potato peelings lay all over the floor. He was trying desperately to get her off him.

'Alex quick…. get this mad bitch off me.'

The boys nudged each other.

'I've seen two dogs trapped together like that in our school yard once. Mr Foley had to throw a bucket of water over them.' Jac laughed out loud.

'Well I'm not fucking touching that ugly thing,' Kinsey indicated without shame, looking for a bucket.

'Quick, come on, before the rest of them swarm all over us like Zulus,' Lusty said, bringing some reality to the situation.

They grabbed wherever they could and pulled. After a short while, the alleyway lovers became unattached. The smell was rancid. Lusty started to heave. The rest of them joined him especially when they saw a white blob running merrily down her inner thigh, and plonked onto the floor. A starving dog raced up and licked the substance off the stonework.

Jac instantly imagined, the dog having a small litter of puppies, that would look like Alex's granddad, all in little wheelchairs and holding shovels.

Before they had the chance to make their getaway, Rita lowered her skirt, her knees buckled slightly, as she sauntered over to her lover in the metal seat. She kissed him on his head, and gave him his money back, (she had never done that before).

The boys hurriedly transported him out of the lane and drove away. They had to open the window to fit Alex's granddad's grin inside, before driving away.

'Come back Mister… Come back… I think I love you.' She called after him, (she couldn't believe what she was saying).

Alex's granddad felt torn in two. Half of him was glad that he had got away from the smelly, piss stained whore. His other side, knowing that the vision that he'd had inside of him for all those years, had just died.

'Fair play to you Mr Davies, that was impressive. What did you do to her?' Jac spoke for the others. Even Lusty nodded his approval.

'Fuck me, Mr Davies, what did you do to her?' asked Kinsey.

'It's all in the hand and wheel movement boys.' He said with pleasure. 'What about some grub and a pint?'

'Only one or two for me,' Lusty said. 'I have my special date tonight.'

'With who, my boy?' Alex's granddad enquired.

'I don't know. It's a surprise.' Lusty commented.

The other boys whistled, and purposely looked away.

Thirty minutes later, they were sat in a quiet pub, sipping their second pint. A caged bird, sang a cute song above their heads.

'You haven't got any of that Bob Hope left have you?' Alex's granddad asked.

'What Bob Hope Gramps? We don't use the stuff.' Alex hurriedly denied.

'Come on, don't lie. I could smell it in the car when I came back. Who do you think I am, your mother?'

Lusty looked at Alex to get acceptance, before revealing a five skinner from the inside of his jacket pocket. He checked that the bar man was out of sight, and they lit it up.

The conversation drifted around playfully, as the dope kicked in. Even the bird sang in slow motion. Alex was amazed how his granddad seemed to handle the joint, like it was second nature to him.

'You like that then do you Mr Davies?' Lusty asked, watching him hog it a little too much.

'No disrespect, but I'm used to a bit better shit than this,' he replied, passing it on to his nephew. 'I've got an ounce of pure Moroccan back at the ranch.' They all stared slowly at the old man. 'It kills the pain boys. I have it on prescription off Doctor Ernie.'

'What happened to them anyway?' Again Lusty piped up, more interested in the fact that the old man could get a shed load of good stash on the National Health. Alex gave him a vicious stare.

'No, the legs are OK!' He answered. It was now the boys turn to appear confused.'

'So if your legs are fine, then why the wheelchair and why have we been pulling maggot ridden old tarts off you all fucking day?' Kinsey didn't hold back.

'I've got the disease.... you see. The Deep Navigation '51 disease, to give it its full title.

He told the boys to pull their chairs in closer, and he started to explain his story. He explained, that after the war, he worked in Deep Navigation Colliery, extracting coal from the bowels of the earth.

'It was hard graft boys. The water was cold, the place was dark, and the rats would eat the shit as it flowed out of your arse.' The vivid pictured that he painted sent a nasty bitter image through the boys' bodies.

'How old were you Mr Davies?' Lusty asked.

'Too young my boy. Too young to know better.'

'Do you really know what happened to the great Deep Navigation pit?' he gestured thoughtfully.

'Yeah… it's coal seam dried up, and the whole town went poor again,' replied Kinsey. '

'Not quite. The council decided to flood the place, to stop the damage it was causing.'

The boys were speechless. They had all read in history classes how the discovery of the coal seam had produced a source of much needed wealth and happiness for the area, and most of the people that lived there. Overnight, the mine thrived, and the rich deposits of coal were being exported all over the country. The population swelled at a massive rate. Prosperity was hanging from every tree, and decadence was dripping from every rooftop. The pages of history had also told them, that just as quickly as the coal seam had helped to make their fortunes, it soon dried up and their fortunes all withered away.

'Hang on a minute Mr Davies,' said Jac. 'We were told that it was the saviour of the whole town at the time.'

'It was the saviour, but it then nearly turned into its damnation.' His eyes grew large, and his nostrils flared.

He then told them, that in the year 1952, they opened a new seam face, on the west side of the pit. One day, someone came across a jet of warm water at the bottom of the shaft, that spurted up about two foot in the air.

'At first we used it like a bidet. There's no toilet facilitates down there you know. So we thought that it was a gift from God himself. But then men started to use it for more sinister things.'

'Like what?' None of them could imagine what he was referring to.

'They started to use the warm water to... let's say... satisfy their animal desires. We started a secret club.'

'What was it called.... the bum washers anonymous club?' Kinsey laughed, but stopped when he felt the rest of the people around the table, including the caged bird, stare coldly at him.

'I was saying,' the old man continued. 'I was young and foolish, and I had feelings like you boys. Feelings that spread down below. Feelings that took over my body. Feelings...'

'Ok Gramps, we get the picture, but what happened?' Alex said impatiently.

'It was lovely boys,' he continued. 'No one had ever felt anything like it before. Of course, we still had to dig for the black stuff, so we worked faster to make our quota, so we would have longer to sample its delights. The secret club grew bigger, and the 'sit-ons' went on for longer.' Old Mr Davies closed his eyes in its memory. He relived the time he had squatted over the geyser, trousers around his ankles, wriggling in pleasure.

'What the fuck is wrong with that?' Jac asked feeling rather jealous of the old git and his secret club.

'Quiet boys, there's more. Then they started to appear,' the old man whispered.

'What started to appear?' asked Jac.

'They were small at first, and no one noticed or talked about them, but then they started to grow.'

'What started to grow?' they asked.

'The more you used the geyser for your own personal pleasure, the bigger and faster they grew.' Alex's granddad closed his eyes.

'What started to grow faster?'

'There was no stopping them.'

'Stopping fucking what!' They were now all jumping up and down, swearing and spitting like banshees.

'Tell that fucking bird to shut up,' screamed Kinsey, whacking the cage.

'Poor Jenkins was the first to go. We had to carry him around in a wheelbarrow, before he passed away.'

'Why... What was growing?' The fever in their voices had reached its peak.

'The piles!' he said at last 'The piles started to grow.'

'The piles?' said Jac. 'Everyone's got fuckin' piles, Mr Davies, Even my three year old niece has got piles... It's part of growing up in this cold climate.'

'Piles just come and go Mr Davies' Lusty said diplomatically.

'Not like these piles... these were different. These were evil piles, sent by God to cleanse our souls.'

'And your arses by the sound of it. You are starting to sound like Father Clancy,' Lusty said.

Kinsey butted in, 'You are telling me, that just because some horny coal miners, washed their arses now and again in a jet of water, (he was going to add fresh water, but he thought that a sentence with arse, washing and miners, shouldn't have the word 'Fresh' anywhere near it), that God sent down a plague of piles to punish everyone... fuck off.' Kinsey realised, that although the old man was Alex's blood and bones, this was too far fetched for words.

Alex, the normally sensible one, had to reflect on this statement for a while. He had always imagined various forms of nasty plagues sweeping over the land in many guises. He could picture a plague of locusts swarming down from high. Maybe a sky full of birds, like in that Hitchcock movie, but an infestation of killer red piles

171

spreading down below, well, that was too much. He knew that piles were not classed as a disease in this part of the world. Cholera was a disease. Small Pox was a disease, and now something called Aids was mentioned in the same breath as the previous two. But piles were a just way of life, just like the cold, the damp, and the massive rats. The women folk in the town swore by them. In fact, a woman was not a real woman, until she could show her peer group, that she had at least a small bunch of grapes growing out of her backside. Now, for a woman to become well respected in the town, she could only reach those dizzy heights, if she had a bunch of piles for at least ten years, she was minus the smoking tooth, had a moustache like a Polish sailor, and skin so tough when she died they could use it to resole the underneath of working boots with.

'You can mock if you like, but it is the truth.' Mr Davies looked genuinely hurt by the boy's lack of faith in his message. 'Ok…. I'll show you. But you have been warned.' He raised himself up slowly from the depths of his chair. 'Just brace yourself, and take a look at these beauties!' A joint still stuck between his lips.

The boys looked in disgust, at the sight of the old man's empty love sack.

'But that's because you just had your end away.' Kinsey shouted.

'No no…. not those… look at these!' With that, the old man turned around, and bent over to reveal a pair of piles that hung from his behind, like a set of balls outside a pawn brokers shop. They must have dangled down for over two and a half feet, and had heads on them like small ripe melons. He had them conveniently tucked into his ankle socks using bicycle clips.

The boys, screamed out in horror, and made a mad dash to the safety of the fruit machines. The small bird had a heart attack and keeled over.

'Put them away Gramps. We believe you. Put them away.' They all yelled pleadingly.

172

Chapter 12

'The three of shovels'

The detective in the raincoat, from the big city, was slightly taken aback by the hordes of people, that were wandering through the grey precinct as he disembarked from the early morning train. The first thing to strike him, was how normal they all appeared to be. They seemed to just be getting on with their daily lives, with little, or no fuss.

This wasn't what he had expected at all. The perception from the more affluent half of the country was, that folk from this God-forsaken area, skulked around on all fours covered in boils, and carried their bastard, uneducated, half-witted sprogs in their hairy pouches, while queuing all day to sign on.

Before he continued on his journey, he double checked with a shoeless beggar, that he had actually arrived at the correct destination. He handed the poor man a handful of berries, before heading to the busy hub of the town centre, to search for some clues to the puzzle.

He didn't have a plan, or the faintest idea of where he was going to start to unravel this mystery. He had missed that particular lesson when he was in detective college, due to a heavy cold. He decided, that perhaps the best place to begin the investigation, would be at the local public house, that the weight watching criminals that he had arrested, had told him about in their police statements.

He walked up and down the high street, but failed to spot the bright pink coloured pub, with a ten foot sign outside, dangling over the boarded up window, and a commemorative plaque on the pavement, which marked the exact spot of Arthur's landing. He finally asked a man, who pointed straight at the pub. The man shouted angrily after the misinformed policeman, and told him that he could stick his berries where the sun refused to shine.

The Detective ignored the man's advice, and after checking his pockets, he wished that he had brought some more berries with him. As he entered the drinking establishment, which was strangely subdued for this time of day, the policeman hoped he wouldn't have to stoop to dishing out hand-jobs, when the real interrogating began.

There was no apparent reason for the detective to flash his police badge, and inform the regulars that he was a highly respected and decorated officer from the city force, but he did. There was definitely no need for him to boast, in a loud voice, that he was working undercover on a secret hush-hush mission, and that no one including his boss, knew where he was, but regretfully for him, he just happened to mention that too.

The reason the regulars hadn't required these titbits of useful information, was that they could smell a pig from five hundred yards. They instinctively knew when an undercover copper had joined their midst, just by the stench of arrogance that followed behind them. The pub crowd had already concluded, that this big-headed little piggy, probably didn't even have any friends on the force.

'I bet his colleagues don't even know when his birthday is,' one man whispered to his mate.

'So no one knows that you are here then?' the barman checked that he had heard him correctly.

174

'No one knows… not even my Super. I'm completely undercover. The invisible man.' He replied laughing. They all laughed back. He was starting to quite like these valley people. They were definitely not half as bad as they were portrayed on Crimestoppers.

Unfortunately, what the detective had failed to detect, while happily chatting by the bar, was the front door being shut and bolted. He had also missed the Mickey Finn, that had deliberately found its way into his fourth bloody Mary.

The locals all knew exactly what was coming next. They rubbed their hands with glee, as the swaying detective tried hard to stop himself from seeing double.

'I don't feel too well,' he muttered, as he bumped heavily into the space invader machine. He tried to focus on the door of the toilet, with the aim of swilling his flushed face under the cold tap.

The barman put the knock-out drops back under the counter next to the shot gun, and shouted to the drugged policeman, 'So you are undercover are you?'. He then sang out, *This little piggy went to market. This little piggy stayed at home. This little city piggy was never seen again.'*

The laughter from the many sets of mouths seemed to chase him around the pub. Every item became blurred and out of focus. He staggered, and fell head first into the beer cellar. He landed on his back, staring up at the surprised Arthur Cherry-nose, and the ex-Mayor.

'Not another one,' the ex-Mayor yelled. 'There's not enough room in here to swing a dead cat… especially with old big beak and Sneezer over there.' He pointed to the horse, that was drinking a mug of Lemsip and covered in a electric blanket. He then stormed off towards the beer barrels which he had made into a writing desk, complete with ink well, to write another letter of complaint.

'Are you Arthur, the psychic?' The detective reached out and touched the tramps leg, just before

Slaughterhouse Bill kicked the intruder back into the relatively unsafe environment of the pub.

The copper was dragged, still conscious but unable to move a muscle, into the deathly surroundings of the beer garden. Several chickens and pheasants hung upside down from the iron railings, with their throats cut.

While some of his assailants got him ready to meet his maker, the rest jerried up the heavy-duty patio slabs, for the second time that year.

Later on that day, the scratching noises that came from the concrete in the beer garden, were drowned out by the musical blasts from the free jukebox.

'We'd better get rid of the diamonds,' Ronny Mouth-organ said to the barman, who was himself trying on a new ex-policeman raincoat, 'before the pigs send someone next time with half a brain.'

Chapter 13

'She sells sanitary towels'

Kinsey cracked open a cold can of lager from Lusty's fridge and sat down at the small kitchen table.

'Hey, what are you going to cook for her anyway?' he asked, on seeing the good-looking boy prepare something over the cooker.

'Soup to start,' Lusty replied, 'followed by paella.'

'Any chips?' Kinsey enquired.

'With paella?.... Don't be daft.'

'No chips. She'll think you're a right tight cunt.'

Lusty was shocked by his friend's observation, and quickly added 'But I've got some Artic roll ice-cream to finish.'

'Fucking hell... dessert as well. She'll have your pants off before you can say 'cheese and biscuits.' Kinsey laughed.

'I hope not.... don't forget this is my special date. I don't want any of that.' He then asked nervously, 'Who is she anyway Kins?'

Kinsey pretended to do up his shoe lace, and answered 'I really don't know.' He lied through his back teeth, but he kept a straight face.

'Jac told me that she was very nice. Well bred.' Lusty seasoned the Oxtail soup with a pinch of salt.

'Fucking in-bred,' Kinsey thought, but again kept his observations firmly to himself. 'The cast of Deliverance meets, The Hills Have Eyes.' He laughed to himself before muttering out loud, 'Who's plucking the banjo here?'

Fortunately, Lusty was concentrating more on stirring the substance bubbling in the pan to take any real notice. 'He even said that I shouldn't have any trouble with her wanting sex because she's more or less a virgin,' he shouted out.

This made Kinsey crease up. He knew that Jac could be a right vicious twat at times, but even by his standards, this was right up there with the time he superglued a group of OAPs to the table in the Labour club.

'More or less a virgin. How old is she?... Eleven.' Kinsey knew that even Lusty hadn't believed that part of the fairy story. 'You won't get many virgins around here for a pound.'

But Lusty was really looking forward to this night. A proper date. A chance to get to know someone. He had prepared some questions along with preparing the food for the evening. He didn't want to tempt fate or get her drunk, so he had purchased a bottle of non-alcoholic wine. He wanted it to be perfect. A perfect night to remember.

Lois (the Swallow), grabbed Jac firmly by his balls and squeezed with all her might. It wasn't until she could actually see his eyes bulging out of their sockets, that she finally loosened her stranglehold on his old boy.

'Tell me again…. but slowly…. What did he say to you about me?' Her fingers flexed just enough to show him that she was still very much in command.

'Look Lois… honest to God. Lusty came to see me personally, to ask me if I could organise a date with you… no strings attached.' She loosened enough for him to pull away.

'Why me? It just doesn't make sense. The world's going to end and the boy who could get any woman he wanted…. picks me?' She stared deeply into his face. She remembered reading somewhere, that you could always tell if someone was lying from the movement of their eyes. But she couldn't recall if the eyes had to move to the left or the right, or straight up, to catch them out.

'Look, if you don't fancy it…. I'll let him know.' Jac's eyes didn't tell the girl anything anyway, because they moved in all directions at once. This was mainly due to him having a woman touch his genitals (even if the touch had been of a threatening nature). 'He said that he always fancied you, and thought about you constantly when he was away.'

'But I've never spoken to him.' She said suspiciously.

'You don't need words to break down the barriers of love.' He felt like being sick in a bin, but he needed this to sound convincing, or his cover would be blown.

One of her children, dressed in a batman costume, came sliding down the barrister and crashed through the piece of cardboard that was blocking up the hole in the front door.

'Get back up those stairs now you little fucker, or I'll send Nanny Welsh up to see you.' Lois screamed at the little tearaway, 'without her glass eye in!'

She turned to face Jac. 'You better not be jacking me, Jac,' she muttered, 'What does he wanna do?'

'Just cook you a meal at his place, drink some wine, some soft music, and you never know. Don't tell him I've told you, but he confided in me that he hasn't had a woman for ages.' He winked at her knowingly.

Lois could feel herself getting horny, just by talking about the boy. 'If he gives me half a chance, I'll shag that tight little arse off him.' She glanced in the mirror and fixed her wig, that had slipped a little, imagining, how his neck would taste.

'Great, just great,' Jac said to himself, changing his tack slightly. 'But he is very shy. If he plays hard to get, its just because he's quiet and unassuming. Let me give you a tip. He loves his women to be forceful and in complete control.' Jac was enjoying this. He wished he could be a fly on the wall during this battle. 'So I'll tell him that you'll be around about seven, ok?'

He left, with a bag full of smiles in a carrier bag of mischief. She went straight upstairs, to do a couple of light practice rounds with her very own Jungle Jim.

The candles burned brightly, the food smelt delicious, and the soft music drifted in on a magic carpet of romance. Lusty was leaving nothing to chance. He found himself pacing back and fore, and talking to himself all evening. He had decided not to go over the top with his clothes, and plumped for his usual attire of jeans and black t-shirt.

What he didn't know, was that his mates had decided, that they couldn't miss this opportunity to watch the great one trying to fight off the advances of the normally unstoppable Lois. They were parked up opposite. A cigar box full of joints, rolled just for the occasion, together with a few cans of lager.

The three boys ducked down quickly on seeing her appear out of the mist. She drifted passed them, like a ghost pirate ship in high heels and mini skirt. As she walked, her chains glistened in the bitterly cold night, and her skirt rose up to reveal the cheeks of her arse. The boys had to force themselves not to burst out laughing, and give the game away when they heard her crack a fart from her bow, which was louder than any Spanish Armada cannon.

'She's fucking disgusting,' Kinsey said, watching her fan her tiny skirt to get rid of the smell, before knocking on the door.

Lusty tasted the 'home made' tinned soup for the very last time. He didn't know what to expect as he slowly opened the door to his dream date. He nearly swore out loud when he saw who it was. He hoped his expression hadn't given away his true feelings at that precise moment. He quickly regained his composure and said in a civil tongue 'Hello Lois, glad you could make it. Do come in.' He really wanted to just close the door on her and go and beat the hell out of his double crossing mates.

'Can I take your coat?' He could see at a glance that she hadn't just come to sample his culinary delights. She looked like she was dressed for full on hand-to-hand combat. Or in Lois' case, mouth-to-cock sexual combat. He knew that Jac would come up with a girl who would be a bit of a challenge, but picking Lois 'the Swallow' was really below the belt. Her reputation came marching in the door well before her, as she pinched the cheeks of his arse.

'She was definitely going to be a tough nut to handle, in order not to see her crack,' he thought to himself.

If the rumours were to be believed, she'd had more inches of manhood in her than the entire steelwork construction of the Eiffel Tower. Lusty would have to be careful, that he wouldn't become the last eight inches on top of the French steeple.

He pictured Jac and the other two, pissing themselves to the point of no-return, at his expense. 'I'll have my revenge on them.' he promised himself.

'That smells lovely. What is it?' Lois asked.

'A special surprise. You'll have to wait and see.' Lusty replied.

'It smells like tinned sardines on toast.'

At that moment, Lusty wished he had stayed in Spain and fought for the hand of Francesca, even if had meant a hot chip-pan bath.

He led Lois into the front room, and then went into the kitchen and tipped the non-alcoholic wine down the sink, and poured himself a stiff whiskey.

'It's not going to warm up in there for about an hour,' Kinsey suggested. 'Let's go for a quick drive around. See what madness is going on down in the streets tonight.'

'I don't know. We don't wanna miss anything.' Jac interrupted. 'Lois is a fast worker. I bet she's already down to underpants as we speak.'

'Lusty's cooler than that. Lets go for a quick spin.' Alex piped up.

The blue van turned out of the street, and into the wet and wild world. A bonfire was raging on the common behind the comprehensive school. Its flames must have reached up to touch the moon. Hundreds of kids were dancing around it, and shouting at the top of their voices. They were all ripping pages out of their textbooks, and feeding the hungry fire with knowledge. Several teenagers had broken into the school premises and had gathered up chairs, tables, and blackboards, to ensure that the bonfire would burn long into the January night. The caretaker was tied to a lamppost.

'That's what I call a bonfire. I wish we could have done that when we were in school.' Alex commented.

'We would have burnt the fucking teachers and all.' Kinsey entered the conversation in his very own 'down to earth' way. 'Especially that Mr Brown. I still haven't forgiven that twat for saying I was off-side in that football match. He would have been my Guy Fawkes.' His warped mind drifted back off in time.

Alex laughed. 'Who would you have put on top of the fire, Jac?' he asked.

Jac thought for a minute. 'I know, Mr Stephens. He hated me.'

'No wonder he fucking hated you. Didn't you set his hair on fire with that Bunsen Burner?' Kinsey jumped back in.

'It was an accident.' He replied innocently.

'How the fuck can you say it was an accident? He was your fucking woodwork teacher. The fucking Bunsen Burners weren't even used in that classroom. They were locked in the cupboard in the science lab.'

'Ok. Perhaps it was a premeditated burning accident. But he deserved it. How could he have only given me a C+ for my wooden model ship?'

They recalled how all the school had nicknamed the teacher Niki Lauda, as he sulked through the corridors in his bobble hat until his hair grew back.

'What about you Al, who would you have sent to that firey grave?'

Without hesitation, Alex told them it would have been Mrs Chicken. 'She was a real bad egg.'

'Mrs Chicken.'

'I would have doused her in petrol myself. Frigid cow.' Alex remembered the time she had purposely shamed him in front of assembly, when she accidentally informed them all, that the reason he was absent was because he was being circumcised. The stick he had when he finally came back, was unbearable.

'Is it because of the circumcision thing?' Jac asked.

'Of course it is.'

'Remember everyone called you Oliver Cromwell, because of your new round head.' Kinsey laughed.

'It's better than having a fucking cheesy head though.' Alex spat the words back in temper.

A loud explosion caused them to search for the source of the noise. They watched in disbelief, as they witnessed a gang of fourteen year olds drive a stolen car into the centre of the flames, and run away for cover, just as the vehicle exploded. Bits of steel door exterior sailed high into the night sky. The three boys moved on, as the gang of joyriders searched around for another car to torch.

Lusty dished out the first course to his unusual guest. The night wasn't turning out as bad as he had first imagined. The conversation between the two had been patchy in places, and in some parts as dry as a desert, but she had made him laugh once or twice, especially when she showed him her impression of a light bulb in a Jewish wedding.

Inwardly Lois was panicking. She wished she had gone on this date, with slightly more protection on than her current pair of flimsy underwear, was providing her with. The material itself was definitely nowhere near substantial enough to hold back the raging love storm brewing on the horizon. It was turning out to be a big mistake. Her knickers were so damp; she could wring them out with a mangle. Her juices were seeping through, and she was so wet between her legs Jacques Cousteau could have set up a diving school, and his pupils could have plunged into the deep salty sea from off the side of her swollen love lips, in full aqualung equipment.

In spite of this, it was the best night of her life. Her host was class, a real gentleman with an arse to die for. She hoped that he would let her eat strawberries from between his tight cheeks on their second date.

'This is really lovely soup…. what is it?' she asked, extremely complimentary.

'Oxtail, with just a touch of oriental spices.'

Lois had always been a soft touch for a spot of sophistication. At school she would go weak at the knees when she heard someone say words like, 'Pythagoras' or, 'Algebra'. No one had ever told her what the words had actually meant, but what the hell? Talk like that really hit the spot. Her flood defences, that normally protected her shoreline from the raging waters of love, were at bursting point. 'If he says anything else sexy, I'm going to spray a jet of love juice, all over the carpet like Sammy the seal juggling a ball in Sea World,' she thought worryingly.

Lusty asked her many questions, about her chains, her tattoos, her children. He had decided, that since she was here, he was going to have his special sex-free night, and really upset, his so-called best friends.

In return, she enquired about what he had done in Spain. He told her some of his adventures, but held back the intimate bit about his Close Encounter of the Cheese Family Kind. She was going to ask the gorgeous hunk if he smoked straight after sex but she decided to wait to see for herself.

She studied him while he talked. She watched every muscle in his well-designed face move in harmony. In a strange sort of way, he reminded her of a white Jungle Jim. They were both perfect in every dimension. They were both things made by a superior being, just to satisfy women. Only difference was, one was made in the garden of heaven, the other in a cramped sweatshop factory in Taiwan. She hoped that God's angels had matched the little Korean's, when it came to the knob department.

'Oh shit,' she suddenly thought, remembering that she had put Jungle Jim in the coal shed last night, just in case her mother came across the rubber man when she was doing the monthly clean. It wasn't a case of her mother objecting to the use of artificial sex objects. She had a small rubber sausage dog with a life like tongue herself. She just didn't like black people!

'He'll be cross.' Lois thought. Over the last few months, he had become her rubber husband. They'd even discussed the possibility of kids.

Lusty had spent a great deal of the last few years living the high life, and educating himself about the many different cultures that existed on the planet. But he now realised, that perhaps he had found a species that most resembled prehistoric man, as he observed his guest munching her way through the paella, without bothering to take the shells off the prawns. He noticed, that her eyes were searching all over the table for something.

'No chips, what a mean cunt!' she thought.

He got up to change the record that had completed its intended journey across its vinyl road. He shuffled through the stack of LPs, trying to decide what track would sum up the mood. He wished he still had that song 'Monster Mash', which would have fitted nicely. He finally plumped for some underground Reggae instead.

The incredible sight of him in his ripped jeans, released a gush of juice which flowed from her body, copious enough to have destroyed a row of terraced houses, if they had been foolish enough to stand between her and her man.

The chair she was sitting on, became extremely slippery. Unexpectedly, she skidded straight off landing on her backside underneath the table. She quickly clambered back to her feet, looking like one of the zombies, rising from the grave in Michael Jackson's Thriller video. She wiped the sticky stuff off the seat with her sleeve.

After her third helping of Artic Roll, Lusty suggested that she retired into the other room, while he would follow with the coffees, before he walked her home.

While she stared at her face in the mirror, Jac's words came floating back to her. 'He's very shy... He'll play hard to get. It will be up to you to make the first move.' She plotted her attack.

Kinsey, Alex and Jac, agreed they had been driving around for long enough. They had quickly decided to head back to Lusty's flat, after they had witnessed a gang of middle aged women smashing every shop window in the high street and pilfering the window's contents. Some of them were actually changing their old clothes, right there in the street. But, most couldn't make up their minds what to nick, and eventually found themselves going back to the first shop that they had ransacked.

The boys, waited outside, until they saw a female shadow roaming around the lounge of the flat. Kinsey had volunteered to climb the ladder to spy on the couple.

He balanced on the top, while the other two paced around underneath.

'What can you see?' Jac hissed at his mate.

'Nothing yet... but hang on a minute... wait... she's stripping off.' He informed them.

Now normally, if three boys with sexual appetites that were as big as a blue Whale, had the opportunity of peeping on a female peeling her clothes off, Father Clancy with a machine gun couldn't have stopped them all from climbing that ladder. But, this was not any ordinary girl, this was Lois. They had all seen it before. They still had nightmares. They still had the faint love-bite scars. No one moved.

As she squeezed a blackhead in the mirror, she noticed a face at the window. She didn't panic or show any signs that she knew she was being watched. This was not a new experience to her. Many boys and grown men would press their faces up against her window pane, either looking for a good time, or waving goodbye to their long lost underpants.

She finished her facial repairs, stepped out of her panties and pretended to go to the bathroom.

'What's happening now?' Alex shouted up.

'Shuush.' Kinsey put his finger to his mouth. 'I can't see anything. I don't know where she's gone.....'

Just as the words escaped from his mouth, Lois appeared at the window, in the nude, without her wig and an expression on her contoured face that would have made the little evil boy in The Omen shit himself violently.

'Fuccccccckinnn... heeellllll' Kinsey tried to scream, as he reached out, for any kind of emergency exit. Unfortunately, the ladder had also seen Lois and had taken it upon itself to get the hell out of there. It tried to run, but soon realised that it didn't have any feet. Both the ladder, and its occupant crashed to the ground.

'Go and pester someone else you pervert,' Lois yelled out, and thankfully closed the blinds.

Jac and Alex had heard the screams, and were half way down the street, when they decided, that they had to go back to try and retrieve their mate. They finally uncovered Kinsey, face down in a flowerbed. They turned him over. There was a look on his face that could easily have belonged on a man, who had just been told that the surgeons, had mistakenly removed his penis, instead of his in-growing toenail.

'Are you Ok?' they both queried.

'It was horrible. I've never seen anything like it before in my life.' They both knew that this was serious shit, because Kinsey, who worked for the council, had seen many disturbing things, while helping to rewire the council houses in the Gurnos estate. He had, unfortunately, talked to Grandmothers who's skin was so tough, it could have been used to transport potatoes halfway around the world: He'd also seen small children suffering from chronic asthma, because they had been forced to enter smoking competitions before they could actually walk. So, the boys knew, that whatever Kinsey saw in the window, must have been the dog's bollocks as far as bad was concerned.

'Get me away from here.' Kinsey staggered to his feet.

'Cool down Kins.' Alex muttered.

'We've got to go and rescue him.' Kinsey insisted. 'She'll damage him beyond repair.' He imagined a Lusty doll with one arm missing, and with his glass eye poked out, sitting in a discarded rubbish bin.

'You set him up Jac,' Alex turned on his friend, and added 'It's up to you, to unset him up.'

'And quickly Jac,' Kinsey piped up. 'That poor boy is going to come out of the kitchen carrying the coffees, straight into the clutches of a fully formed Penis fly trap. We have got to warn him… he doesn't stand a chance.'

'Ok,' Jac snorted. 'Leave it to me. I'll be back in two seconds.' Jac rushed off into the night.

He returned several minutes later in his uncle's pick-up truck.

'What the fuck are you going to do with that thing?' Kinsey enquired. 'Smash through the fucking walls and run her over. Our best friend is up there with that creature,' he pointed to the third floor then added forcefully 'and you pull up, thinking you can just drag

188

her off to the nearest garage for a quick tyre change and MOT. Don't you understand… he's in great danger? I've seen her in the nude.'

'So what?' Jac uttered impatiently. 'Over the years we have all seen Lois in the buff…. even you!'

'Yes, but not with the fucking light on.' He broke down into tears. The others shivered at the thought.

'No… no…. you'll see.' Jac turned and jumped back into the cab.

Upstairs in the kitchen, Lusty felt, that the next five minutes would decide the outcome of this love tennis match. If he served up the strong Colombian coffee, and she returned the compliment with some playful banter, then he knew that the game would be his, and he would be walking her home soon. But, he was also very much aware, that if she came back aggressively and asked for new balls please, then it was curtains to his big plan, for a romantic, sex-free night.

He picked up the tray, making sure that his love racket was tucked out of sight in his underpants, and he re-entered the lounge.

He found the lights had been dimmed to the point of darkness. She had changed his choice of music. The low sultry strains of Barry White's voice, strolled around the room in tight red trousers, covered in the great smell, of Brut.

'She must have brought that evil music with her,' he thought, trying to make out where the strange purring noise was coming from.

'I'm over here darling.' He saw her lying by the fire, completely naked, with her left leg over her head. Her hand was busy stroking herself down below.

'Was this the mating call of some black widow spider?' He asked himself.

'Look Lois, you don't understand. I just wanted, a romantic….' She halted the flow of his sentence, with a flick of her hand.

'Hush now darling, you know you want to!' she crooned. 'Jac told me all about you being shy and not having a woman for ages,' she squawked, putting her overworked wet finger into her mouth.

Lusty realised that he had been done up like a kipper. 'Bastard, I'll kill him,' he said under his breath, looking for his best escape route.

The continued silence forced him to speak up again. 'Please Lois, put your clothes back on before you do yourself a permanent injury.' He saw, that she had now placed her other leg behind her head.

Lusty quickly thought, that if he could tape her feet together behind her neck, he could perhaps throw her into a pot of boiling water, like a crab with its claws safely secured out of harms way.

'I'm waiting lover... I need to feel you inside me.' Her well-worn speech, was suddenly disturbed by a voice that came from her stomach.

'Lusty.. Lusty... it's me Jac. Look I'm sorry mate... if you can hear this.... RUN... run for your life. We'll see you outside.' Jac shrieked into the CB radio that was in the pick-up truck.

As Lois, regretfully, watched the man of her dreams disappear out of the door, she realised that it would be Jungle Jim again tonight, unless she could pick someone up on the bus ride home.

Chapter 14

'Everybody wants to screw the world'

Cyril dreamt that he was being held captive in a dark room, and a spider was crawling all over his unshaven face. A moment later, he woke with a slight jump, and found that he was tied up in a small dark room. A spider in a furry mohair jumper, Che Guevara slippers and a belly full of eggs, was in fact shuffling across his cheek heading for his ear. He moved sharply to dislodge the creature from his skin, before it unloaded it's cargo of unborn offspring into his lobe.

'Hey TV detector man.... are you awake?' came a quiet voice from somewhere in the room.

Cyril strained his eyes against the black curtain of darkness that draped in front of him. After a while he could just make out the silhouette of the bunking officer with his Mohican haircut.

'Where are we?' he asked.

'We're in the attic. They must have shoved us up here when they caught us trying to escape' said the bunking officer who crawled up closer, and accidentally squashed the pregnant spider.

'He was a big one,' frowned Cyril, remembering the drainpipe, and that seven foot Indian in a two-tone tracksuit.

'Who was?' asked the bunking officer vaguely.

'That seven foot Indian in the designer sports wear. You must have seen him.'

'I didn't see anyone.' The bunking officer made a face that was full of innocence. 'I thought that I must have fallen awkwardly off the roof, and next thing I knew I was waking up in here.'

Cyril didn't feel like pushing the subject of their escape attempt, which must have been the shortest in history any further, so he quickly changed the conversation.

'I thought you said that there were a family of Mormons living up here.'

'There are,' the bunking officer replied confidently. Suddenly a match was lit, and Cyril could see at least fifteen faces smiling back at him through pearly white teeth.

'Jesus Christ,' the words tumbled out of his open mouth.

'There's no need to blaspheme Mister,' a voice rose out of the darkness.

Cyril made sure that his eyes hadn't been playing tricks with him, before he asked the older man of the group, who he assumed to be the elder and father of this strange race. 'Sorry.. but how long have you been here?'

'About six to nine months,' the old man replied cheerfully.

'Bloody hell,' he thought, 'Imagine spending nine months couped up with the Osmond family.' He didn't think he could stick that and added. 'How the hell did Pablo capture fifteen of you?'

'On no,' the old man laughed, and the rest joined in. 'He only caught three of us at first, and imprisoned us in the attic.'

Cyril looked quite confused, and it showed on his face.

The old man quickly went on to explain, 'But he treated us well, and it's a lot safer in here than where we live. So after a while I moved my extra wives in, and some of our friends came for a weekend, and liked it so much, that they decided to stay with us.' The entire family flashed the whites of their dentures, which illuminated the attic darkness.

Cyril was speechless. He always knew that Mormons were a funny breed of people. There was definitely something odd about the way they knocked doors on a Sunday afternoon, expecting to be invited in for tea and cup cakes. The way they smiled all of the time. Nothing in life can make people that happy, even if they did have a famous family that ruled the British pop charts in the seventies. No one normal could be that clean cut and fresh faced, and what was the story with the neat suits and rucksacks?

'It's quite a good arrangement really,' the old man continued, after realising that the TV detector man was shaking his head in disbelief. 'They feed us well and we're allowed to hold prayer meetings here every Tuesday.'

'Have you ever tried to escape?' Cyril asked.

The old man was now the one shaking his head. The rest of the group nudged each other and giggled. 'We don't want to escape. We like it here. Mr Pozzoni has even had a couple of front door keys cut for us, in case we come back late from house calling.'

'Fucking front door keys cut. You're telling me, that you can walk out of here and come back of your own accord. Is there something wrong with you? You are imprisoned. Your children are locked up. This is no place to bring up your kids. It's cold and dusty, can't you see that?'

'There's no need to curse and cuss Mister,' a woman chipped in, while breast feeding a new born baby.

Cyril caught his breath and continued 'But how do you manage to get out of the ropes?'

'We're not really tied up.'

Cyril thought that this was getting weirder and weirder as the minutes ticked away. 'But why have you got your hands behind your bloody back then?'

'We're just being polite.' The old man admitted. 'We didn't want you to feel the odd one out.' They all removed their hands from the invisible ropes, and placed them in the air, offering their forgiveness to Jesus.

'So could you untie me?' Cyril enquired.

'We don't know about that. We wouldn't want to make him, and especially his son, mad.' The old man said looking towards the trapdoor.

'But they are all fucking mad already,' he thought but this time he kept his observations to himself. 'Even the Mad Hatter would have declined an invitation to this tea party.' Cyril considered his strategy for a moment and added 'Look, I promise that if you untie me, I'll become one of you. I'll even walk in front banging the tambourine. I have always dreamt of being a Mormon, ever since I saw Donny Osmond singing on Top of the Pops.' He then burst into a verse of, 'Puppy Love'.

The Mormons had a quick conflab, then the old man turned and said quite poker-faced, 'Ok then, but we'll have to wait until the time is right, and we will need to make several adjustments to you and your friend.'

They then held hands in a large circle, prayed for peace and love, and Sunday afternoon cup cakes.

The head honcho of the Post Office Workers Union, (one of the most powerful and militant unions in the country), sat solemn faced in the works canteen, facing his equally worried members. The hot steam from a mug of Typhoo tea swirled up in front of him. He took off his cardigan and proclaimed, 'This is a sad day for the Post Office Workers Union, boys.' He talked; they listened, while quietly passing around a tin of assorted biscuits amongst themselves.

'You are all aware by now, that one of our colleagues has gone missing in action.' He dunked a chocolate digestive into the boiling liquid.

'But what are we going to do about it Boss?' someone shouted out.

He rose up as fast as his tired bones could operate, and he pointed towards the masses. The soggy end of the biscuit dropped onto the floor. 'Look,' his voice boomed out. 'No one takes our little Kieran. No one takes Postman 661321, off the street, in broad daylight, without us knowing.'

'That's right Boss,' the masses replied in a common consensus.

'No one messes with the Post Office Workers Union without a damn fight on their hands.' He banged the canteen table. A salt cellar toppled off the end and dive-bombed onto the wooden tiled floor.

'Can't we go to the police, Boss?' another voice spoke up, obviously full of concern.

'They are much too busy boys. The town appears to be losing its marbles, and the police are all out of alley bompers!' The members looked at each other in complete confusion, but they understood the gist of his passionate address. They all knew that the boss had a habit of using words, or phrases, that shouldn't really be allowed in the same story, never mind the same sentence. He continued regardless, 'The coppers are trying their best to uphold law and order, but most have phoned in sick over the last couple of days, to spend more quality time with their families.'

'And their mistresses,' the same person who had asked the previous question piped up. 'Most of them lot think that they are God's gift to women. Just because they get issued with bloody truncheons and handcuffs.'

It was obvious from the reaction of the audience that there was no love lost, between the boys in blue, and the shiny pole brigade. This had been made worse, with the introduction of a council-run annual initiative competition, to find the Best Emergency Service Unit. The rivalry between all the town's uniformed departments was extremely intense, to put it mildly, especially leading up to the day of the award ceremony at the town hall.

The union boss was handed a black bin bag. He reached inside, and pulled out Kieran's delivery sack and his clipboard. The appearance of these items without their owner, was met with loud groans throughout the compact canteen.

'We found these boys discarded in a rubbish bin up on the estate.' The boss looked disturbed. 'It doesn't look good.'

Concerned questions were bombarded at the man on the platform. 'What do we know boss?' someone asked. 'Have we got any leads to go on?' and 'What's for dinner?'

'Ok… but one at a time.' He turned and started firing answers back to the crowd. 'We don't know much at this time.' He pointed to where the first question had come from. He added 'Sorry, no leads at the moment, and, I think it's chicken and chips followed by sponge and white custard.'

'Oh, not chicken again Boss. We've had it three times this week already, and it's only Monday?' He could see everyone deep in thought. He was definitely going to get these bloody canteen facilities improved, with some decent nosh for his loyal members.

'What if they've got him Boss?' the comment from the little man in the front, sent a wave of muttering and dissent amongst the crowd.

The boss quickly made his voice heard. 'Look boys, I've already spoken to the Ambulance Service, and their union representative has assured me that they haven't started to take hostages yet; but he did say, that if we didn't give them their two ambulances and defibrillator back soon, they would not be held responsible for their actions.' He continued, 'So I think it must be someone else who has stolen our young lad.'

'It's not those bloody Traffic Wardens is it?' someone else chipped in forcefully.

'I don't think so boys.' he indicated. 'Kidnapping is not their style. They are more into knee-capping these days. I believe, it is some other bastard that has our boy, and we want him back. I can feel it in my blood, and it's making my water boil. And I'll tell you all something for nothing; I bet that our baby Kieran, wasn't taken without a damn good fight.' Tears welled up in his eyes. He held up the post sack, showing Kieran's number sewn on the side, and he pointed to a red stain in the material, which he wrongfully assumed was the brave Post Office worker's blood. Actually, it had been the remains of a dollop of tomato sauce, that had found its way out of the boy's sandwiches.

He completed the rally cry, by shouting out 'We are going to find our boy, boys.' he punched the air, and the Post Office Workers Union members fell into a frenzy. The whole room jumped up and down wildly. They were all completely oblivious to the fact, that young Kieran, was, at that moment, dressed in a yellow and green summer smock, with thigh length white leather boots, and a long blonde wig, and was getting chatted up by Alex's granddad in Buffaloes.

The boss signalled for them to quiet down for a minute. He read out the last entry that had been entered on the missing boy's clipboard, which had informed them that Keiran, had delivered a large plain brown parcel, to a Mr Pablo Pozzoni of 32 Acacia Avenue.

There was a bigger groan this time around. The boss didn't know, if it was because of the news of Pozzoni parcel, or that the rather attractive dinner lady was bending down to mop the floor.

'Do you think that scrounger's got him Boss?' He was asked.

'I really don't know. I don't know anything anymore.' He shook his head despondently, 'But what I do know, is that the signature on the delivery note was fake. And we all know, that any Post Office Delivery Worker worth his weight in vinegar, wouldn't leave a package at a residence with a false signature on the paperwork.' He shivered at the thought, or he could have been shaking at the sight of the canteen girl's skimpy knicker-line through her white uniform.

'I've heard that Pablo's done something like this before,' a man spoke up.

'Are you sure?' the boss demanded, trying to peel his eyes away from the girl.

'Yes, I'm positive. Last year, he was charged and convicted of holding the gas-man, against his will for two days in his outside toilet, he had only come to read the meter!'

'That's just the information that broke the camel's leg,' he mistakenly said, stormed over to the gun cabinet, and started to hand out the rifles to the incensed union members, who were all waiting in orderly file. It reminded him of the last time they'd got fully tooled up; when they had a dispute with the Dustmen about who had the biggest and baddest vehicle. That ended with several troops from both sides getting seriously injured. Unfortunately for the Postmen, the Ambulance Service refused to treat them because of their little disagreement, and left them battered, bruised, and bleeding on the pavement.

'Let's go and get our man back,' his battlecry bellowed through the megaphone, as a convoy of red Post Office vans snaked their way out of the depot towards Acacia Avenue.

Colette, the newly appointed Mayoress, was taking to her role like a duck to water. Everyone was so nice to her at the newly built council offices. She was unsure if this was because they really liked her, or due to the fact that they actually despised the ex-Mayor so much.

'We'll save a fortune on stamps and stationery paper, now that he's gone,' her new secretary told Colette as she showed her around the council office on her first morning.

'What am I supposed to do?' Colette asked the woman solemnly, when she returned with a tray of coffee and biscuits.

'It's easy really. There's nothing to do. Today you just need to sign these three official top secret documents, and then decide what sandwiches you would like from the sandwich van that comes at 11am. There's a meeting you need to attend at 11.05am until 11.23am, to discuss 'The End of the World' party, and the most important decision of the day is what to pick for lunch? Then after lunch the afternoon is free. The ex-Mayor normally spent his time wandering around the stationery section in WH Smiths.

Colette sipped the coffee and said, 'Well that sounds easy enough. It was a lot harder waiting tables in Hing Hongs.' She picked up the documents in her in-tray, and started to browse through the pages before she signed them.

'There's no need to read them.' The secretary smiled at her, pushing a biro into her hand.

'Well, what are they all about?'

'Don't know. To tell the truth, no one knows.' She topped her new boss' cup up and added, 'No one ever bothers to read them, because by the time they are passed around all of the councillors, who insist that they need to sign them, they are out of date anyway.'

'Do the councillors read them?' Colette asked.

'Who... the councillors? Don't make me laugh. Most of them can't read or write. Some even need an interpreter to help fill out their expense forms.' She could tell by Colette's expression, that she needed to explain in a bit more detail how the wheels of the civil service turned through the corridors of bureaucracy. 'Look, it's simple. The forms are passed around to all the overpaid knobs. They sit in their in-trays for at least two months, until they finally snake their way through the red tape and get signed. But, by that time they've gone passed their approval date, so then the sequence of events starts all over again.'

'That doesn't sound efficient,' Colette rightfully observed. She pondered on what would happen, if this lot worked at Hing Hongs. No one would get served.

'Of course it's not efficient, but it keeps us busy, and stops us over spending our budget. Or it should stop us from spending over our budget, but by the time you take into account all the expensive meals and foreign visits, it all adds up.'

Colette didn't feel in a strong enough position at the moment to challenge the system, and anyway she was meeting Malcolm in the afternoon. He was taking her to see him perform at the New Theatre. Apparently, someone had told him that he could do a slot between performances.

Not only did she now have an extremely interesting job, she also had an educated and talented new boyfriend as well. She found Malcolm to be a very special person. Wherever they went, people would stop and stare at them, and she was beginning to like it.

Last night he had taken her to a little restaurant in the country, where he entertained the customers all night. She was amazed how much they clapped. She knew that they really liked Malcolm's poems, they hardly touched their food, and when she went around later with a hat for a tip, all the people emptied their pockets. Some even gave their expensive watches and wedding rings.

She floated on cloud nine that morning, even when someone had told her that they had been mentioned on the Nine 'o' Clock news last night. Her life was definitely on the right side of the track, for a change.

She went to add her signature to one of the top secret documents, which proposed that a victory parade and celebration, for the Penydarren under ten's football team for winning the trophy, should be organised as soon as possible. She stopped reading after noticing the date on top of the form.

'Is this right?' she asked her secretary curiously.

'What?'

'This victory parade and reception for the under tens football team.'

'Yes of course. What's wrong with that? It sounds a great idea to celebrate the little fellers success.' The secretary retorted. 'And to tell you the truth I have a bit of a soft spot for us to get this passed, my younger brother was the full-back for the team.'

'There's nothing at all wrong with it. In fact I think it's a great idea. But it says here at the top of the form, that they won the cup in bloody 1973.'

'Colette, it takes time. It just takes time. The world wasn't built in seven days.' The secretary said, shaking her head. She obviously hadn't heard Father Clancy giving one of his creation sermons.

Colette tried to work out in her mind how old the boys would be by now. She gave up after running out of fingers, and wished she had gone to school instead of spending her childhood working for a chimney sweep. 'But most of those boys will probably be in jail, or drug rehabilitation clinics by now.' She said seriously.

'I think that's a very small-minded attitude to have, especially for someone in your position,' the secretary answered, obviously upset by the woman's last remark. 'By the way, my brother was framed for that burglary, and should never have been remanded in prison for three years.' She snatched the china cup out of her hands and put the lid back on the tin of biscuits.

'Sorry, I didn't mean anything by it. But, when do you think that this document will get sanctioned?' Colette asked.

'Only another couple of years at the most.' The secretary muttered back, handing her the sandwich menu.

By the time Colette reached the second document in the pile, she had made a conscious decision to just sign the damn things and get them over with.

The meeting to finalise the 'End of the World' disco was making good progress. Apparently, an entire floor of the building had been given the task of organising the event. There was the usual hold up, while waiting for the mounds of paperwork to be signed, countersigned, and checked, but there were already lots of things in place. They had finally agreed the proposed design of the invitation ticket, after just a sixteen hour emergency brainstorming meeting. They had also arranged some great entertainment for the night, and had even booked the world famous Motown band, 'The Temptations' to end the show of all shows.

Colette's final duty of her first day, was to decide between the duck or the pheasant for lunch. She plumped for the duck in a light pale ale sauce. She wasn't actually sure what type of fish a pheasant was.

Both of the TV presenters, on the morning breakfast show, tried desperately hard to keep a straight face, even though one kept kicking the other under the desk, during the report that showed the savage demise of the once popular Bobby Wilson.

Since his outbreak several days earlier, he had not only been beaten up seven times, and his wife had filed for divorce, demanding a seven figure settlement (even though she knew that he only had four thousand pounds to his name), but he had a mild angina attack due to the stress. The pictures that were beamed into every household in the country, showed the frail shadowy figure of the defunked front man of Final Score, being sadly led around the garden of the hospital, in his goalkeeper gloves.

The cheer from the red half of Merseyside, could be heard ringing around the rest of the country.

'And now for a story on the lighter side of life,' the presenter changed her expression to suit the mood of the next feature. 'Just imagine that some old tramp has just predicted that the world is going to end in five days time, and everyone in the town believes it's going to happen. That's right, everyone in the town, including the newly elected Mayor believes it.'

'That's got to be right up there with that story we covered last month, about those dancing squirrels and their noisy nuts,' Her male companion chipped in.

'But it's true. There's a small old mining town in the valleys, that is bracing itself for the final days before the world ends. It's supposed to be all coming to an abrupt finale on Wednesday, at exactly midnight GMT.'

'Let's go now to the scene of this extraordinary story, and our reporter Tracy Paris.' The camera panned to a busy high street.

'Hello Richard. Hello Jane. I have just arrived at this drab town, and I must say that it seems like just another run of the mill industrial grey town.' A wino with the morning shakes interrupted the proceedings briefly, when he demanded that the cameraman swapped shoes with him, (even though he didn't have any shoes to give back in return).

Tracy turned to try to catch someone's attention. She stopped an old couple who had a shopping trolley full of cat food.

'Hello, my name is Tracy Paris from the BBC breakfast morning programme. Do you mind if I ask you a few simple questions?'

'If it's about the killer piles love, I'm afraid you are wasting your time. My husband was too poorly to work in the coalmine at the time.' The old woman spoke. 'And if it's concerning who shot Santa, we told the police everything we knew at the time… and they believed our alibi.'

'No, it's not about the killer piles, or Santa,' she hesitated, but noted the strange comments in her memory banks, for perhaps another world exclusive. She added 'No, can you tell me if you know if something out of the ordinary is going to happen soon?'

At first, the two old wrinklies appeared conveniently not to fully understand the question.

'Oh yes,' the woman finally piped up. 'Are you talking about how the world is going to end? I think it maybe tomorrow, or the day after that.'

'Who told you that the world will end?' the presenter smiled patronisingly, turning to get her mug-shot onto the screen.

'Cherry-nose.'

The reporter talked back into the microphone 'Who did you say?.... Berry-nose.'

'No, Cherry-nose. His nose is much too big to be a berry.' The couple cackled to themselves. 'And anyway there's already a Berry-nose living in Bedlinog, with the Stuck-together twins.'

'What did this Cherry-nose predict? And why do you and your husband believe that it's going to happen.' She asked, just as the wino started to try to untie the camera - man's laces, of his hush puppy shoes. The cameraman was having difficulty in keeping the image still.

'He said the world was going to end, after that horse kicked him out of the window with stockings on.'

'Cherry-nose had stockings on?' Tracy asked.

'No, not Cherry-nose.' They laughed louder. 'The horse had the suspenders on. Cherry-nose doesn't wear women's clothes. He's not a pervert.' She then turned and told a passer-by, that the out-of-town reporter thought that Cherry-nose wore suspenders. The passer-by gave the reporter a cold stare.

'Tracy, Tracy,' the manager of the outside broadcast units yelled into her ear. 'Look Tracy, try and talk to someone else will you, these two have obviously got

Alzheimer's, or they are high on some drugs or something.'

The old woman continued 'Well love, Cherry-nose always predicts things… and he's never wrong.'

'Where is he now?' asked Tracy intrigued, just noticing the cans of Whiskas cat food in the mesh trolley.

'He's locked in the cellar with the ex-Mayor.' The old man stared at the portable camera, sticking his row of medals, which sat with pride on his jacket pocket, into the lens.

'What's he doing locked in the cellar with the Mayor?' the cameraman actually asked, to the annoyance of Tracy and the broadcast manager.

'Hey, you are only here to take the photos monkey boy,' she stared at the red faced cameraman. She then repeated the exact question word for word.

'He's not with the Mayor. She works in Hing Hongs. He's locked up with the ex-Mayor. He's not the Mayor anymore. He lost the privilege in a raffle.'

'Tracy. I'm pulling the plug on this broadcast. It's too bloody weird. We are having lots of phone calls complaining that it's frightening the kids. It's well before the watershed. They'll take our licence off us.' The station manager voiced his concerns.

'Ok Boss, but I just need to ask one last question.' She turned to the old woman and enquired 'If the world is going to end, why have you bought all of that cat food?'

The old couple looked at each other in disbelief, and both shook their heads. 'It's for our cat love. What do you think we were going to do with a trolley full of cat food… eat it ourselves? We may be old, but we can tell the difference between steak and shite.' The old woman looked disgusted at the well-dressed reporter.

'No sorry…. I didn't mean that. But can you tell me what good thirty cans of Whiskas are going to be for your cat… if the world's going to be destroyed?'

'The cat will survive. Cats always survive any disaster.' The old man butted in again. 'Remember

Pompeii? Only the cats lived. The great fire of London…
Dick Whittington and the rest of the city folk burnt to
dust… the cats in the city didn't even singe their fur.'

'Tracy.' The manager was now really annoyed 'If you
ask them how the fuck the cat is going to open the cans,
I'll fucking sack you on the spot.'

Tracy cut the interview short and wandered around,
trying to find someone who looked normal enough to
discuss the issues of the day. Unfortunately, the whole
broadcast was aborted when the cameraman fell into a
man-made underground tunnel, that had just opened up in
the ground, outside the Chinese restaurant. He landed on
the struggling man, who had a mouth full of sweet and
sour mixed with dirt, and a earless puppy.

Back in the studio, Richard joked to his co-presenter.
'Well that looks an interesting place to visit. What would
you do if the world was going to end in five days?' He
asked Jane.

'Get away from your continual arse pinching and your
bad breath,' she thought to herself, but didn't let her
thought escape out of her mind. 'Go shopping,' she said
instead, living up to the dumb blonde image that the
studio insisted she portrayed for the morning ratings.

Percy had thought, that his self-enforced release from
slavery, and his first days of freedom, would somehow
taste better than they did. He had been handed the
lifestyle that he had craved for, which was without the
bickering, but he hadn't quite realised how conditioned
he had become to it. It felt as if he had been let out of
prison after a thirty-year stretch in the penile system,
without any understanding of how this new world
operated. He didn't know how to re-adjust to every day
existence on Civvy Street.

He was fifty-five years of age, and it was not the right
time to be starting it all over from scratch. He wasn't
quite sure if he regretted what he had done to his wife, or

hated the fact that it had taken him all this time to be man enough to do it.

Demons had begun to talk to him, and he could not hide the fact that people were asking questions about where his wife was. Or was she coming to the dance? And what would she be wearing? He knew, that although these people had the habit of looking as dull-as-fuck most of the time, when it came to sizing up the situation, they had been bred with a knack, of instinctively knowing the score. And the score in their eyes was that he was up to no good. Some had already started to suspect that something was amiss, at number 36 Acacia Avenue. Percy Norman wandering around without his wife… just didn't ring true.

It had been the same, the time that Mother Theresa had been wrongly accused of shoplifting in the Gurnos shops, after she came to the borough to open up a new Convent, which had been fitted up with all the modern religious mod cons. The church insisted that she was innocent, and the department store sent its deepest apologies, (and a Christmas hamper) after realising their mistake. But, deep down, the people knew she had done it. How else would you explain the two tins of sardines in her hold-ups?

Percy felt remorse. He touched her ice cold body lying there. For the first time since he had known her, she was silent. Even in death he somehow pictured her despatching words, at a mile a minute. He pitied the Devil, when she walked into his pit of eternal damnation. Old Nick wouldn't have a moment's peace.

Her mother phoned daily, and he palmed the old witch off with some story. This had kept her happy for a while, but he also realised that she would soon get suspicious, and probably fly over on her broomstick after dark to find out for herself. To be on the safe side, Percy had covered the doors and windows in garlic bread and crosses.

He went to the pub. It felt strange. No one knew who he was anymore, and he felt as though he had been left behind in some nineteenth century world. He tried his best to join in the meaningless conversation about football, without knowing really who played for who. He didn't even bother to enter the daily debate about, 'If they came back as a girl, would they be a lesbian?' He didn't know where to start.

Soon, the forced conversation between the men dried up, and Percy would make his excuses and leave.

In the cold light of day, he found himself worrying that someone would find her. He was stressed, in case, they took one look at her mutilated carcass, and point the finger sharply at him, without understanding the provocation that led him to take someone's life.

He needed to get rid of the evidence. To bury it or cut it up and flush it down the drain. He knew that he didn't deserve to go to jail. He had bloody well spent most of his married life in one, enduring the worst torture known to mankind..... A bossy, overweight wife, with a degree in nagging, and plenty of time on her hands.

He woke up sweating. He went back into the murder scene bedroom and apologised to her, which made him feel better for a while (but hadn't impressed his wife for a moment).

He then came up with a plan. It was simple, but he needed to bide his time. He picked up his bowling bag and went to the Labour club, to ask them what the hell a Lesbo was anyway?

Chapter 15

'Hit me with your reality stick..beat me whip me'

Lusty sat on the armchair waiting for Kinsey to appear from upstairs in his bedroom. He'd been sitting patiently for about twenty-five minutes. In that time, he couldn't help but take sly glances at Kinsey's dad, who lay stretched out on the settee still dressed in his pyjamas. The boy knew that he'd been away for a while in Spain, but he couldn't help but notice that there was something odd about the man. He couldn't quite put his finger on it, but he just looked different.

'Everything going well Mr Kinsey?'

'Just grand my lad… just grand.' He got up to switch the tele over.

Lusty decided to dig a little deeper. 'You're looking very well Mr Kinsey.'

'I'm feeling well son… feeling well. Call me Danny son, call me Danny.' Lusty remembered that Kinsey's dad was never the type of dad to hold a meaningful conversation with. The man had developed a communication process, that revolved around speaking in bullet-points rather then full sentences.

Mrs Kinsey entered the room in a very smart long evening dress, with an extremely larger than life black hat balancing on her head.

'Where the bloody hell are you going?... Ratting?' Kinsey's father hissed loudly. Lusty tried hard not to laugh.

'Hello Lusty, I bet you are glad to be back.... especially with the world ending and all.' She looked in the mirror and straightened her headpiece, completely disregarding the comment from her other half.

The dark haired boy shrugged his shoulders nonchalantly and added, 'You're looking extremely lovely today Mrs Kinsey... off anywhere nice?'

'He's a little charmer that boy,' she thought 'More bloody observant than that lazy slob of a husband that I married.' She stared at the man who was picking the remains of his Rice Krispies out of his teeth.

She informed Lusty, that she and her best friend were off to Ladies' Day, which had been hastily arranged by the women's section of the Labour Club. Normally, every year they would all troop off to Ascot races dressed up in their best finery, to experience for one day only, a world they only saw in magazines. So due to the little matter of the earth being blown to smithereens, they had decided to fast forward this year's event.

Lusty heard the loud elephant footsteps of his mate bounding down the stairs.

'Come on Lust.... let's go!' Kinsey said, but suddenly stopped in his stride, turning to ask his old man 'Dad, have you dyed your hair?'

'That was it,' Lusty thought. 'He looked about twenty years younger.'

The father didn't answer, but by the shade of red that his face turned, he had already informed them of the answer.

'Mam.... has dad dyed his hair? He looks like Superman.' Kinsey spurted out, before they all burst out laughing.

'Up….. up and away Mr Kinsey.' Lusty made the superhero's gesture. 'You better watch out that Lois doesn't get you. She'll suck you dry of all your kryptonite.'

'Leave him alone son. Apparently, they all had it done in the club last night. They must think that they are bloody teenagers… not middle aged men.'

'You'll be having a tattoo next Mr Kinsey,' Lusty commented.

Kinsey could see by his dad's expression, that he already had something else to show them. His old man got up and exposed, a drawing of a 'Skull and Crossbones' on his chest. He muttered proudly, 'Hey, nothing wrong with trying to look your best. The world's going to end the day after tomorrow, so there's no harm in it. The girl who gave out the tote tickets, told me it made me look the spitting image of Sean Connery.' He posed in the mirror.

'Da…ad, what the hell are you doing? What are you going to attempt for an encore,…. having your ears pierced?' Kinsey shrieked.

'The daft twit has already got something bloody pierced, but it's not his bloody ears,' his mother confessed.

'Hey…. I don't know why you are so uptight.' He pointed to his wife. 'You weren't complaining last night. Hello, the name is Bond…. Danny Bond.' He tried a Scottish accent, and winked at his crimson coloured wife, who tried desperately to hide under her hat.

Kinsey covered his ears up in disgust, and went in search of a quick exit through the front door. Lusty followed behind saying his goodbyes.

Outside in the street, Lusty asked Kinsey, if he had decided what he would like to do for his one wish.

'Yep, I've got it all planned. But we need to go and see the Red Indian up on the hill.' He replied.

They headed off to meet up with the rest of the gang.

The taxi dropped Kinsey's mother and her best friend, just outside the large building which was holding the event. Already, a mass of women of all shapes and sizes, were queuing up dressed in evening gowns, with a variety of hats. All clutching hand bags full of make-up and small bottles of vodka.

The two ladies entered the well decorated room, just as Colette was standing on the stage officially opening the proceedings for the day. She finished her short speech by adding, 'And don't get drunk and try to shag the barman.' This was received with a massive cheer by all, except the barman himself, who checked that the door leading to where he carried out his duty was securely locked, and that his baseball bat was close to hand.

On first impressions, the day had been arranged very well. There seemed to be something for everyone. All tastes were apparently catered for. Well, nearly every woman's tastes were catered for. Lois 'the Swallow', on the other hand, (and probably many of the other sexual frustrated females present) would have been more than happy to have had Lusty blindfolded and tied to the bingo machine on the stage, covered in sticky toffee pudding.

No expense had been spared to ensure the success of the day. An open-air market had been set up at the far corner of the room. Lucky-Lucky men had been flown in from treading the beaches of Spain, with black hands full of shiny things that mesmerised their female audience. One of the most ingenious alterations that was evident, was a 'one-for-all', and 'all for one' (no number twos were allowed), communal toilet which had been erected, so that all the women could go en-mass to the bog without the fear of getting talked about. In theory, this was an excellent concept, but the women still talked about each other, by using hand signals while they reapplied lippy to their cracked dry lips.

The dance floor had been constructed in the shape of a giant handbag, so they didn't feel obligated to boogie around their own. Mirrors that made everyone appear thin and fat-free, had been screwed to every spare part of the wall.

Topless male waiters were employed to serve up fancy cocktails, and they were made to jump up onto the tables and shake their tail feathers, when anyone shouted 'House' during the bingo.

Everything was going down a storm. While in the real world, husbands were frantically searching for tin openers, or trying desperately to work out how to switch the oven on, while the rest of the household cried out in hunger.

Hairy Mary and the rest of her lesbo chain gang were also out in force. Even they had delved deep into their more feminine side, and were all dressed up for the occasion. One or two of them even had long dresses on, which the other, more traditional, long trouser clit ticklers, found quite amusing.

Hairy Mary herself, was decked out in purple leggings with a matching purple halter neck top, and a 'Kiss my Twat' hat on, which she had bought whilst up in Blackpool for the lights.

'Hello gorgeous,' Hairy Mary said, slamming a pink Russian in front of the new girl that had just appeared on the block. Mary had been eyeing her up from across the room, lightly stroking her 15inch dildo that splurged out of her tight fitting purple leggings.

'Hi, and thank you.' Kieran the postman answered the lesbian back, but in a well-disguised womanly voice.

'I'm Mary. What's your name.' she stretched out her rugged hand in the direction of the Post Office deserter.

'I'm Kier... Keri.' He hesitated before shaking her hand. He stared at the home made tattoo's, that spelt out 'Love', and 'Hate', across the knuckles of her hands.

Mary invited herself to take the seat next to Kieran. 'Keri.... that's my favourite name.' Mary flew into her chat up technique.

Across the room at the lesbian table, Hairy Mary's current piece of stuff, a seventeen year old student that had fallen in love with her big butch lover, turned her back in hidden rage.

'What brings an angel like you, to such a God-awful place like this?' Mary asked, sticking to her old tried and tested chat-up routine.

He didn't tell her the real reason was that he had just bought a new leather bag from one of the market stalls; instead he lied, and answered in a suggestive manner 'Just came to meet some interesting ladies.' Kieran was enjoying this.

'Are you a meat and two veg girl, or are you a succulent juicy prawn and melon, sort of lady?' Mary asked, a glint in her eye, followed by a lick of her lips.

'It's all according how hungry I am. Normally I like both.' Kieran hadn't cottoned on, to the sexual undercurrent that had been swirling around in the loaded question.

'That's my type of girl,' Mary indicated, knowing that she had enough supply of both types of food, to satisfy any girl's cravings. She pulled herself closer to the fake girl, and accelerated her effective method of seduction.

After a short intense conversation, Hairy Mary reached across and her lips found Kieran's, who was a little unsure at first, but surprisingly, found himself enjoying the experience. He felt weird, because he had gone through a stage, of not knowing what type of sex he really liked. He'd tried a girl once, but he had found the whole two minutes and twelve seconds precisely, sticky and rather painful. He had even had a few brief male encounters, normally, in the less than romantic environment of the bus station toilets. He had also found the act of five-finger shuffling the guy in the opposite cubicle, just as unrewarding. At one point, he believed that he was sexless, just like a slug, or Cliff Richard.

Mary was also enjoying it very much. She felt as though she was in heaven. The hairs on her shins stood on end, poking out of her thin cotton trousers like a wire hairbrush, that had been designed for King Kong. She finally unwrapped her tongue from around the head of the postman, and went in search of a suitable cocktail drink to impress her new lover with.

Kieran took this opportunity to rebalance himself. His penis, which he had Sellotaped to his thigh, had broken out of it's shackles and was bobbing around in his silk panties, demanding attention.

Kieran was just starting to realise what it felt like to miss a heart beat, when he suddenly found himself thrown to the floor, by the weight of Hairy Mary's current and jilted lover, who had sprung onto his back. They landed on the dance floor in a ball.

'CAT SCRAP,' someone shrieked out, informing all the other women who were tucking into their baskets of scampi and chips.

'This is more than a cat scrap,' a slightly drunk nun muttered. 'This is the best type of cat scrap. This is a JEALOUS LESBO LOVER CAT SCRAP.'

What people hadn't realised, was that when Mohammed Ali fought Big George Foreman in that memorable rumble in the jungle boxing match in the seventies, the epic encounter was only the warm-up fight to the main event. The real match, that people from all over the world had paid large sums of money to see, was the return grudge match between 'Mad-as-Fuck Alison', and her bitter rival 'Helen-the-Hatchet Woman Jones', over the licking rights to the beautiful Italian lipstick lesbian, who had broken both women's hearts.

The scrap lasted thirty-six gruelling rounds, and only concluded, when Mad Alison, who had had her tongue bitten clean off in the previous round, gouged both Helen Hatchet's eyes out, and stamped them into a pulp on the canvas.

Back in the Labour club, the women crowded around the two fighters like an army of school kids, watching a first year fight in the yard. The women standing at the back found their view was obscured, by the array of tall hats that were worn.

Kieran was taken aback by the ferociousness of the attack. He finally managed to kick the little gremlin off him. He got to his feet, checking that his wig hadn't slipped off during the melee.

'I'll fucking kill you…. you blonde slut.' The incensed student screamed, eyes bulging and claws flashing. 'She's mine… Mary belongs to me.' She hurled herself head first back at the Postman.

She attacked, scramming both his cheeks to the bone and pulling a chunk of hair, (luckily for him, it was from his wig), that could fill a cushion.

Kieran was afraid. This was an unfair contest. Even Kieran, who had been ABA boxing champion for two years, was finding that even with all that training in the noble art, it was useless when faced with a love crazed Lesbo in a frenzy, with switchblade fingernails, and who was tanked up on Pina Coladas. Luckily for him, he was saved by his guardian angel, that came in the shape of Hairy Mary. The burly woman sent his attacker clean across the polished floor, with one slap of her open fist. Mary then ran over and stamped on her girl's exposed face, breaking her nose in two places.

The whole day was in grave danger of exploding, until the DJ came to the rescue. He had been brought up on a diet of female roman wrestling matches, and he knew how vicious they could get. He flicked through another of his emergency 45 record collection entitled, 'How to get women united against the rest of mankind.' There was only one record worthy to sit at the table. The DJ quickly slapped on, 'I Will Survive', by Gloria Gaynor. Within twenty-five seconds, the fighting had all been forgotten, and every flat cock in the building was on their feet, (or tables), singing loudly to the women's unofficial national anthem. All the men serving on the market stalls packed up their gear, and legged it.

216

To try and keep the mood going, the organisers made a snap decision, to ask the topless waiters to perform an impromptu strip tease for some extra cash. The young men agreed, and started going through some basic routines.

Hairy Mary soaked the flannel in cold water, and gently applied it to the battle scarred cheeks of Kieran the postman. She had grabbed his hand after the fracas, and led him to the relative quiet of the kitchen at the rear of the building.

'They look nasty, but they'll heal' she told him. 'Sorry about that, but she's such a jealous bitch.'

'Oh... Oh,' Kieran who wasn't the bravest tool in the box, whimpered back. In fact he was a big baby, who had refused to deliver mail to any house, on the estate, with a dog, or pet wolf.

Hairy Mary's touch on his skin felt good. It stirred something inside of the pretend woman, which he had never felt stirring before. Mary, on the other hand, had never been shy in coming forward; she squeezed his cheeks and kissed his lips again feverishly. Her tongue tickled the roof of his mouth.

'Oh... Oh... Oh.' He said again, but this time it was a mixture of both pleasure and pain, as she let go of his face.

In one movement she stripped her top off. Two large pierced breasts with the words 'Bitter' and 'Mild' over the nipples, were launched at the surprised postman's face.

In the main room, the topless waiters, hadn't realised, that their provocative act, had exposed them to serious danger. What they should have thought about before they agreed to gyrate their tight butts, was that these normally, half decent cats, were all under the illusion that their world was going to end soon, and so they didn't give a fuck about their actions.

The men hadn't noticed the women inching their way towards the stage. Lois led the attack from the front. It took less than a few seconds for the first wave, of sex-crazed, rampant females to storm the platform. The loss of their trousers, converted the topless waiters into completely buck-naked men. The women were now on the rampage. They could taste flesh. The five fellows made a quick retreat when the barman caused a small distraction, by firing off a flare. They locked themselves in the toilet and barricaded the door. The women could smell knob, they appeared from everywhere, like cock-eating zombies in the 'Living Dead.' They soon turned their attention to the lucky, lucky men and the DJ.

The barman, who was concerned for his safety phoned the police, as the enraged pack of females pulled down the wooden lamppost from the car park, and started to ram the toilet door, which was quickly buckling under the strain. The screams from the cowering waiters inside, were easily drowned out, by the mass chants of;

> *'Come out, come out... just open the lock,*
> *Come out, come out... and show us your cock.'*

The police officer on duty who had received the SOS call thought it was a practical joke. And even if it was true, that a gang of sex crazed women had cornered some men in the toilet, and were demanding a rogering, he didn't have any spare officers to send anyway. Most of them had either phoned in sick, or had been despatched for a revenge attack on the Traffic Wardens, who had knee-capped Sergeant Morris of the Flying Squad last week in the school playground.

Hairy Mary pushed Kieran's head down towards her never, never region. The commotion outside didn't distract the two lovers from continuing with their passionate journey.

Kieran was worried, not only due to his limited experience of oral sex, but the more pressing matter of when their roles were reversed, and Hairy Mary would find out, that her supposedly feminine girlfriend, was hiding the 'Last Turkey in the Shop' in his pants. He knew that she would probably murder him, right there amongst the pots and pans.

He remembered, that when he was an apprentice working in the franking room at the PO, an old timer told him, that licking a pussy was no different to licking a stamp. 'You just need to be careful afterwards,' the old timer confessed, 'That you don't attach the wrong one to an envelope, and send it to your favourite aunty in Dundee.'

Kieran was pondering this, as Hairy Mary stepped out of her leggings. He tried hard not to let out a scream. He had heard the rumours of how she was covered in black hair downstairs, from her toe to her belly button; but he honestly thought, that he had accidentally come face to face with a gorilla with a Rastafarian wig on, when he stared at the place where her minge should have been. The only thing he could think of, was Tarzan swinging through her jungle roots. He also noticed, the weapon, that she had strapped to her leg. Even that was covered in a bush of black hair. He made the sign of the cross, closed his eyes, and jumped in, tongue a blazin'.

Mary let go of a scream, her breathing deepened, and she sucked him further into her. His head went out of shape as her powerful thighs crushed his skull, and he could feel his eyes bulging, ready to pop.

She reached down and pulled his head back up, nearly dislodging his blonde wig. She kissed him, tasting herself on his lips. Her hands slowly started to explore his body. It was now or never for the postman. Bravely he pushed her up onto the draining board. The aluminium pots crashed to the floor, causing an almighty clatter. In a split second, he hitched up his smock and sent his normally redundant tool into the wet cave of this hairy, prehistoric creature that lay before him.

She stiffened for a moment. He froze. She looked into his eyes. She roughly snatched at his head, knocking the blonde locks onto the kitchen floor. He stopped momentarily expecting the worst, but it didn't come. She kissed him harder than he imagined physically possible. It felt as though she was trying to climb head-first into his mouth. His wisdom teeth nearly came out.

She pulled back, gasping for air and panted 'You fucking tell anyone Postie and I'll kill you, and your family.' She kissed him again, thrusting her pelvis into his. A shiver of ecstasy rose up from their toes, and covered them both in a series of mind-blowing orgasms.

Chapter 16

'It's a kind of tragic'

The after-shock, caused by the publicity and exposure, due to the screening of the small news clip on the breakfast programme, had a mixed effect on the town. By 9am the following morning, sightseers and tourists started to appear over the mountain in droves.

The first to arrive was a convoy of travellers with matted hair full of street-wise headlice. They set up camp, and played loud music at the edge of town. Not far behind, was a mini-bus of religious fanatics, who parked behind the college car park, and got prepared to hold some kind of giant baptism in the river.

By lunch-time, the streets were teaming with new arrivals, of every shape, size, and weirdness. Each of them seemed to be on separate missions, to either save the world, or just chill-out waiting for the party to begin.

Circus performers entertained the crowds with fire balls, that shot into the sky. Hundreds of depressed, failed suicide cases, with sleeping pills and razorblades, camped outside the nightclub, hoping to be the first in line to get killed. They sat around eating fig-rolls, and showing each other the scars of passed botched suicide attempts.

Helicopters and small planes circled overhead, full of curious passengers with cameras taking snap shots of the masses. Street traders instantly discovered a roaring trade in selling tee-shirts and souvenirs, that either said

'I've been to Merthyr and survived'
or
'Hey Cherry nose... I believe you... bang!!!!'

Fortune tellers were all of a sudden the new face of Vogue. Old hags from the gypo camp on the Bogey Road, with green and white tea-towels on their heads, and crystal balls made from fish bowls, sprung up on every available corner. Palms and Tarot cards were read, and the news of death and destruction was shelled out to morbidity seeking customers.

Kinsey and Lusty walked through the chaos. It reminded Lusty of Saturday Acid nights in St. Antonio bay. During the short journey, the boys were offered everything imaginable, from a good time for less than a tenner, to smokin' potions that claimed to cure baldness in thirty-five minutes.

The street was becoming a contradiction of itself. Outside the Buffaloes pub, on the left hand side of the road, the anti-Cherry-nose brigade had hundreds of voodoo dolls of the poor man, and were all proceeding to pierce the cloth skin with sharp pins, demanding that the no-good, big nosed tramp be hung by the snout, until pronounced dead and buried in an unmarked grave.

Over by the sweet shop, being held back by the overworked police cordon, were the lobby for the protection of the rather misunderstood hobo. They were out in force with tee-shirts and balloons. They were asking passers-by to sign a petition for the immediate release of Arthur Cherry-nose, and to get him Knighted by the Queen in the New Years honours list.

Every now and again, someone from either side would sneak through the thin blue line that separated the two factions, and a scuffle would break out.

To add to the chaos, large amounts of illegal bets were being placed, on *'How was the world actually going to end?'*

The money taken was equivalent to the sum of cash exchanged on Grand National day. Everyone, including grandmothers were having a flutter.

'Blown to pieces by a space meteorite,' had been the favourite at first, but there must have been some insider dealing, because out of nowhere, an unusually large amount of money was put on a rank outsider, (led mainly by the Irish, who had a couple of bucks left over from the Cheltenham horse racing festival).

The new, 'two to one' odds on favourite was:-

'The world to be destroyed by a tidal wave after the Chinese, (including those working in Hing Hongs), all jumped up in the air on a secret instructions at exactly the same time, causing a massive tidal wave to flood most of the United States. The Yanks in turn, (who were always ready for this type of terrorist attack), would have all of their fatties, eating hot-dogs in a circle in Central Park, ready to send a retaliation wave back in their direction.'

Kinsey was stopped in the street by a rather downtrodden deformed old woman, who asked if he knew a man in a wheelchair called Marty something? He could see her eyes were full of tears.

'Yeah love.' He replied without thinking. He then recognised the woman as no other than Rita Flood from the docks. He quickly added 'Sorry love, he died this morning.'

'Of what?' He could hear the panic in her voice.

'Of the clap,' he squawked. She screamed out loud and ran sobbing in the direction of the nearest bridge.

Next the boys stopped to watch a load of people getting off a bus. The strange looking individuals were all walking like they had shit themselves.

'I wish we had taken another route.' Kinsey muttered to his mate, as one man staggered up and asked them about the special place where they could a buy the magical cure for Haemorrhoids.

'Who said that you can get your piles cured around here?' Lusty shrugged sceptically.

'Haven't you heard, it's all over the news?' the man replied. 'Merthyr, the town for miracle pile cures and a place where cats never die.'

What the two boys hadn't notice, were the hordes of bewildered cats that had been dumped off at the edge of town, with a trolley of tinned food, and a Swiss-army knife.

'Are you sure you wanna do this?' Alex turned and asked Jac.

'Positive.' He replied grinning wickedly.

'Well I could think of a better fucking way to spend our last days on this earth.' Kinsey snapped back.

Jac stopped pulling on the yellow wellington boot and said 'Look, we all agreed that each of us would decide on something to do, and the rest of us wankers would do it. We've seen Alex's granddad hump some old flame. We've rescued Lusty from a fate worse than death, and we don't know what the hell you want to do yet. So now, shut the fuck up, and put the uniforms on, and let's get going.'

'I know.' Lusty gestured to Kinsey 'But we did make a promise.' Throwing him a helmet from a locker.

'Yes I know... but this is plain stupid. Who the hell wants to be a bloody fireman? It's just daft. What if someone sees us?' Kinsey reluctantly did up his belt.

Jac clapped his hands in eager anticipation.

'What if there are no fires?' Kinsey gulped, still feeling the need to make his point until the bitter end.

'I'll fucking burn you instead. Is that OK? Now shut up or one of the lazy bastards will wake up and catch us.' They looked across to where all the real firemen were fast asleep in their beds, snuggling up to their teddy bears, (that were also in little firemen's uniforms). The captain of Red Watch was sound asleep in a four poster bed, with slices of cucumbers covering his eyes.

The four boys stood in a circle and faced each other. They all started to giggle.

'Are we ready? Let's go?' Jac asked eagerly.

They took it in turns to slide down the pole, landing inside the area where the fire engine was waiting at the ready.

Jac, who had been banned from driving any kind of motor vehicle since the mishap with the coach and the brass band, started up the engine of the machine. Lusty quietly activated the roller shutter doors, and the red beast crept out into the daylight.

'Then the fire engine crept in…. crept in… crept out again.' He sang the old seventies song. His hand was itching to make its way to the horn that was invitingly positioned in the cabin.

'Not yet Jac. Wait until Lusty's back on board.' Alex commented, making sure that their mate had climbed safely up onto the side, before shouting 'Ok NOW!'

On that command, Jac pulled the cord with all his might. The noise of the siren reverberated around the station house. Upstairs, the firemen automatically bounced out of bed. Some got straight into their uniforms and in one movement greased the poles with their thighs. While four of them looked bemused as they searched their lockers for their already stolen stuff.

'Where the hells bells has our fire engine gone?' one bleared eyed fire fighter cried out, still holding his cuddly Paddington Bear toy.

225

'There it is Chief.' Another answered on spying the big red metal animal turn across the Iron Bridge, all lights and whistles blazing.

'Quick phone the police.' The chief demanded.

'They are not talking to us Boss, since we filled their panda cars up with foam.' He was swiftly informed.

'If that's the case, bugger it. Let's go back to bed. I'm doing some moonlight window cleaning this afternoon and I need my sleep.' They all trooped back up the pole, one by one.

The newly named 'Wankmobile' which had been christened by Kinsey, drove around the estate for a couple of hours, giving kids a lift, or spraying others with jets of freezing water from the cannon. Even Kinsey '2 amp' was enjoying it, especially when he soaked a gang of skinheads who were marching in single file down the street. He sat on top of the machine; legs spread-eagled, water gun at the ready.

'Can we go back now?' Alex asked Jac who was still beaming about their adventure, and the fact that he was fulfilling his life-long ambition.

Suddenly, an old woman stepped into the road and was attempting to flag down the red shiny machine, when a sharp blast of icy water picked her up and deposited her into a near-by garden.

'Kinsey you prick,' Lusty yelled 'She was in distress. You idiot'

'Well she's in a wet dress now,' Kinsey laughed.

They apologised to the woman, but not before she whacked Kinsey (the golden shot), over the head with the rake that she had landed on. She then went on to tell the fake Emergency Service Officers, that her cat was stuck up a big beech tree, and she was worried that it would fall off and hurt itself.

'And I have just been to Liptons to buy it some cat food,' she told them.

Kinsey aimed the water cannon at the animal that clung to the branches saying its prayers. He was just about to open fire, when Alex turned the water supply off at its source.

'No. we'll have to go up for it' Alex added.

'You must be joking' Kinsey showed his annoyance. 'It must be about forty foot.'

Jac again rubbed his hands in glee. 'Come on boys, lets get the ladders out.'

Reluctantly they struggled for about twenty minutes to get the bloody things out their holder. During their struggle, the aluminium ladders went out of control, smashed into a telephone booth, and nearly tipped a mini metro onto its side.

'Who's going up then?' Alex asked, indicating that he didn't like heights and that he would take control on the ground.

'Well I'm not going up. I'm not risking my life for a sly fur ball that's probably more content with licking its own arse.' Kinsey walked away.

'I'll go.' Lusty bravely said, noticing a couple of lovely looking girls who had stopped to survey the hunks in uniforms.

A short while later, Lusty was back on firm ground with the unharmed and uninterested cat in his arms.

'Hey handsome,' one of the observing girls shouted from across the street. 'You can come and rescue my pussy anytime…'

'Where is it stuck?' the handsome fireman called back, handing the cat to the old woman.

'It's hiding here… in my big black bush.' She smirked, her eyes undressing him as she spoke. 'But fetch your hose pipe with you… because it's on fire.' The entire crowd smiled at the sexual connotations in the conversation.

They reactivated the ladders into their casing and were waving goodbye to the females, when a call came through on the radio intercom in the cabin. 'Hey you

227

thieving little pricks,' the voice barked. Jac ignored the mystery caller and fired up the engine.

'Hey, you little fuckers that have stolen our engine. We have just had a 999 call, that there's a house fire at number thirty-six Acacia Avenue. So because some dopey, selfish bastards have stolen the only working engine in town, you better get your arses down there now and put it out.' The boys could hear lots of additional screams from the other firemen in the background 'Hey, and by the way, if our little Berty comes back with as much as a scratch, we'll track you down and make you pay. Now we're off to have grub and give each other a full body massage. And before you go, I hope you get your skin burnt off.' The intercom went silent.

Alex turned to the driver and said, 'But Jac we can't.' Sadly he knew it was too late. The excitement that filled his mate had already made him swing the big machine around and switch the siren on full blast. They headed towards the thick billow of smoke that danced up into the wild winter sky.

They arrived five minutes later to see the house ablaze. Most of the windows had cracked under the intense heat and the flames that lapped out of every available space.

'Thank God you've arrived,' a neighbour shouted towards Alex and Jac. 'His wife is still in there. She's trapped. We are sure we can hear her screaming.' She pointed to where Percy Norman was stood quietly in the front garden, still holding his bowling bag. He was staring up at the bedroom window.

Before the boys had time for their feet to touch the ground, Jac was strapping on the breathing equipment, in anticipation of tackling the flames.

'Are you mad?' Kinsey screamed.

'I'm going in.' Jac replied firmly.

'Jac get a reality grip. You're a fucking carpenter from the flats, not Barney McGrew from Trumpton,' said Kinsey looking for Alex to agree with him. 'What the fuck are you going to do in a burning house? Plane the doorframes or try to chamfer the fucking kitchen work surfaces.'

'Look, this is beyond my wildest dreams. Not only have we rescued a cat from a tree, but I have the opportunity to become a hero and bring Mrs Norman out of the burning building.' He pushed passed and wrapped the smoke visor around his eyes.

'I'll get her out Mr Norman. I'll get her out alive.' He shouted across the garden.

'I would like to see you do that,' Percy said straight faced, as a loud bang from an upstairs window heightened the drama in the street.

The hands of the flames engulfed the house in its grip, as the brave carpenter kicked the front door off its hinges. He entered the passage way. It was just as he pictured, but he could never have imagined the intensity of the heat. The smoke formed a thick black screen whichever way he tried to go. He eventually traced the stairs, more by luck than judgement and carefully manoeuvred himself blindly to the top. Although everything around him was white hot, he actually kept his cool rather well, considering the circumstances.

He found the master bedroom. His sight was impaired, but he could just make out the shape of a woman lying on top of the mattress. He reached out to shake her. She didn't stir.

'I hope I'm not too late.' He said loudly to himself. 'Perhaps she's just fainted due to the fumes.'

The smoke spiralled around her head. He accidentally touched her breast. It felt nice. His other hand reached over automatically to cop a feel of the other one. He played around for a few seconds. Just then, the reality of the situation smacked him hard across the face.

'You're are in a burning building, pretending to be a fire fighter and you are more interested in feeling a bit of old woman's tit.' He told himself. 'For fuck's sake… just sling her over your shoulder in one of them fireman's lifts and get the hell out before the roof caves in.'

He grabbed her arm and tried to lift her up. 'Just hold on.... Mrs Norman, I'll get you out.' He didn't really appreciate how icy cold she actually felt. He just thought it was the contrast to the warmth of the embers.

He could see the flames edge ever so close to the bed, with hatred in their coloured fingertips. He couldn't see his hand in front of his face. As he swung around to escape, her body smacked into the cupboard.

'Sorry Mrs Norman.... hope you didn't hurt you head.' He tread blindly back down the stairs, continuing to bang and bump their way all the way down.

He appeared through the front door, out of the thick coat of smoke. People cheered when they saw the boy with the woman on his back. He gently placed her onto the grass in the garden. The cheers and congratulations soon turned to gasps of shock and horror.

Jac tried to catch his breath, and cough the fumes out of his lungs. His triumphant smile soon fell unceremoniously off his dirty scorched face, when he turned to see why the rest of the observers were opened mouthed. He examined the woman on the ground in the blood stained dressing gown. It took him several moments to take in the brutal fact, that Mrs Norman was headless.

'Bloody hell Mister Fireman, the flames must have burnt her head... clean off.' A small boy cried and ran to the arms of his shocked mother.

'Oh no,' Jac thought, taking his helmet off. 'I must have knocked it off when I banged into that tall-boy.' Although it was a logical assumption, the feasibility of that happening was lost on the now physically, and mentally shattered teenager.

A path opened up through the silent crowd like the Red Sea did for Moses, as poor Percy reluctantly strolled to see the remains of his wife, sprawled amongst the flowerbed.

No one uttered a word. They watched as tears rolled down the husband's cheeks. He knelt by the side of the headless corpse and kissed her hand. People cried with sadness and pity at the widower's grief, until Percy unzipped his bowling bag, reached inside and pulled out the perfectly decapitated head of his wife. The feelings of the crowd turned completely through a full 180 degrees of emotion, as he positioned it lovingly on top of her shoulders, where it once fitted.

The sound of a police siren heading in their direction still didn't drag people's attention away from the scene.

'Quick….. let's get out of here before we get nicked.' Alex said to his mates.

The pretend firemen threw off their clothes and legged it out of sight.

Percy stood up, wiped his eyes, and straightened his tie. He then picked the body of his wife up in his arms. But during the excitement, he momentarily forgot that her head was not attached to the bit he had just snatched up from the icy ground. He tried unsuccessfully to bend his knees to pick the head off the floor, and due to her weight, he nearly toppled over. A woman walked forward, picked the dead woman's head up by a few strands of matted hai,r and tucked it under Percy's arm like a football referee carrying a ball before a big game.

The crowd of people moved back, not knowing what to expect next. Percy walked towards the burning house. He didn't turn back around; he entered the blazing shell. Two seconds later, the roof caved in.

Chapter 17

'They fumigate council houses, don't they?'

Later on that afternoon, Alex tried to offer some crumbs of comfort to his distraught mate, who had partially rescued the already dead and headless woman from the burning house. 'Look Jac, it wasn't your fault. Apparently Percy had already hacksawed it off days before. So I don't know why you are still feeling so bad about it. You tried your best.'

'But I caressed a headless woman's breasts.' He remembered back to the way he had expertly tweaked her ice-cold nipples. 'And I bloody liked it!' He hadn't mentioned to his friends the erection he had at the time.

They continued walking through the High Street. Two figures suddenly appeared from out of the doorway with their heads covered by their coats.

'Hey Fireman... you haven't seen where I've put my head have you?' Kinsey jokingly shouted from underneath his jacket.

'You wouldn't give these a little squeeze for me?' said Lusty pretending to cup a pair of tits.

'Fuck right off you two.' Jac kicked out at his two unsympathetic friends.

'What's wrong with Fireman Jac?' Kinsey added, popping his head from beneath his jacket.

Alex shot a glance towards Kinsey and Lusty.

'Don't look at me like that.' Kinsey's eyes returned the stare. 'It was his fault. He's the one who wanted to rescue the bloody world.'

Jac finally saw the funny side, and then went on to inform them, that he believed that the experience had cured him of his sex addiction. That morning he had destroyed all of his dirty books, even the one that he had since 1974 with the French girl on the trampoline. He had emptied his supply of baby oil down the drain. His parents were fuming. They had spent thousands of pounds on supposedly miracle sex cures devised by Doctor Ernie, who they later discovered was an unemployed fisherman from a village in Cornwall.

The main casualty of Jac's self-imposed masturbation strike, was the Indian restaurant and their loyal customers, who had all of a sudden found themselves without a regular supply of their tasty home made starters.

The four boys respectfully stopped to observe a funeral procession, that snaked its way in front of them. The death march was for the boys from the Labour club who had decided to bring forward their imminent funeral, and organised a two-day wake for themselves. After the short ceremony and a quicker resurrection, they all quickly raced back to the club dressed in shrouds, just in time for the starter's orders at Haydock Park.

'Where are we going anyway?' Alex asked.

'To see Pablo Pozzoni.' Kinsey's answer was clear and concise.

'Pablo…. why are you taking us to see him?' the other three stopped in their tracks.

'To borrow some horses from him.'

'Horses!' Jac muttered.

'Yeah, you know, four legged things. I decided that I would like us all to go horse riding.' Kinsey informed them.

'And you took the piss out of me for the fireman thing, and now you want us to trot around like Lady Godiva?' Jac issued his manic mate with some of his own medicine.

Alex joined in 'So what do you want us to do with Pablo's horses?'

'Just ride around for a bit. I've always fancied riding around the mountain side on the back of a horse.'

'You are not thinking of using them as a get away if we robbed the bank.... are you?' joked Lusty. Kinsey's stare was enough for Lusty not to continue down that path of humour.

They all finally agreed to have a go, Lusty added that after this was over, could they all just go and get pissed?

The boys made their way through the streets, towards the swirling Indian smoke signals that puffed into the sky.

Ten minutes later, they opened the wooden gate to the garden and carefully strolled up to the council house. The whole place had been designed in the style of a ranch. (A reminder of the time, when Pablo was a fully paid up member of the Gurnos Cowboy Club). On the wall, carved out of wood, were the simple words *'Welcome to El Rancho'*. Next to it, Pablo had painted a picture of a chicken nailed to a fence post with his throat cut.

'Go on then, knock.' Jac whispered.

'I'm not fucking knocking.' Kinsey informed them. 'Apparently, last week Pablo leaped off the shed roof and scalped the trumpet player from the Salvation Army band.'

'So, how the hell are we going to get to ride his horses then?' Jac sneered back.

In the meantime, as the two argued, Alex rang the doorbell, but as a precautionary measure, he waved a handkerchief through the letterbox as a symbol that they had come in peace.

Several minutes later, Romana opened it slowly, holding a boiling hot chip pan.

'What do you want?' she cried.

'We would like to speak to Pablo,' Kinsey quietly said, noticing the leather moccasins on her feet.

'There is no one of that name here, only Great Chief Giro-cheque.' She added.

'Is he your Dad?' Alex asked.

'Yes'

'Well he'll do.'

The rest looked at each other slightly confused. Romana slyly took a second glance at the tall, dark haired boy standing at the back. White boys normally didn't do anything for her, but the handsome stranger was absolutely gorgeous.

She ushered them into the front room. They stood in bewilderment, nudging each other as they stared at the tepee that took centre stage in the lounge. Romana smiled at Lusty, as she closed the door behind them.

'What the hell is this?' Kinsey whispered, on seeing a shop window dummy tied to the wall with two arrows in his eye sockets.

They saw the shadow of a plump figure rising out of the tent.

'Hooooow!' Pablo held the palm of his hand up.

'Hooooooooooow!' repeated Jac.

'Hooow!' The other three sluggishly followed their mates lead.

Pablo re-entered the tent, indicating for the boys to follow him. They dutifully obliged. Pablo sat cross-legged on a Swap Shop beanbag. In the corner another mannequin lay headless.

'Jac, you haven't been rescuing more people have you?' Kinsey smirked unsympathetically.

Jac felt like crying. He realised that it was going to take a while to out grow the stigma of the headless corpse rescue.

The pot bellied fake apache asked 'What does white boys want?'

'Pablo… we would like to borrow your horses.' Kinsey said. The boys could see the knackered animals grazing in the back garden.

'No one of that name lives here.' He said. His eyes were cold and ruthless.

Suddenly, the noise of a rattlesnake rose up from the far corner of the tent, startling the boys. Pablo jumped up and grabbed the snake and snapped its neck. Unfortunately for the Chief, the boys could actually see that it was made of rubber and the hissing sound was coming from a portable cassette.

'Bloody infested with rattlers,' Pablo announced. The boys were holding on tightly to fits of laughter that were building up inside of them.

'Look Mr Pozzoni… we can give you money.' Kinsey informed the Indian who had plonked himself back down on the beanbag.

'Money,' he raised his voice 'Me don't want white man's dirty money. Have you got any coloured beads, or thick woollen blankets?'

Pablo's wife, who was in the kitchen skinning a badger on the pool table, yelled back 'Pablo, take the bloody money. We have enough bleedin' blankets in the airing cupboard to keep the entire population of Alaska warm. And make sure it's in fifty pence pieces, so I don't have to change it at the fruit machines.'

'Ok.' Pablo conceded as the woman's voice died down 'I'll take your blood money. A monkey will do.'

Lusty wondered if the real Geronimo would have let his wife get involved in such important matters.

'How much is a monkey worth nowadays?' Alex asked.

'A monkey is worth a monkey,' berated Pablo.

There was silence as they all looked at Kinsey.

'What,' he said, feeling their eyes burn into him.

'Well it was your idea,' Jac said.

Kinsey spoke again. 'A monkey Pablo is a bit steep. We only want to trot around the block. What about a pony?'

'That's what the cost of hiring my horses will be. It's either a monkey or nothing.' The man stared menacingly at the boy and added 'And if you call me by that name again, I'll cut your bollocks off.'

Money exchanged hands, and then Pablo summoned Romana to bring in the traditional peace pipe. Jac coughed from way down in his boots on sampling the hidden delights of its contents. Kinsey declined at first, but reconsidered when Pablo reached for his hatchet.

The tepee soon filled up with smoke, and the conversation between the occupants wandered around without a clear purpose or direction.

Then out of the blue, a rock smashed through the front room window and bounced off the tightly strung tent material. Glass splinters showered the room.

'Attack…. Attack.' Pablo sprung to his feet bellowing out instructions to his tribe, who were quick to assemble in the passage way.

'Trust us to be sitting smoking a peace pipe in a Red Indian tent, when the fucking cavalry turns up,' Kinsey said, as the four boys cowered behind the 48" TV set.

Pablo asked Romana to read the note which had been attached to the brick.

'What does it say?' he demanded.

'It just says…. We've come for our boy. It's been signed the P.O.W.U.'

'Who the fuck are the P.O.W.U?' Pablo was angry. 'Well if they want a war…. let's give them a war.' He blasted out commands to his loyal family.

Suddenly, a red Post Office van smashed into the front door, denting it. The driver sprinted back towards the safety of his union troops, but not before Luke pierced his back with a six-inch dagger. Footsteps could be heard clambering on the rooftop.

After the initial panic had subsided, the Pozzoni's soon got into battle station formation. Booby traps were activated. Snares were set, the dogs were unleashed.

Up in the attic, Cyril could hear the commotion coming from downstairs. The house was full of the sound of gunshots, petrol bombs, and bows and arrows being fired. The noise of battle filled the dark room.

'Hush.' He signalled to the Mormons, who were in the middle of another wedding ceremony, to stop singing. 'What's that noise?'

'They've come for me at last,' the bunking officer shouted out. 'Finally, thank the lord.'

'Who would honestly waste their time and come to rescue you?' Cyril asked coldly.

'There are lots of people that would come to rescue me,' the man replied, looking around the room for encouragement.

'Like who? You have only been put on this planet to stop kids mitching. No one likes you. You have as much chance of being rescued as the Rent-man, and everyone hates him. The only way someone would consider saving your type, was if they wanted to use your kidney to give to someone higher up in the food chain, like a taxi driver.' Cyril savagely told the poor man.

The bunking officer's lip started to quiver, and he buried his head into the bosom of a large woman.

Cyril stood up. 'Those are my boys. I can tell by the sound of their rifles. That's the TV detector's new model army. They are only despatched for VIPs. They normally spend their time training the SAS.' He told them all.

The bunking officer stopped crying and faced up to Cyril, pushing him in the chest. 'I've had enough of your comments. Just because you think that you're a big shot detector man, that's no excuse for being rude to everyone.' Before he finished his words, Cyril slapped him hard across the face and jumped on his back. They rolled about into the water tank. While they fought, the

239

Mormon's were dishing out Colt 45 revolvers, plastering war paint on and climbing out of the pull down attic door to go and protect their new found home.

'Follow me.' Lusty said bravely, diving out of the little toilet window that was obscured from the fighting. It led to the alleyway. They still found themselves in mortal danger, because the Post Office Workers Union, unfortunately, couldn't hit a barn door with a cannon. Bullets whistled around their heads, ricocheting through the garden. The boys motioned quietly, for the four horses that had been left to roam around Pablo's backyard, to come over. But they couldn't attract their attention.

'Have you got any sugar cubes handy?' Jac asked Kinsey.

'Of course I've got some sugar cubes,' Kinsey answered rather calmly, before streaming full throttle into the punch line. 'They are right here in my pocket next to Lord Lucan reading a copy of the fucking Doomsday Book. What the fucking hell would I be doing carrying sugar cubes around with me for?'

'Just in case we needed some!'

'Just in case we needed some,' Kinsey spat out the words which were closely followed by a stream of salvia. 'You mean just in case, we get fucking trapped in a alley way, while some Red Indian warthog and some other lunatics are fighting to the death.''

'I was only thinking out loud,' Jac replied.

'Well fucking don't, unless you can think of something more constructive to say.' Kinsey felt like nutting his mate.

The resistance from the occupants of the council house surprised the union boss of the P.O.W.U, as he observed the struggle from his position on top of a delivery van.

'I thought you said that there were only four members of the Pozzoni household,' he expressed concern to his number two in command.

'That's what our surveillance records indicated.'

'So if that's the case,' he said, in between barking directions to his members. 'Who the hell are all those smug, smiling, dull looking bastards firing at us from upstairs?' He had to put sunglasses on to reflect the glare of the Mormons teeth. He was still waiting for a reply, when a stray bullet from one of his own men found a resting place in his derrière.

'Urrrgh…. They've got me boys…. they've got me,' he cried out feeling warm sticky liquid trickle down his leg.

His screams caused a momentous pause to the fighting.

'Sorry Boss,' a red faced Post Office member said. 'I was aiming for the boy on the roof, the one that looks the spitting image of Jimmy Osmond.'

The boss stared at him in disbelief. 'What are you doing Jones? I bloody well saved you from getting the sack last year, and you repay me by… Urrrrrrgh,' he screamed out again.

'Sorry again Boss. I was sure that I put the safety catch on.' The man apologised for the second time. This time the bullet had ripped through his shoulder blade, knocking him off the bonnet into the gutter.

His concerned members stopped firing, until they received news about their leader.

'Quick,' said Alex, jumping onto one of the horses. The other three were quick to follow.

'Giddy up,' Kinsey shouted, digging his heels into the underbelly of the animal. The horse raced forward and crashed through the wooden ranch fencing, swerving to miss an ice cream van selling drugs.

The four horsemen of Merthyr, escaped to the safety of the hills, as the boss of the P.O.W.U. called for extra bandages and reinforcements, as the siege of El Rancho intensified.

'Hey this is the life,' Billy 'the kid' Kinsey shouted as the four mates cruised through the field on the back of their mounts. They had unanimously named the horses, Joe, Mick, Paul and Topper, after their favourite band.

The saddle-less horses were proving to be quite tricky to manoeuvre, as well as stay on. Kinsey had fallen off twice, to the great amusement of the others.

'Hey Gringos' Jac called out. 'Let's park-up for a while, and sample some of this tasty grog we have.' He pointed to the shopping bag full of Strongbow and Embassy Regal, that was tied around the beast's neck.

They dismounted, and watered the horses in the near freezing stream. They sat on the edge of the mountainside, discussing trials, tribulations and other such matters.

A noise startled them into turning around. They saw Malcolm Knuckles wandering aimlessly through the wild heather, holding a bunch of dead ferns and reciting a verse at the top of his voice. His hair was set in a quiff to the side, and he was dressed as a young Oscar Wilde.

'Quick, hide, before he either beats us to death or limericks us to boredom…. then proceeds to beat us to death.' Alex gestured.

'I heard that he gate crashed a Mason meeting yesterday, and wouldn't let any of them go, until they performed a short play that he had penned about glue-sniffers,' Lusty spoke out.

'How can someone that used to be so violent, now be so lovey dovey over night?' Jac asked, swigging on the apple juice.

'It's a big sham,' Lusty insisted. 'A leopard never changes his spots. Mark my words. Especially a leopard with psychotic tendencies.' To keep himself warm he sucked hard on the fag nip.

As if Lusty had cast a spell, over the moment, the new Poet Laureate chased after a sheep that had the audacity to stroll away while the big man was halfway through telling it about his idea for a TV mini-series, set in 18th

Century Britain. He finally cornered the petrified creature, and proceeded to kick it straight over a farmer's boundary wall.

Lusty smiled and stubbed out the end of the cigarette and added 'Another sheep bites the dust.'

'It's quite scary really.' Jac commented.

'What, Malcolm's temper?' Alex lit another fag.

'No.... not knowing what the hell is going to happen tomorrow,' said Jac.

'Well we can't do fuck all about it.' Kinsey re-joined the conversation in his very own special way.

'What if we camp up here for a couple of days? Perhaps it's just the shitty cities, or the terrible towns that the tidal wave will hit.' Alex indicated hopefully.

'Did you also put a bet on the tidal wave ending it all?' Kinsey asked him.

'Of course. Those slanty-eyed bastards have been dying to get one over on us. It's a dead cert.' They all smirked at the unintentional pun.

'Imagine, that due to some freak of nature, we were the only ones to survive,' Jac quipped.

'But that would mean, that if we survived, then Malcolm would survive,' added Alex. They turned to observe the big man whacking a bull over the head with a branch of a tree.

'Fucking hope not. He would turn us into some Shakespearean theatrical company, and have us travel around the country performing for theatres full of cats.' Again, a loud spate of laughter raced up the valley.

'We'd have to rope some women in,' Lusty interrupted.

'There's always the sheep.' Alex interjected, as they watched the animal that Malcolm had launched stagger back over the wall, holding it's bruised ribs.

'Well I'm not having a sheep,' Kinsey was adamant.

'You've had worse.'

'Fuck you.'

'Perhaps we'll ask Lois if she'd like to come,' Jac joked.

'She does,' Lusty recalled to his regret. He'd had to throw the kitchen chair out because of her.

They discussed the possibility of living without the fairer sex. Alex sat in quiet retreat, throwing stones into the twisted path of the river.

'I was thinking,' he spoke up. 'I always thought that I would live until I was old and grey.'

'What... until you were thirty?' Jac again joked.

'That age doesn't seem too bad in the present climate. We're only bloody nineteen. It's not fair. I haven't seen most of the things that I want to see. I haven't been further than London.'

Kinsey muttered 'London. I don't know what the fuck you are moaning about, I've only been as far as Meredith's the butchers.'

'Imagine reaching the big 3..0. I wonder what we would be doing.' Alex stayed on the subject that was obviously playing on him.

'Probably we wouldn't even see each other by then. We will have out grown each other.' Lusty wisecracked.

'You'll never reach thirty,' Jac said pointing towards Kinsey 'Especially with your stress levels.'

'Me. You can fucking talk.' Kinsey let rip. 'You'll end up wanking yourself to death.' Nodding in Lusty's direction 'He'll fuck himself to an early grave and Alex will be planning his death in minute detail.'

'Let's make a promise.' Alex urged seriously.

'Not another of your bloody plans,' Kinsey was discouraged.

Alex skipped over the last comment and continued 'Look, if tomorrow comes and goes without us being drowned by a tidal wave, or getting hit by a killer meteorite.'

'Or having twenty stone frogs land on us,' Jac added.

'Twenty stone what?' Lusty stood up.

'Apparently, there's been money put on by some mysterious middle-eastern consortium.' Jac informed the rest.

Alex shook his head. 'Ok, or if we survive being squashed by fat frogs.'

'Do they mean twenty stone French people, or the slimy pond things?' Lusty was curious.

'Look boys. I'm trying to get my point across here. Can you stop interrupting for just one minute?' Alex pleaded. 'If it doesn't go the way that Cherry-nose predicted, can we promise that we become strong friends again? Lets start doing things again, like when we were at school.'

'So you want us to go bunking off work, eat half a bread loaf and chips, go to Jac's house and light our farts all day?' Kinsey asked sarcastically.

'If that's what it takes…. then yes.' The silence was even more powerful than his thought provoking message. 'Let's do things together,' he pleaded.

'Like what?'

'Travel around the world? I don't know!'

'Hey,' Jac added 'We could form a pop group. I'd like that.'

'I'll be the singer then.' Kinsey mimicked the actions.

'Singers need to be good looking. Not short, stocky and ugly boys.' Jac wrestled the idea back. 'If you were singing we would be known as the group with the pig-ugly singer.'

'Lusty will have to be the singer.' Alex acknowledged. 'I'll be the guitar hero.'

Jac jumped in quickly, 'I'll be the bass player….. Paul Simoneon eat your heart out.'

'Well I'm not being the little fucking drummer boy, stuck at the back, sweating like a hog.' Kinsey was not a happy bunny.

'Well I was going to suggest, that you become the roadie,' Jac laughed, before a bottle of cider hit his side.

A while later they sat on the ridge of a small hill, looking up to the sky. All the drink and grab had gone, but packets of fags still burnt bright.

'I'll tell you what, this hill would have been great for playing best man's fall when we were kids.' Jac commented, sizing up the incline.

No more words were needed. Without a second thought, they jumped headfirst back to their childhood,

'Right. I'll be the Jerry with the machine gun in the watchtower, and you lot have got to attack. I'll judge who does the best fall.' Jac was already in position, while the others sorted out their strategy.

The newly appointed British commandos gathered at the bottom, pretending that they had just disembarked off a 'U' boat on the beach of Dunkirk.

Alex was the first to attempt to storm the defences. Jac was ready, and shot him with both barrels. Alex clutched his chest, spinning around and fell flat onto his face.

'Fucking terrible,' Kinsey screamed 'Your sister could do better than that.'

Lusty was the next in line. The boy glided up the mound of grass, ducking and diving, occasionally firing off a round of ammunition, but the German gunman had him in his sights and blasted him with everything he had. Lusty toppled back theatrically and slumped backwards to a shallow grave.

'Pathetic,' Kinsey added, 'Boys…. look and learn.' Kinsey took everything very seriously. He pretended to load up his imaginary handheld bazooka, throwing a hand-grenade to pave the way. He sniped across the grass. The other two watched, shouting out catcalls at him.

'We can see your big arse sticking out from here.' Lusty cried, as Jac threw stones at him.

'Shut up…. I'm on a mission.'

Jac's aim was true. The rattle from the pretend gun knocked Kinsey sideways several times. He landed on his knee, but managed to clamber back to his feet and charge at the enemy once again.

Jac fired several million bullets into the on-coming boy's body. Kinsey finally conceded, and rolled backwards all the way to the foot of the hill, where he lay motionless for several moments.

Jac announced, 'I think that the winner of the best man's fall competition is …. Lusty followed by Alex.'

Kinsey was on his feet in a second, racing up to the brow of the hill to protest and to demand a recount.

For the rest of the evening they played like little children, until darkness stepped in to spoil the fun and games. Importantly, they played until they laughed. Laughed until they cried, and they cried until it hurt.

They headed off back towards the town, and sadly back into their teenage lives. Their last action was to line up on the football field, and have a winner takes all horse race. Lusty riding Joe won by a big margin.

'Strummer was always the one way out in front,' he informed the bad losers, as they trodded back through the concrete wasteland with only the lamplight to show the way.

They arrived back at Pablo's house. All seemed quiet on the council house front, but the siege was far from over. A cease-fire had been agreed, while medics attended to the wounded and Doris Pozzoni went to the fish shop for supper for everyone.

'It may be war, but even soldiers have to eat,' she told the Mormons as she dished out the rissoles and chips.

Red vans circled around the house. Post Office workers sat warming themselves over oil drums that housed make-shift fires, while silently wondering what tomorrow would bring.

Chapter 18

'To cut a long story in bits (and hide the remains in a bin bag)'

It felt just like another typical, cold, lazy Sunday morning, as the first rays of the sun slowly straightened themselves up into position in the skyline mirror. What most people hadn't fully appreciated, as they soaked up the laid-back weekend atmosphere, was that it wasn't Sunday at all. If the truth was known, it was, in fact, a miserable bloody Wednesday. And what made it even more depressing to the masses, was that on this particular midweek morning, there would be no dole cheques being delivered through letterboxes to lighten up the gloom. Neither was there any half eaten madras chicken curry in the fridge waiting to be finished for breakfast. For today, was a day, like no other. As the minutes ticked away, everyone was expecting the imminent arrival of the angel of doom on a charabanc from hell.

The high pitched drone of the church bells rang out from the steeple, engulfing the town with a sense of doom. Its chimes broke the strangely subdued silence, that had taken refuge on the deserted street corners.

Jac and his three mates sat in his bedroom, very much awake but extremely quiet. They had spent the whole night equally spaced, between smoking dope, listening to their favourite music, and soaking their bruised thighs (from the horse riding), in bowls of hot water. At one point during the long night, Kinsey's dad had popped in, dressed in faded jeans and a Jimi Hendrix tee-shirt. He had stayed for a while fully embarrassing his son, as he pretended to play air guitar with his teeth, and telling them about how they couldn't possibly understand proper music, because their generation had been born several decades too late.

The sound of the bells rocked and tolled for the town, way off in the distance. The four best friends all looked tired, but this wasn't a day for falling asleep. They were literally sick to death of talking about past glories and past conquests, but it seemed more appropriate, at this moment, than discussing what the future held in store for them.

As they gathered in the kitchen, opening up the fridge hoping to find some things to eat, the rest of the town was also starting to contemplate, what unusual ingredients would be sprinkled onto their last supper meal of this day.

Arthur Cherry-nose stretched out his short legs, hitting his feet against the new delivery of beer barrels that covered the majority of the floor space in the cramped cellar. He felt an irritating tap on his shoulder blades.

'Look,' he subconsciously answered. 'I beat you fair and square all day yesterday. I think it's about time you faced the facts. You may be seven foot tall, and pretty adequate at making fire by rubbing two Newcastle Brown bottles together, but you can't play one on one cabbageball.' He knew these words would cut the Indian to the core, but sometimes it was better to be cruel than be kind.

'No, it's not that stupid Indian. It's me,' said the ex-Mayor, who was kitted out in a newspaper editor's outfit, along with peaked cap and arm bracers. He went on to inform the tramp that he thought that the other roommates had legged it.

Arthur quickly came to his senses, backing away from the man who he didn't like or trust. He groggily asked 'Who's gone?'

'That tall, mute Apache, and that annoying sneezing animal.'

'They'll be back. He's probably gone down the local leisure centre for some extra dunking lessons.' Arthur swilled his mouth out with the dregs from an out of date Double Diamond beer barrel.

'No I don't think so... look.' The ex-Mayor pointed to the door, where Cherry-nose saw the Indian's shell suit and white trainers, placed neatly by the fire exit.

'We won't see those two again, mark my words,' the ex-Mayor muttered, scurrying off to compose another protest letter, demanding the immediate return of Crossroads to daytime television.

Cherry-nose looked around the dark beer cellar, and sadly felt all alone yet again. He had enjoyed the company of the seven-foot Indian, even though he was a terrible basketball player and an even worse loser. He knew that he would also miss the horse. He had become big pals with the sickly animal, and they would stay up until dawn, discussing many issues. Now since it seemed that his two companions had decided to ride out into the sunset to nowhere, he wasn't looking forward to the prospect of spending his final day, cooped up with a letter writing freak, who had somehow during the night, knocked up a home made typewriter out of candle wax, a first aid box and several dozen old bottle tops. As the tramp listened to the tapping of keys, he placed his head into his hands, and broke down into a flood of snot and tears.

Colette woke up semi-naked in the tiny bed-sit, surrounded by plastic rose petals. She struggled at first to make out the person in the French striped tee-shirt, beret and string of onions around his neck, painting on a six foot canvas.

'Don't move, love,' Malcolm cried holding up his thumb and paintbrush to ensure that he had her perfectly to scale. He mixed some more flesh coloured paint on his easel, and finished applying some water colour around the section where the image of her nipples began to come to life.

'What are you doing, darling?' she asked the man who had swept her completely off her feet during their short time together. She had fallen head over heels in love with this person.

'I just decided, last night, to capture your beauty for eternity.' He attempted a French accent, that was so bad, even the flowers cringed.

'Can I see?' she asked excitedly.

'Not yet… I haven't quite finished,' he told her, as he removed the string of onions from around his neck.

Although she had found every single minute of this wondrous experience very rewarding, she was starting to get a little bit tired of Malcolm's constant thirst for the Arts. Yesterday morning, she had come around to his flat bright and early to cook him a breakfast, only to find him halfway through sculpting a sixteen-foot dinosaur out of papier mache. As she started the fry up, he serenaded her, by playing the classic song 'American pie' on a banjo, which had only one string. She smiled weakly, and thought it sounded more like a 'beef and onion pie,' but she didn't let on.

'Come and sit Mal.' She patted the side of the bed. 'You'll wear out all of your artistic cells if you carry on at this rate.' She noticed that he was in bare feet, and his toenails were painted black.

He finished off his last stroke of the brush, and ambled over to where Colette lay.

'You look so beautiful in the early morning light,' he told her, kissing her naked arm. He stopped at a safe enough distance from the pissy smell of her armpit.

'Malcolm, can I ask you something?'

'Anything love, anything.' He said, starting to sketch her with chalk on the headboard of the bed.

'Please Mal…. stop. You need a break.' She took the chalk out of his large powerful hands and said, 'If the world doesn't end tonight, do you think there's a future for us?' There was a hint of desperation in her voice.

'What type of future?' he said, thinking to himself, that if the world didn't end, he was going to buy a decent camera, and travel around the Lake District taking photos of wild birds.

'I don't know perhaps get married…. maybe have some kids. Perhaps just have some kids, and not bother about getting married. That would probably be better, because we could still claim off the social,' she added.

'Colette.' He took her hand. 'You won't want to marry me, I'm rotten. I've played dad before, and it doesn't suit me. I'm an animal. I've done nasty things.'

'That was before you became the town's artist. Everyone loves you Mal. Look at last night, when that man went down on his one knee and kissed your hands,' she said with feeling. 'That was pure adulation…. pure adulation.'

Malcolm knew it was adulation, but not because of his new lifestyle. What he didn't tell her last night, was the man was a complete nutcase, who had been his number one fan during the violent years.

Malcolm spoke up 'I don't know. I've got so many things to do. I'm a new man. I've got to finish off that dinosaur, re-string that lousy banjo, and there's also the auditions for my new musical to organise.'

'Mal, can we do it one step at a time. Do the rest tomorrow Mal. Please do it all tomorrow. Come and audition for me for a while,'

He took off his beret, skimming it across the room. She removed the thick mayor's chain, letting it drop to the floor. They held each other tightly and rubbed noses.

Cyril Beaverman was unaware of what was going on in the real world, as he took a five-minute nap. At this point in the proceedings, he was more concerned with conjuring up ways to escape out of his personal purgatory.

The fighting between the P.O.W.U. and the occupants of 32 Acacia Avenue, had ceased for the time being. Although the fighting had been sporadic, it was quite ferocious when it did kick off. He had regrettably witnessed, the amputation of the mutilated right leg of one of the younger Mormons, who had been run over by a Post Office tank. Unknown to Cyril, this loss of the boy's limb would probably mean his immediate expulsion, not just from the attic, but from the Mormons itself. This was because Mormon law, stated that under no circumstances, was a deformed or crippled believer allowed to knock on someone's door. It had been proven by research that any deformity in the slightest, would have a massive negative effect when trying to convert someone to Christ on Sunday afternoons.

The remaining members of the religious sect, who were too young to get involved in the fighting, had been tasked with preparing Cyril and the bunking officer, to be initiated as fully paid up members of the Mormons Club. They had already started the cleansing process. To begin with, they had given the two men short back and sides, followed by a clean shave. They ordered them to brush their teeth ten times a day, and fifty minutes of deep flossing was compulsory. They had been measured up for new suits by the local tailor. Personal handcrafted bibles had already been delivered. But during all these proceedings, unknown to the two men, the four phase plan of brainwashing had already started.

Cyril had been sharply woken up, by the loud noise of drilling in the attic. He opened his eyes to find the Mormon children hard at work, trying to polish and buff his teeth.

'What are you doing?' he shouted, spitting out bits of plaque.

'Sorry Mister,' the young girl spoke, 'You cannot be a practising Mormon with sheep teeth. We need to fix them straight away. Our kind will never get invited into someone's house for cup cakes, with gnashers like those.' They covered his nose with the chloroform, and went back to working on his dentures. While he slept, the headphones were placed over his ears. The button was pressed. Soon, the monotonous cheerful tones of a man could be heard, who announced 'Hey...my name is Randy. Have you been awoken to the power of JESUS,' the voice on the cassette swirled around his head, burrowing its way into his inner psyche.

Hairy Mary stared at the reflection in the bathroom mirror. She could feel the light stubble which protruded out of her chin. Normally this would be considered a healthy sign of masculinity amongst her gang, but Hairy Mary was starting to look at herself differently.

She picked up the Bic razor, and removed the offending hair from her face. After she finished, she looked at the rest of her body. She wondered what it would be like to be smooth all over. She instinctively covered herself in shaving foam, and started the long process of removing her body hair. Six bin bags later, and plastered in small pieces of toilet roll which helped to stem the flow of blood from the little nicks from the deadly razor blades, she felt like a new born baby again.

She lowered herself into a nice hot bath full of her favourite scent, (Old Spice), and let her dreams take over for a while.

Kieran waited patiently for the love of his life to finish doing whatever hairy bisexual lesbians did in the bathroom. But he was happy to wait. He felt he had turned a major corner in his life, and he was well on the road to Damascus. He couldn't actually believe that sex between two consenting adults could be so earth shattering.

For the first time ever, he felt like a proper man. He didn't need to hide under a blonde wig. And he definitely didn't need to dress like a woman to gain the thrill of life. What he did like though, was the feel of the silky panty material on his skin. So he decided, that he would perhaps still keep wearing them under his trousers, just in case he changed his mind.

He lay on the bed in his girlfriend's house, whistling joyfully to himself. The room was a torture chamber of sexual devices. He physically shook when he picked up the thing that Mary had in the bedside cabinet drawer. He was positive that it could be used to unblock drains with.

But he didn't care. He was in love. His girlfriend was great, and the world was going to come to an abrupt end in less than twelve hours. What more could a Postal worker, who only yesterday thought that he was a transvestite, really expect from this life. He picked up a copy of the gay hard core porno magazine called, 'Butch women with eight-inch sideburns on home made go-carts', and relaxed back in between the nice warm sheets.

The four friends collectively decided to do a bit of a round robin, and visit all their respective family and friends, before heading off to get a good seat at the disco, (for possibly the last dance).

Obviously during the house calls, there were lots of tears, and mountains of hugs and kisses. The houses they visited were either like funerals, where everything was sombre and people talked in short black sentences. Or front rooms which were alive with music and laughter, like a grand family wedding, (before the arguments began).

Whatever the mood, people looked at each other differently. They could sense that this was a scary time. Grown-ups held their children tight, and cursed the big nosed tramp for wishing this event on them.

Alex tried to study the many faces that they came in contact with. He saw many different expressions, ranging from sheer pain and sadness, to pure relief that this day had finally arrived. He felt that only now was the place starting to spring into life. It was bursting with a nervous energy, which they had all done well to contain on the inside.

Alex kissed his little sister goodbye before the school bus came, which was taking all the little ones away to the cinema, where it had been arranged for a Tom and Jerry cartoon festival to be screened until the midnight hour. Crisps, sweets and ice-cream were all free. Again, another gem of an idea from the new and caring Mayor.

The last stop was to Alex's granddad's house. They arrived to be greeted by the old man in his dancing wheelchair, and a glimpse of mischief in his eye.

'Hello lad, quick, there's a swift drink of rum for us all, then it's off to the disco.' His words were merry.

'But gramps, I thought you were off to the other dance at the Labour club, for the OAPs? What do have they call it? The Armageddon foxtrot waltz.'

'Bollocks to that,' he barked back with some bite. 'I wanna be where all the action is. I'm feeling lucky tonight.' He pulled out a pack of three and sprayed some WD40 on the wheels of his love machine.

They all looked each other in the eye for the umpteenth time since this day had started, then headed off to the land of the plastic palm trees, and the night to remember.

Chapter 19

'Do they know it's doomsday time at all?'

Since her surprise appointment, Colette was really making her mark, as a first class ambassador for the town. She was giving numerous interviews to various worldwide TV channels, and other than the occasion where she flashed her tits, and chased the fresh faced reporter from CNN down the street like a baboon chasing a chicken, she was doing a grand job.

She had been consistently bombarded with a variety of awkward questions, and asked to comment on the unusually strange behaviour of her town members. But unfazed by it all, she just shrugged her shoulders, and told them that it was all in a days work and in her opinion, this was probably the sanest she had ever seen the town. 'You should have been here when Santa got shot, now that was really strange,' she told the Austrian journalist.

Since she had announced the great, 'End of the World Bash', her secretary had been inundated with sad stories of individuals, who couldn't attend because they had been banned from entering the pearly gates of the nightclub. Of course, Billy '2 amp' Kinsey was included on the list of offenders. So in her wisdom, and after negotiating with the owners of the club, she had secured a twelve-hour amnesty for all those people.

So due to the great gift of bargaining, by the new and now extremely popular Mayor, Kinsey sat up by the bar in Tiffany's with his three mates. The clock had only just struck six, and the place was already swinging.

They sat back, slightly high on life, but a lot higher on the white chemically enhanced substances, that they had purchased off a boy in a doorway, who was a one-man chemist shop. On the table in front of them were plates of sandwiches and scotch eggs, that had been supplied by the council.

Over by the chicken and chips in a basket enclosure, sat the owners of Hing Hongs, who had decided to give themselves the day off. Everyone else in the club was slyly eyeing them up, waiting for any suspicious signs or sudden movements that indicated that they were ready to cause the initial tidal wave. But unknown to everyone, on the next table was a party of CIA agents, disguised as CIA agents, waiting to retaliate.

The boys overheard a new arrival at the club, telling someone she thought that the beginning of the end had already started, because she had heard a loud explosion, and flames shooting high into the night sky from the middle of the council estate.

The head boss of the Post Office Workers Union, had discharged himself from the casualty department, and was again leading the troops from the front, in their quest to free their man from the evil clutches of Pablo the Tyrant. Perhaps leading from the front was an exaggeration, more like slightly to the left of where the actual action was taking place, and definitely nowhere near where his members were situated. Just as a precautionary measure, the boss was sitting way down in the bowels of the Post Office company issue Chieftain Tank, and he had borrowed a bullet-proof flak jacket from the local lollypop lady. He wasn't taking any chances this time. He had made it quite clear to his members, that he would sack anyone, that turned and pointed a gun anywhere in his direction.

The earlier explosion that had resounded across the town, had been caused when the Post Office explosive expert had blown up the Pozzoni's outhouse. The force of the blast killed a Mormon sniper, who was up on the roof, and two Meals-on-Wheels workers, who had been imprisoned inside since last June. The Union boss had called for reinforcements, from another vastly experienced branch, who were fully trained in this sort of urban combat.

Inside 32 Acadia Avenue, the short cease-fire had given Pablo enough time to reconsider his battle strategy. He had decided that full out attack was the only form of defence. He had reassembled his family and his merry smiling band of mercenary Mormons, inside the tepee. War paint made from beetroot juice, was dabbed on all the brave warriors for perhaps the last time. Luke and a hand selected band of Mormons, (who had blackened out their teeth with shoe polish), sneaked out of the downstairs toilet window for an all out offensive assault.

Back amongst the disco lights, people wandered around smiling and winking at each other, which only acted as a thin veil to disguise the anxiety that was boiling up deep inside of them.

The token street protestor was waltzing around with his placard on, informing everyone that the future couldn't be better and all the wars in the world were going to end immediately, (especially the Chinese verses American tidal wave fracas), and everyone was going to live life, in some kind of 'Happy Days' TV programme.

Colette had sprung another major surprise, when she had a large Christmas present wheeled onto the stage. The house lights were put on, and Alan the Midget was asked up to unwrap it. To everyone's amusement, underneath the wrapping paper, was a one foot, ten inch girl midget, who Colette had hired from a escort agency, that specialised in finding love mates for circus performers, unusually deformed ugly characters, and farmers from West Wales. Alan seemed to immediately grow by three foot as he paraded his new girlfriend, around the now sweaty nightclub, with his little arm locked firmly around her little shoulders.

Love was definitely in the air tonight. Apparently, Lois 'the Swallow' sauntered into the nightclub, and had thrown her knickers onto the wall by the cloakroom and shouted out 'I'll pick them back up on the way out. I'm going commando style tonight.' The bouncers looked on in disgust, as the discarded panties stuck firmly to the wallpaper.

The only real animosity, seemed to be coming from the table where the uniformed Police Officers sat staring across at the Firemen, who in turn, were eyeing up the Ambulance Service, who themselves, would have been staring at the table of Post Office workers, if they had been there, and hadn't been involved in the siege up on the hill.

After much debate, it had been decided that Cherry-nose would be invited to the party. This had pleased lots of people, and as expected, angered many others. Despite this, Cherry-nose entered the bear pit, and was positioned in the centre of the dance floor like some freak in a medieval show.

'Elephant nose, they should have bloody called him,' someone shouted out, before throwing a hardboiled scotch egg at the poor hobo.

As an extra special treat, the council had organised for a Christopher Lee look-a-like dressed as Rasputin, to show up, and have his photograph taken shaking hands with the disgraced tramp.

'The atmosphere is great,' Jac said dragging on his second menthol fag in as many minutes.

'Yeah it is. Pity it's stopping at 12 'o' clock exactly. I feel a bit like Cinderella dancing at the ball.' said Alex adding some humour into the conversation. 'It's a wonder the nightclub owners didn't ask God for an extension until two.'

Another loud explosion rocked the nightclub to its very core. Glasses shot off the end of tables. The record on the turntable jumped back to the beginning and an unconscious student Musketeer was dislodged from the plastic trees.

'Meteorite,' Lusty announced to the rest.

Automatically everyone glanced over to the table of Chinese cooks, who had all decided to stand up on their chairs, pretending to make the sign of the cross. Women screamed, and reached into their bags for snorkels and flippers, but the incident was saved, when the CIA agents (disguised as CIA agents), sprayed pepper spray in the cooks' faces, and proceeded to sit on them until given the all clear.

The actual noise from the second explosion, had nothing to do with meteorites falling from the sky or Post Office workers blowing things up. In fact it was the noise of a recently stolen rogue space shuttle, that had lost control and crashed head first into the Buffaloes pub, killing all the Graham family, and the Russian monkey called Darren. Sadly, the ex-Mayor, who was the only person in the cellar, and had just finished putting his signature to a two hundred beer mat letter complaining about the poor conditions of the street lights, was also blown to smithereens. The only survivor of the shuttle crash was the Graham's family cat, called Mister Toby-jug.

The force of the impact ripped the public house apart, sending rubble sailing high into the night sky, which rained down onto the roof of the nightclub.

'Fucking hell,' yelled Kinsey. 'They were bloody right after all, we are being attacked by twenty stone frogs.'

Everyone took refuge under the cover of the tables, until the noise, of either the imaginary fat slimy creatures, or the sound of garlic eating foreigners subsided.

263

'When we die, do you think we'll go to heaven or hell?' Jac asked Alex, as they dusted themselves down while taking their seats.

'I think I'll go to the one with the shortest queue or the one the nicest looking girls are in.' Alex replied.

They watched a lovely looking thirty-something woman take Lusty by the hand, and lead him to the ladies toilet.

'Well, wherever he ends up,' Kinsey joined in the conversation pointing towards their departing mate, 'Be it with God or the Devil, they will have to have their wives fitted up with chastity belts when he walks into the room.'

They sat there hoping that some thirty-something woman, or any woman (except Lois) would come up to them and take them to see the hidden mysteries of the inside of the womens toilet.

'What should we do when we meet on the other side?' Jac again aimed his question at Alex.

'I know exactly what I'm going to do,' Alex replied regimentally.

'I bet you've made a fucking list already,' Kinsey quipped, he then added sarcastically 'Monday, meet God. Tuesday, get my wings. Wednesday, learn to fly.'

Alex turned his back on Kinsey and said to Jac, 'I'm going to manage a pop group.'

'A fucking pop group. They don't even allow guitars in heaven, only harps,' Kinsey again butted in.

Alex's granddad wheeled himself up to their table, and started to take the middle out of the scotch egg.

Jac loved meaningless debates like this, especially when they were high on speed. 'Who's going to be in your group then Al?'

'Moon on drums.' They all nodded their heads in approval, at the obvious inclusion of the first proper wild man of rock.

'Lynett on bass, Hendrix on guitar, and I think Bolan on vocals and rhythm.'

'Good group,' Jac said quite impressed.

'What are you going to name them?... The fucking Hair Bear Bunch?' Kinsey shot his words from the hip.

Alex again ignored Kinsey's comments and asked 'So who would you have in your heavenly pop group Jac?'

'Easy. Moon, Lynett, Lennon. A three piece, with lots of talent and oodles of bad attitude.'

'What a crap line-up,' Kinsey spoke up.

'So who would you have then clever dick?' Jac took offence.

'Ok, Moon on drums, Vicious on bass, that guy who played on Free bird on lead guitar, and the one and only King on vocals.' He threw a scotch egg across the room.

'Who's the King?' Alex's grandad asked 'Henry the Eighth.'

'Elvis Gramps.... Elvis.'

'Elvis is not even dead. He's living on an island with Bruce Lee, practising karate kicks and shit like that,' Alex started the easy process of winding Kinsey up.

'Of course he's dead. I've seen photo's of him in his coffin.'

'Anyway, if he is dead, there's no way they would let a fat pervert like him through the pearly gates.' Jac wound the hands of Kinsey's clock a little tighter.

'He may have ended up fat, but Elvis wasn't a pervy.'

'He was. He used to watch women change behind two-way mirrors, playing with his hound dog,' Alex laughed. 'I bet he's singing in a two-bit band in the fires of hell.'

They all looked across at Jac, who would normally be frothing at the mouth at the slightest mention of sex. He didn't flinch.

They all then turned to the dance floor, where someone had accidentally thrown Alan the Midget's new girlfriend across the room, and into the lights on the stage.

'Ok,' Kinsey finally conceded. 'I won't have Elvis. I'll have the singer from the Doors..... *So come on baby light my fire,*' he tunelessly sang.

'What about you Mister Davies?' Jac brought Alex's granddad into the surreal debate.

The old man thought for a while, and told them all, that he would have Tommy Dorsey doing all that rousing big band stuff. Someone who called himself The Big Bopper playing guitar, and Duncan Edwards singing.'

'Duncan fucking Edwards. Wasn't he that footballing bloke who died in the Munich plane disaster?' Kinsey called out.

'Yeah, but what a great footballer he was. He could do anything. He had a head like the Merthyr to Newport dock coal train.'

'But could he sing Gramps?' His Grandson asked, laughing.

'Sing! He could sing like a bird.'

The conversation died out over time, just like the members of their imaginary heavenly pop group had. Alex turned and saw Malcolm Knuckles up by the toilets, offering to draw caricatures of people for free.

Outside the streets were empty. Even the news reporters had split after hearing the first explosion.

Back in the heart of the siege, the body count was rising. From across the street, Kieran and Hairy Mary strolled arm in arm through the fighting, making their way to the party. They had been late, because Kieran had finally come to the conclusion that he wasn't really a cross dresser, and had spent longer than normal trying on some of Mary's clothes from her wardrobe, to find something manly to wear over his silky panties. Mary on the other hand was radiant, in a spangle top, short mini-skirt and not a black root in sight.

'Hey, what's up Rich?' Kieran asked one of the P.O.W.U. members who was down on his knees giving one of his colleagues the kiss of life.

'We are trying to rescue you from that evil house Kieran,' he replied, as blood shot all over his face from the wound of the dying man.

'Why are you trying to rescue me?'

'Because you have been locked up and you are in grave danger. If I was you I would get away from here in case you get hurt.' He made the sign of the cross as the man on the ground breathed his last breath.

'I hope you get me out safe,' Kieran said and walked away, thinking it was a joke.

As they picked their way through the wreckage and devastation, someone asked if the lady on young Kieran's arm was Hairy Mary, the queen bee of the lesbians.

'Hey small dick,' Mary shouted. 'Less of the nickname. I would like you to call me by my proper name from now on. That's Hairless Mary Marshmallow-Smith.'

Wolf whistles accompanied them on their journey.

The boss of the POWU stuck his head gingerly out of the tank. 'Hey Kieran… What the bloody hell are you doing? You are supposed to be locked up in that bloody house.'

'Hello Boss. I've never been in Pablo's house.'

'So where the hell have you been, and why did you desert your post bag?' the boss yelled, taking off his helmet.

'I just needed to sort my head out Boss, but you'll be glad to hear that it's sorted thanks to this lady, and I'll be back on the beat on Monday morning, unless we all die tonight.' He put his arm around Mary. They kissed. The troops smiled. The Mormons hugged each other. Luke shot an arrow which hit the union boss in the eye. He tumbled off the tank into a pile of cat shit.

Someone then happened to mention, that if Kieran was safe, that meant that they could all go to the disco. The words were quickly followed by a loud cheer from the union members, who proceeded to drop their weapons, and race towards the town centre.

The battle appeared to be over; except for one soldier whose war had only just began. The recently scalped trumpet player from the Salvation Army band, who had been savagely attacked the previous week by Pablo, had different ideas. So as the fighting ceased, and the Mormons stood in the garden saying their prayers, he aimed his revolver at the kitchen window. The single shot sailed through the air, missing its intended target of Pablo, but sadly the bullet hit Romana. She cried out, as she dropped to the floor. A scream from Doris was not far behind. The Mormons chased after the man disguised as a Post Office worker. They finally cornered him by the shops, where they beat him to death with their bibles.

Pablo lifted his only daughter up into his arms. She was bleeding heavily. He positioned her carefully across the rump of his horse, and slowly walked her the mile to the hospital. She was seen straight away while Pablo and Doris sat nervously in the waiting room. An hour later, a doctor told the quiet parents that their daughter would be fine and the bullet had gone straight through her shoulder. As the relieved couple walked out, Doris head-butted the cocky porter who had had Pablo arrested earlier that year. It made them both feel good.

'Hello…. Hello… is there anybody there?' Cyril called out down the hatch of the attic door, which had been left unlocked during the fighting.

He couldn't hear a sound. There was no movement, and nothing stirred in the small terraced house.

'Where are you going?' asked the bunking officer who had been Mormonized so well, that he looked as clean cut as Liberace in Sunday school.

'There's no one down there. It's our chance to escape.' Cyril said. The silence was welcome but strangely frightening. 'Are you coming?'

The bunking officer hesitated for a few seconds, and slowly added 'No… you go ahead. I quite like it here now. You were right; no one likes a bunking officer anyway. All I do each day is nab mitchers. What's the fun in that? I think I'd rather be a Mormon.' He smiled through a much healthier set of teeth, and climbed in the makeshift coffin, which had been set up for the initiation ceremony.

Cyril said his goodbyes with genuine feeling, and he mentioned that he hoped that he'd get the chance to slam his front door in his face, when he and the rest of the Osmonds turned up at his front door on a Sunday afternoon.

'That's the nicest thing you have ever said to me,' the bunking officer filled up. He gave him a memento.

Cyril tied the yellow scarf around his head as he climbed down the aluminium stepladder. He stepped over a fatally wounded Mormon, who was unfortunately on a fast track to meet his maker. Bullet holes decorated the plaster board walls. Cyril closed the man's eyelids.

He reached the ground floor without interruption. The front door to freedom was wide open. He followed the fresh trails of blood that lead the way out onto the pavement. Cyril ran outside. He breathed in the air which was a mixture of death and smoke, but it smelt miles better than that over-populated attic, especially after one of Doris Pozzoni's badger curry nights.

Suddenly, something inside him snapped. Perhaps it was the pent up anger, of him being imprisoned against his will for so long. Perhaps it was the memory of those long nights, being brainwashed by the Mormons. Or it could have been the simple fact that someone had stolen his company issue van, which had made him turn and walk back into the house. He had some unfinished business to carry out.

He entered the kitchen, carefully selecting a meat cleaver, and a lump hammer, from the array of deadly instruments that were hanging above the pool table. He had fire burning in his eyes, and a belly full of hatred, as he burst into the front room.

He proceeded to slash and hack at the large tent, like Norman Bates in the shower scene from Psycho. He stood back to admire his handy work, the tepee was cut to shreds.

He broke Pablo's peace pipe into a thousand pieces and stamped uncontrollably on the portable cassette player, which up until that point, was still playing rustic sounds of the big country.

He hadn't planned for this outburst, but it didn't half feel good. He then remembered what he had originally come to the house for in the first place. He raced around, cutting all the pre-moulded plugs off the fifteen television sets that were dotted around the house. He felt invigorated, and extremely nervous at the same time. He needed to use the toilet. Cyril smiled manically to himself and laughed out loud as he squatted over the flap of the video recorder and took a dump.

'What are you doing?' the bunking officer asked, literally frightening the shit out of the TV detector man. 'He wouldn't like you doing that.' His face didn't hide the disgust that rose inside him. He held his nose tightly.

'Fuck him, and fuck his family,' Cyril wiped his behind with Pablo's moccasin slippers.

He viewed the devastation that he had caused. As he was leaving, he accidentally kicked over a tin. Out fell a pile of videotapes onto the floor. Cyril noticed the word 'Jaws' written on the front of one of the tapes.

'I'll show him,' he said to himself. He pulled the black tape out of the cassette holder, and danced around the room, mimicking Pablo's Indian war cry.

He unwrapped the miles of videotape around one of the shop window dummies, then ran out into the street, still making Indian noises. Like a kid lost in a sweet shop, he bounded merrily down amongst the rows of houses, too excited to notice that he was all alone. Front doors were wide open. All the lights were switched on. No cars occupied the tarmac. No humans were anywhere to be seen, only gangs of cats strolled around looking thoroughly pissed off.

'Ladies and Gentlemen,' Phil Haddock announced over the nightclub's PA system. 'Please put your hands together for the main act tonight... all the way from errrrrr... where are you from boys?' He shouted behind the curtain.

'Detroit,' one of them answered in a brummie accent.

'Detroit. Are you sure?' Phil shook his head and continued 'Ladies and Gentlemen, all the way from Detroit....it's ..... 'The Temptations.'

The curtains were opened and applause filled the room. There stood five figures in the darkness. The stage lights lit up when the first note of 'My Girl' made its way over the sound system. The audience swooned onto the dance floor, with partners to love and to hold.

Fifteen minutes into the set, Jac appeared and said to his mates, 'Not bad are they?' tapping his hand on the table.

'Not bad. Have you noticed anything unusual about them.' Kinsey mumbled, necking his pint.

Jac shook his head.

'They're fucking white,' Kinsey piped up in pure disgust.

'Oh yeah... I didn't real notice that. So were the Temptations actually black or white?' he asked stupidly.

'Black, of course,' Kinsey added. 'The fucking Temptations, What a sham. All the way from Detroit, all the way from fucking Darlington more like. This council couldn't organise a piss-up in a brewery. Look at that singer, second from the right,' he pointed to where the group were clicking their fingers, down on one knee. 'He's got a mop of fucking ginger hair and a beard like that guy from ZZ Top. The one on the end looks like a bottle of gone off milk.'

'Oh relax and enjoy it,' Lusty muttered, finally re-joining his pals after another trip to womanville. 'There's only one hour to go.'

'It alright for you,' Kinsey shouted back. 'You're been off shagging all night. I'm telling Father Clancy about you.' Kinsey didn't mean the sentence to sound as childish as it did.

'Isn't it exciting,' Jac stated. 'I wonder how it's going to end. It's got to be the tidal wave.' Kinsey was dangling on the verge of hysteria; one more stupid comment would be enough to tip him over the edge. He stormed off to find the token street protestor to punch.

Pablo held the meat cleaver to the bunking officer's throat, and ranted in the poor man's ear. 'Where is the Kimo Sabi with TV badge gone?'

'I told him not to shit in your video recorder... honest but...but he just wouldn't listen to me.' He sobbed uncontrollably, staring over Pablo's shoulders at the Mormons, who for once were not smiling. 'That must be a bad sign,' he thought.

'I don't care what you told him. Which way did he head?' Pablo suddenly let out a massive shriek on seeing his wife pick up the destroyed film case, of his all time favourite video. 'Oh no... not my film.... where's my fucking gun? I'm going to kill the bastard and peel off his skin. I'm going to feed his eyes to the birds and cut off his manhood.'

In one movement, he threw the bunking officer clean out of the window. He marched out, stuffing his pockets with shotgun cartridges. He mounted his horse and rode off towards the town centre.

Cyril wandered into the High Street. It began to rain heavily in between the bouts of thunder and lightening. He suddenly realised that he hadn't come across any people since he had escaped. He knocked on several doors, but no one came to see who was there. The streetlights shone aimlessly onto the empty pavement.

As he walked around he started to regret smashing Pablo's house up. 'What if we are the only people left in the world?' he said to himself. He kicked out at the cats who tried to attract his attention.

'What the hell is going on?' he said to one of the creatures. 'Where have all the people gone?'

The cat looked back and said in return 'They are all in Tiffany's, because the world is supposedly going to end.' Of course Cyril couldn't understand the cat's translation but he was sure that the last meows sounded like 'You couldn't do us a favour and show me and my mates how to use a can opener!'

He turned into the high street. He stopped in amazement at the sight of Buffaloes pub on fire, with a NASA space shuttle sticking out of the side of the building. A dead monkey in an astronaut suit lay face down in the street.

Cyril felt like crying. Was it all a bad dream? Had he been given too many sausage and batter suppers that had scrambled his brain? He heard a faint noise. He could just make out the low beat of music coming from the precinct. He felt relieved. There must be people. There must be life. He headed off to find whoever was responsible for the music. The lightening forked across the blackened sky.

Pablo was too upset to notice the lack of people on his journey, and too angry to worry about the rain. He didn't even glance at the space shuttle embedded in the burning public house, as his horse stepped on the dead monkey.

Then, from behind the betting office, he saw what he was looking for. Cyril let out a scream, as the window of Mothercare exploded around him. The second blast from the Indian's weapon, blew apart the sign that hung above the Sports shop doorway. Cyril ran, closely followed by Pablo on horseback. Shots filled the concrete shopping jungle. Cyril hid in Ferraris cake shop, hoping the rain would shield him from his assailant. But he soon cried out in pain, as the shrapnel from the exploded glass window ripped into his leg.

Pablo momentarily stopped the pursuit, to refill the over-worked gun chambers. Another two live cartridges took the place of the now dead empty shells, that fell lifeless onto the pavement.

Cyril limped up the steps towards the nightclub and banged on the door. He could hear the strains of, 'Celebrate come on', coming back to meet him. He wondered did they ever play anything else in that bloody establishment. And anyway, he didn't feel like celebrating, especially as he saw the shadow of Pablo trotting up the stairs on his trusty stallion. A bolt of lightening struck Pablo's gun, making his eyes glow a strange shade of red.

The bouncer took one look at the state of the TV detector man, and gleefully shook his head, indicating that he couldn't come in without shoes on his feet. Fortunately for Cyril, the blast from the shotgun missed him completely, but left the solid oak doors of the club in tatters. The bouncers scattered in all directions, thinking that the Grim Reaper had started his rounds. Cyril clambered past the paying booth, up the few steps and into the main hall. Pablo on his horse, ducked underneath the doorframe, and proceeded to follow the bleeding man into the main dance hall, firing his gun at will. Everyone assumed that it was just firecrackers going off, as they all assembled around the edge of the dance floor, waiting for the last and final countdown.

Tears rolled down people's faces as they started to kiss and hug each other. Alex, Lusty, Kinsey and Jac stood by the bar, which was lined up with shorts. Lois was backstage giving the ginger haired Temptation the blow-job of his life.

Cherry-nose sat quiet in the centre of the floor, staring vacantly at the faces that surrounded him. He felt like shouting back at them all, but he didn't. The DJ began the countdown. In the background, 'Reet Petite', played quietly through the sound system.

Cyril tried to hide in the crowd. Pablo sat bolt upright on his horse, aiming his gun at the moving target. Cyril was pushed into the middle of the floor. Pablo dismounted, and stormed towards the dance floor, knocking people over as he marched on. Tears streamed down his face, making his war paint run.

Cyril saw the lonely figure of the tramp tied to the banquet chair. He raced across, using the disco lights as a distraction. He snatched the hobo's cane off him, and swung it wildly in thin air. But Pablo had him in his sights. He aimed, stepping forward for a better shot, at the person who had for ransacked his home.

Pablo squeezed the trigger, but as he inched forward, he tripped over Alan the Midget, who was snogging with his new, titchy girlfriend. The noise of the bullet rang out, but its direction was wayward. People screamed and ran for cover. Half of them held their nose, expecting a two hundred foot tidal wave to come crashing through the door at any second.

The DJ was on the last three seconds. The bullet ricocheted off the speaker hitting the chain that held the giant disco mirror-ball in position. The impact snapped it, sending the ball, designed as a globe, spinning to the ground.

The DJ yelled into the microphone, 'One….. Happy End of the World!!!!' just as the disco mirror-ball landed squarely on Cherry-nose's shoulders. All the party celebrations were met with complete silence, as the town's clock struck past the hour mark.

'It's after midnight.' Jac opened his eyes and reminded his mates that they were still in one piece.

'Yeah but look,' Alex indicated to the dance floor, where the tramp was motionless, with the disco ball positioned on his shoulders. Only is nose was visible.

No one moved. The zookeeper raced over in crocodile shoes and checked the tramps pulse.

'I'm afraid he's dead,' he informed the masses, closing the poor man's eyes.

'Hurrah.' Everyone screamed. Glitter and balloons dropped from the sky. A giant human conga started.

'It's not the end of the world at all.' Alex continued. 'It must have just been the end for the disco globe ball, and poor old Cherry-nose who was sitting underneath. Remember he told us that he was watching everyone, and then, bang.'

'Thank Christ for that. Let's get another pint.' Kinsey showed no sympathy at all towards the deceased tramp.

Suddenly, like a flash, the seven foot Indian appeared from behind the curtains and attacked Pablo, who was still holding the smoking shotgun. The table of policemen rushed to the scene to try to control the disturbance, and pulled the large Indian off the smaller Indian. The Firemen, who only needed another ten points to win the Best Emergency Service Award, decided to intervene. A massive fight broke out amongst the officers from both sides. Not long after, everyone (as usual) joined in.

Malcolm McCormick stopped sketching the woman, and took off his painter's overall, throwing his easel onto the ground. He clicked his knuckles loudly. He tapped Phil Haddock, the part time actor, on the shoulder.

'Hello, Malcolm the poet, how can I help you on this glorious day when the world is not going to end?'

'It's Malcolm Knuckles to you. Didn't you once say that my poem was crap?' Before the actor could answer the fully loaded question, Malcolm had punched him clean out of his leather loafers and across the room. The big man could taste blood, like a shark swimming in the cold ocean. He again strolled slowly into the middle of the dance floor and took up his fighting stance next to the dead tramp.

Just before a petrol bomb, thrown by a Traffic Warden, blew up the sound system, Alex and his mates escaped out of the fire exit with his granddad in his wheelchair.

'I knew the world wasn't going to end. I told you so,' Kinsey barked, as they entered the High Street.

'You didn't. You were crapping yourself on that final countdown. You were squeezing my hand like a little girl,' Lusty joked.

'Fuck right off Mister Nostredamus.'

As they walked up the steep hill to their homes, Lusty said 'This is one hell of a nutty place. I think it is probably safer in Beirut!'

Back in the nightclub, the roof blew off, just as a gang of Auxiliary Nurses spilled onto the street, fighting bare-knuckled with a section of the Special Police Constables.

'You lot need to find yourself a hobby,' Alex's granddad muttered.

'Like what Mr Davies?' Jac raised an eyebrow.

'Not like you and your perverted mates, sitting on an underground arse-washer machine,' Kinsey chuckled out loud.

'No. My old mate Sid, told me he was going to start a rebel rugby club up in Dowlais. He's looking for players.'

'Up in Dowlais. Fucking hell Mr Davies, even the sheep wear knitted hats and gloves up there,' Jac commented.

'But boys, look at this town.' They all stared down to the anarchy that was overflowing into the High Street.

Alex's granddad continued 'It will get you away from all of that madness and keep you all out of trouble.'

'We'll think about it Gramps, but I'm not making any promises.'

They turned to look at the town for the last time before they headed home to bed. Fireworks were shooting high up in the sky. The alarm from the bank was going off, indicating that Luke Pozzoni had finally blown up the safe.

Then from across the street they saw Lois 'the Swallow' and the Christopher Lee look-a-like walk past them, hand in hand.

'Goodnight Lois,' Jac shouted 'Watch your underpants, Mr Lee.'

They all laughed, and decided to go home and watch a good Carry-On film.

Chapter 20

'Oh Oh... the tongues of Merthyr'

The Station Arms Hotel was deadly quiet, as Gary Churchill finished the end of the story, and took a sup out of his now warm beer.

'Bloody hell,' Chris slowly commented. 'Was that all true?'

'As true as I'm sitting here. If it wasn't all true, I bet you would have thought that I'd made it all up.'

The old storyteller again, shouted across the bar to Ronny Mouth-organ. 'Ronny, was that true?'

'Every single word. Cross my arse and hope to die.' He laughed, blowing on his instrument again and flashing a black bag full of uncut diamonds.

'To be honest, I did exaggerate slightly,' Gary admitted. 'It was concerning the Avon lady locked in the cupboard.'

'I thought that bit was a bit too much,' Chris added.

'No, the Avon lady locked in the cupboard was true. I just made up the part about her believing she was Colonel Gaddifi. Actually she thought she was the saxophone player from Bruce Springsteen's band, but I can never remember his name.'

'Well, what happened after that?' Chris asked.

'Well Mister Inquisitive, when the lights came on in the nightclub, and the Police had finally stopped scrapping with the Firemen, Cherry-nose's body had disappeared, along with the seven foot Indian that everyone thought they had seen, but wouldn't swear on it. All that was left was the TV detector man, still swinging the old tramp's cane wildly at the shadows.'

To the great amusement of the pub crowd, the barman mimicked the frightened detector man with a pool cue.

Gary added, 'Of course, over the following days, there were the sightings. Many claimed to have seen the seven foot Indian, carrying the body of the hobo up towards the old ancient Indian burial ground.'

'The old ancient Indian burial ground. You're pulling my leg,' Chris looked around at the stony faces that were still crowded around.

'No straight up. It's over by the ninth hole on Morlais Golf Club, in the rough, by the side of the trees.' Gary continued. 'Well no one ever saw Cherry-nose or the Indian again.'

'How did the cane get in the lake?'

'Well allegedly, the cane, with the TV detector man still attached, was dumped in the lake by Pablo and his son. But it was never proven. Let's just say that when his body was found, he had a 48" dual surround sound TV, with the plug cut off, tied to his ankle.'

Chris could vividly picture the walking stick in the lake. He shivered, even though the heat from the logs burnt into his skin.

Gary sat back. It was a lot to take in at one sitting. 'What happened to Malcolm, Colette, and the rest of the people?'

'Well Malcolm abandoned his quest for art, and went headfirst back into fighting the street, but this time he was taking no prisoners. We buried him a couple of years ago.'

Gary then went on to inform the pub of what happened to the rest of the colourful characters.

Pablo Pozzoni had been arrested, but all charges were later dropped, because there was no actual body found to use as evidence. He did appear in court on a kidnap charge, but since the jury was made up of Mormons, they not only let him go scott free, but made the council buy him a small holding up the Bogey Road, which he turned into a thriving Indian reservation and Mormon Church settlement. It all started to make sense to Chris, as he remembered seeing a band of Mormons last week, passing his window carrying a totem pole, which had Donny Osmond's face carved into the top.

Colette finished her term in office, but was voted in for another eight years. There, she spent all her time trying to make the council more efficient. She finally started to get somewhere, when she decided to swap her staff with the waiters from Hing Hongs. Apparently, the council became the best and most effective in the country, but sadly, the restaurant went to ruin within three weeks.

Lois married the Christopher Lee look-a-like, who turned out to be quite a decent enough chap called Eric, and was a bit of an explorer in between guest appearances.

'The four friends, (Alex and the boys), did finally go and play for that terrible shameful rugby team up on the hill.' Gary told Chris. 'You may have read about their exploits in the News of the World. It was shameful, bloody shameful.'

Gary then explained, that Hairy Mary and Kieran married but it didn't last. He came home one day, to find her in bed, covered in a pair of home made hairy fish net stockings, with some of the members of her old gang. Apparently the 15 inch plastic cock was in full swing yet again.

'Kieran was distraught, and disappeared once more.' Gary lowered his voice, and nodded towards the dark corner of the pub, where Chris could just make out a blonde-haired figure of a woman with big hands.

'And who do you think they are, over there?' Gary pointed to the table where some rowdy men were playing another drinking game.

'Some sports team that have won a match today?' Gary shrugged his shoulders and replied. He had noticed when he walked into the pub early that night, that some of the men had been chained to prison officers.

'Those, my educated friend, are the Penydarren boys club under tens, who are finally having their victory party. Thirty years after they lifted the trophy.'

Chris was not the only one who felt drained, as he thanked Gary for the story. The entire pub was completely exhausted by the tall tale, which had occupied them all for the several hours.

'And I think that on that note, we will make our way to Sammy's, where the chips will be on Mr Kemish here,' Gary indicated. Chris was more than happy to oblige.

Suddenly the door opened, sending a cold draft waltzing through the public house, and making the fire dance wildly. Eric, the Christopher Lee look-a-like, ran in. He was as white as a sheet. He pointed to the optics on the top shelf, and indicated for the barman to pour him a treble.

'Looks like you've seen a ghost,' Gary bellowed out. 'Or was it Peter Cushion chasing you with a cross.' Everyone laughed.

Eric pulled up a seat next to Chris, and informed the pub, that he had come across the remains of a flying saucer buried in the ground, up by the old railway tunnel.

Gary Churchill shook his head again. 'Are you sure? It could have been an old tram, or a disused train engine.'

'I'm sure… I'm sure,' Eric protested. He then pulled out a pair of tiny silver space boots and a ray gun, from the inside of his jacket.

'Look Eric, we would tell you all about the time that the town had visitors from outer space, but you are not from this area. But, if you can answer one of the following simple questions, I will tell you all about how

ET and his mates came-a-shooting into town, looking to take our womenfolk.'

The man's hands were shaking. He drank the liquid that warmed his inside and nodded his approval.

'Ok, first question. What is my favourite colour?'

'What sort of dumb-arse question is that?' the man said incredulously.

'A fucking good one,' said Chris Kemish looking around smugly, knowing full well, that he was now one of the boys.

THE END

I would like to thank the following:-

Nigel – *for listening to my mad rantings*

Wayne – *for giving me the thumbs ...up!*

Lucy - *for a great cover design (see page 287)*

Carmen, Alison, Greg and Siobhan – *for the proof-reading and for begging me to keep the nasty bits in!!!*

Jane Marie – *for the final check*

And for Wetherspoons on a wet Monday afternoon

I would also like to send an extra special thanks to the *'Dowlais Conservative Club Modelling Agency'* for giving their kind permission for their three top catwalk models to appear on the front cover.

Maxy – *The maddest Red Indian in the world*

Coatsey – *The funniest man in the world*

Gerald – *The best former boxer, now best smoker and cougher in the universe*

Boys... may you always have a tin of tobacco and a double whiskey in front of you....
Best wishes...

Bunko

The Tale of the Shagging Monkeys

Four life-long friends plan a break from the madness of their daily lives.

But unknown to them, Madness is not only packed and sitting on the plane…. It is already tanked up on Tequila.

Would any of them return home Sane?

This hilarious adventure begins, as our four passengers meticulously prepare for the trip of their lives. But, from the very first step it all goes disastrously wrong, with the unknown assistance of a mixture of wild and wonderful characters, a pinch of romance, and a spoonful of skulduggery poured over the top.

Remember that life's journey is 80% fact, and 20% fiction…. The good thing is no-one knows which bits are which?

This is the Tale of the Shagging Monkeys

The Tale of the Shagging Monkeys

Reviews of the first book

"It is ABSOLUTELY HILARIOUS to put it mildly"
**** Four star rating – WESTERN MAIL

"It is a HYSTERICAL tale of everyday valley boy holiday mayhem. Bunko has pace, wit and bags of characters."
The South Wales Echo

"HILARIOUSLY FUNNY... Belly laughs explode out of every page."
Phillip Davies – Blaenavon and area FIRST

"I LAUGHED OUT LOUD from start to finish."
Steve Jones – TV Presenter

"We should have DROWNED him at BIRTH."
Bunko's Nan